TWISTED

ALSO BY K.A. ROBINSON

Torn
Book 1 in the Torn Series

TWISTED
BOOK 2 IN THE TORN SERIES

A Novel

K.A. ROBINSON

ATRIA PAPERBACK

NEW YORK   LONDON   TORONTO   SYDNEY   NEW DELHI

ATRIA PATERBACK

A Division of Simon & Schuster, Inc
1230 Avenue of the Americas
New York, NY 10020

First Atria Paperback edition November 2013

ATRIA PAPERBACK and colophon are trademarks of Simon & Schuster, Inc.

For information about special discounts for bulk purchases,
please contact Simon & Schuster Special Sales at 1-866-506-1949
or business@simonandschuster.com

The Simon & Schuster Speakers Bureau can bring authors to your live event.
For more information or to book an event contact the Simon & Schuster Speakers
Bureau at 1-866-248-3049 or visit our website at www.simonspeakers.com.

Designed by Dana Sloan

Manufactured in the United States of America

10   9   8   7   6   5   4   3   2   1

Library of Congress Cataloging-in-Publication Data
Robinson, K.A.
  Twisted : a novel / by K.A. Robinson. — First Atria Paperback edition.
    pages cm. — (Book 2 in the Torn Series)
  1. College students—Fiction. 2. Domestic fiction. I. Title.
PS3618.O3285T95 2013
813'.6—dc23

                                        2013020234

ISBN 978-1-4767-5216-7
ISBN 978-1-4767-5217-4 (ebook)

To my son, even though you're too young to know.
You've brought so much joy to my life.

To my parents, for dealing with my daily rants and for
supporting me when I thought I might lose my mind.

To my Ninjas and Cougars for just being there and
making me laugh, even on my worst day.

And last but not least, my fans. You have no idea how
much your love and support means to me. I love you all!

PROLOGUE

There are moments in your life that stand out above all the rest—moments of pure bliss, pure anger, pure sorrow. Moments that take your breath away. Most of these moments in my early life were painful firsts. The first time my mother hit me, the first time I felt the sting of a belt against my skin. The first time I cried myself to sleep, the first time I cleaned up my mother's vomit as she lay passed out on the couch.

But the others, the happier ones—they're what makes life worth living.

Early on, these happy moments were simple ones—the first time I ever stayed with Amber, my first Three Days Grace CD, seeing Logan smile at me as he sat down beside me on his first day of class. They were the little things everyone else took for granted.

As my mother's time at home decreased, those special little moments increased for me. I lived for the times when she was gone, when the bruises would finally fade from my skin and my smile would be real.

Both my happiest and most painful moments seemed to revolve around one person, though. Drake. Even saying his name brought a smile to my face. No one else touched my life the way he did. When we had our lows, they were horrible, a whirlwind of pain and regret. But our highs—oh, they could bring me to my knees with joy. I had never felt such total and complete contentment as I did when I was with him. I knew that we were meant to last, that he would stand by my side through any storm I was forced to face.

Sadly, my storm did come. Starting out as nothing more than a small rain cloud, it brought a hurricane with it, not just for me, but for Drake as well.

CHAPTER ONE

CHLOE

My ears were ringing. I looked up as Drake grabbed my arm; his lips were moving, but I couldn't hear anything he was saying. She was here, in Drake's home, my home now. I felt Drake pulling on my arm and I forced my legs to move as he led me to the couch. As he pushed me into the cushions, I caught sight of scarlet dripping slowly down my legs from several small cuts. That was funny; I could see the blood, but I didn't feel any pain.

Drake kneeled in front of me, stroking my hair gently. "Chloe, can you hear me? Snap out of it, baby," he said in a soothing voice.

His voice snapped me out of whatever trance had taken over my body. I blinked rapidly and shook my head, trying to clear the ringing in my ears. It had settled to a dull hum in the background, and I breathed a sigh of relief that I could hear him.

"I'm here. I'm sorry, I don't know what happened." I glanced back at the front door. "Is she still here?"

He ran his hand across my cheek before standing. "Yeah, but I'm going to go get rid of her. Just stay here," he said as he turned to the door.

"No, let her come in. Let her say what she has to and then she can get out."

Drake looked back and forth between the door and me, doubt clouding his face.

"Really, I'm all right. Just let her in," I said as I leaned back into the couch.

Frowning, he turned and walked back to the front door. I could hear both his voice and my mother's, but I couldn't make out what they were saying, only that they were angry.

A moment later, he stepped back into the room with my mother following closely behind him. I watched her as she took in our home with a look of disdain on her face. Andrea Richards, also known as my mother, had aged greatly since the last time we had seen each other. She looked at least ten years older than her thirty-six years. Wrinkles lined the corners of her mouth and eyes, and her skin looked gray and withered. Her hair was still as blond as mine, but it was unkempt and her roots were starting to gray. All in all, she was a perfect picture for the "after" portion of an antidrug commercial.

Our identical blue eyes met as she sat down in the chair across from me. Hers were glassy and watery, but she was still able to show her dislike for me through them.

"When did you get so dramatic, Chloe? You didn't have to put on a show for me—a hug would have sufficed," she said with a smug smile.

"Cut to the point, woman, or get out. It really doesn't matter to me," Drake barked out beside me.

I jumped at the sound of his voice and my mother smiled. "What's the rush? Maybe I want to catch up with my long-lost daughter." She turned her attention to me. "So tell me, Chloe, how have you been? I see you landed a nice guy to take care of you. I wonder how long he'll stay with you until he gets bored?"

Drake jumped to his feet. "That's it! Get out of my house and don't come back. Chloe doesn't need your bullshit."

"Calm your horses—I'll say what I came to say and then I'll leave."

"Then just say it and go, Mom," I said as I grabbed the back of Drake's shirt and pulled him back to me. I didn't want him fighting with her and getting himself in trouble.

"Fine, have it your way. It's about your Aunt Jennifer. It seems she's been hiding her failing health from us. She doesn't have much time left—a couple of weeks max."

For the first time in my life, I saw my mother look truly upset. I had spent only a short time with my aunt, but she seemed like such a kind person, nothing like my mother, and her illness broke my heart.

"What's wrong with her?" I asked.

"Cancer. They thought they had it under control, but it's spread." She took a moment to clear her throat and compose herself. "Anyway, she doesn't have much time and she's asking to see you."

My eyebrows all but disappeared into my hairline. "Me? But why? I've only met her a few times in my life."

"You're her only niece, and for some reason she likes you. You and I both know that Jen has more money than she knows what to do with. She's leaving most of it to Danny, of course, but she wants us to have part of it."

This took me by surprise. Sure, Aunt Jen was a kind soul, but why would she leave me any money? Or my mother? She had to know what kind of person her sister was. And none of this explained why my mother had come here personally to tell me all of this. There was something going on that she wasn't saying.

"I don't want Aunt Jen's money. Let her give my part to Danny or Jordan. They deserve it more than I do."

"Of course you don't deserve it, but she's adamant about it. Since Jordan and Danny couldn't seem to find you, she sent me to do it. We need to leave soon—time is against us."

"Why do you even care if I get any of the money? There's another reason you're here, so tell me what it is. You're not self-less enough to help even Aunt Jen."

My mother's face distorted in anger. "You listen here, you little bitch. You don't get to talk to me like that—you don't have a clue about me."

Drake had settled into the cushion next to me as we spoke, but at these words he shot out of his seat and lunged at her.

I grabbed him and pulled him back as I glared at her. I was usually a calm person by nature, but she had pushed me to my limit. "No, *you* listen to *me*—I can talk to you however the hell I want. Tell me why you're really here or you can get out, and all Aunt Jen will get is a long-distance phone call!" I shouted.

Her face paled as she squeezed her hands into fists. "Fine," she spit out. "You want to know the real reason I came to find you? She won't give me my share of the money if I don't bring you to her. I wouldn't be here dealing with your stupid shit if I didn't have to be."

Now *this* was the mother I knew. All her kindness toward Aunt Jen was for her own gain. She wanted the money so she could run around and do what she wanted with it.

"You have got to be kidding me! How selfish can you be, Mother? Berate me all you want, but don't use your dying sister for your own gain. Get out." I motioned to the door as I spoke.

I'd had enough of her lies. I knew there was something in this for her and there it was: she was going to use me to get money from my dying aunt.

"I'm not going anywhere until you agree to come with me. If you don't, I'll make your life hell. I know where you work, where you live, who your friends are. I bet Amber and Logan would love a visit from me. You know I'll do it."

My stomach knotted as I looked at the vile creature in front of me. She was low enough to not only make my life hell, but everyone's that I cared about as well. If I did this, went one last time to see my aunt, maybe she would leave me alone. Even though I hadn't seen my aunt in years, I thought the world of her. I just hated the fact that I would be accompanied by my mother when I went to see her.

"You stay away from them—they don't need your bullshit. If I do this, I want you gone from my life permanently; you will disappear the minute I walk away from this mess. Is that understood?"

Drake turned to look at me, his mouth agape. "You can't be serious! This woman is mental."

"I'm serious. I'm tired of playing these mind games with her." I turned my attention back to my mother. "Do we have a deal?"

I saw triumph flash in her eyes at my proposition. She had no idea what I was planning. The minute I saw my aunt, I was going to tell her not to give my mother or myself a dime; that money belonged to Danny, and I was not about to let my mother get her paws on it.

"Deal. We leave tonight."

I shook my head. "No, Drake is leaving in two weeks. I'm spending them with him before he goes." She opened her mouth to argue, but I cut her off. "I said no. If you don't like it, I can call Aunt Jen right now."

Her glare was murderous as she stood. "Fine, you spiteful

brat, but I'll be back for you in two weeks if you don't show up. I'll drag you into my car if I have to."

"That won't be necessary; I'll drive Chloe to her aunt's house. She doesn't need to put up with you in a car by herself for hours," Drake said from his seat on the couch. A storm was brewing behind his eyes, and I knew I was in for it the moment we were alone.

I stood and walked to the door, holding it open for her. "There, everything is settled. Now get out of my house before I remove you myself."

She walked swiftly past me and out the door. She turned when she was outside. "I'll be waiting. Two weeks, or I'll be back."

I looked behind her and noticed a beat-up car idling by the curb. A large man was sitting behind the wheel, watching us. He gave me a grin that made my skin crawl as I slammed the door in my mother's face.

"Two weeks," I groaned as I leaned against the door. I looked up to see Drake watching me from the doorway.

"Not now, Drake—yell at me later."

"Are you out of your fucking mind?" he roared.

I walked past him to the kitchen and grabbed a broom and dustpan to clean up the glass I had dropped earlier. I continued to ignore him as I swept up every shard of glass, even though I felt his gaze on me.

"Talk to me, Chloe. What were you thinking? Making a deal with that woman is like making a deal with the devil. You know better than that."

I glanced up at him and saw the worry in his eyes. "I'm not doing this for her; I'm doing this for my aunt. I'll be damned if I let my mother have one penny of that woman's money."

"What do you mean? You're going to see her. If you don't want her to give your mom the money, you need to stay away."

I gave him a small smile as I walked around him and dumped the glass into the garbage. "Not necessarily. I'm going to my aunt's to tell her not to give it to her. I'm sure she realizes my mom is a horrible person, but once I tell her everything that she's done to me, I have no doubt that I can get her to change her mind."

The corners of his mouth turned up in a grin. "Wait, let me get this straight. She manipulated you into going only to have you turn the tables and manipulate her?"

I couldn't help but giggle at the look of awe on his face. "Yeah, that about sums it up. She has it coming to her, and I'm going to personally make sure she gets what she deserves."

Drake was across the room in a flash. He picked me up and swung me around until I started feeling dizzy. "Do you have any idea how sexy you are when you're being evil?"

"Put me down! I'm not going to be very sexy if I vomit on your shoes, and you're making me sick!"

He quickly dropped me and stepped back. I grabbed the countertop to keep my balance. "Thanks."

But before my head could stop spinning, he grabbed me and pulled me into his arms, kissing me deeply. "Come on, I want to show you just how sexy you are."

With that, we made our way to the bedroom, our now cold dinner forgotten. Who needed food when you had Drake?

. . .

"You're absolutely insane, woman!" Amber screeched at me the next afternoon.

I was having lunch with Amber and Logan, and I had just

broken the news about my surprise trip to Maryland and my mother's visit last night. Unsurprisingly, they were not taking it well.

"Chloe, this is insane—you're willingly walking into the belly of the beast. Even if your plan to change your aunt's mind works, you're still going to be stuck in a house with that woman when your aunt breaks the news. I don't see that ending well," Logan said as he looked at me with concern.

After everything that had happened between us, he was trying to rein in his overprotective streak, and I could see how much trouble he was having right now. His voice was calm, but his eyes said he wanted to grab me and lock me in his room.

"I won't be there when my aunt tells her. I'm only staying long enough to convince her not to give my mom the money, and then I'll be in my car on my way to one of Drake's shows. But if things do go bad, Danny will be there to help me, and I'm sure Jordan will be too."

"How long are you staying?" Amber asked as she sipped her coffee.

I twirled my hair as I watched people through the window of the café we were sitting in, lost in thought. If I could pull this off without any problems, I would be there only a couple of days. If something went wrong—well, I wouldn't worry about that now.

"Not long. Drake will be playing shows in Maryland while I'm there, so whenever I'm done I'm going to meet up with him and continue on."

"So you'll still be gone all summer?" Amber asked as she pouted. When I told her about Drake asking me to go with the band, she had not been happy at all. She had plans for us this summer that had involved lots of shopping, along with other things I absolutely hated. I had felt horrible about ruining her plans, but secretly I was glad I could get out of them.

"Yes, I'm still going with Drake. You'll have Logan to keep you company—take *him* shopping," I said as Logan shot me a glare.

"Yeah, not happening. I have better things to do than walk around the mall for six hours while Amber searches for the perfect pair of shoes," he said with a visible shudder.

I couldn't help but laugh at his reaction. If there was anyone else in this world who hated shopping more than I did, it was Logan.

Logan shot me a grin and I felt my heart lighten. After three months, I still took every smile he gave me to heart. There had been a few tense weeks when I thought I'd lost him forever, but Logan, being the kind soul he is, had taken me back with open arms. Even though things would get strained and awkward from time to time, Logan and I were healing together. Drake and he had both agreed to get along with each other, but if I brought Drake around I could easily see the resentment in Logan's eyes. I tried not to let it bother me—the past was the past—but sometimes it did.

"Shut up, both of you. I don't need either of you to go shopping with me; I can have fun all by myself!" Amber said, shooting us both a glare.

"We know you can, Amber," I said as I hid a smile.

"And you'd better freaking call me at least once a week while you're gone! I mean it. I can't go from spending every day with you to nothing for three months," Amber said.

"You know I will. I'm going to miss you guys too, you know—this isn't all one-sided. It's been a long time since I spent any real amount of time without you two and it's going to suck."

"Damn straight it will!" Amber said as she practically pulled me from my seat to hug me.

I giggled as I turned my head to look at Logan, who was watching us as if we'd lost our minds. "Get over here, big guy—group hug!"

He rolled his eyes as he leaned in and wrapped his arms around both of us. "You two are completely mental. How I'm even friends with either of you, I'll never know."

Amber stuck her tongue out at him. "You know you love us both, so shut up."

His eyes met mine and I felt my stomach clench with guilt.

"Yeah, I do."

CHAPTER TWO

DRAKE

I grabbed the last of Chloe's bags and threw them into the trunk of her car. I slammed it shut, praying the latch would catch with so many things crammed inside. Of course it didn't, and I spent the next five minutes hopping up and down on the trunk like an idiot until it latched. I jumped down from her car, breathing heavily, and turned to see Chloe watching me from the front of the car with an amused expression on her face.

"Did you pack for three months or three years? This is ridiculous," I said as I grabbed the overnight bag I was taking with me to her aunt's house and tossed it in front of the passenger's seat. No way was that thing fitting in the backseat with her junk back there too. For a girl who hated to shop, she sure had a lot of clothes.

"Shut up. I'm a girl, which means I change my shirt and underwear daily, unlike some people."

"I change mine daily too, but you don't see my cramming sixty pairs of underwear into a suitcase. I'm sure we'll pass a Laundromat at some point—no need to have an outfit for every day we're gone." I pointed to the back of her car. "You know you're going to have to leave most of this in your car, right? No way is the bus going to hold all that crap."

"Yeah, I figured as much. When are they supposed to be here with the bus, anyway? We need to get going soon."

The band had acquired a small tour bus—actually, *I* had acquired it—and we were waiting for Eric and Adam to show up so I could load my bags before Chloe and I left for her aunt's house. Since our first few shows were in Maryland, the plan was for me to ride with Chloe to her aunt's house and stay with her for a couple of days. Once the band had everything loaded into the bus, they would meet us there to pick me up. I was hoping everything would be settled by then and she could come with us when we left; if not, our first stop was only about an hour away from her aunt's, so she could catch up with us quickly.

"Right on time," I said as I noticed the bus turning down our street.

I caught sight of Adam in the driver's seat and groaned. I'd told them I wanted Eric to drive so that I knew the bus would survive; with Adam at the wheel, that didn't seem like a possibility. I loved the guy like a brother, but I'd seen him destroy more cars than hearts since we had been friends and I knew this couldn't end well.

"What's up, fuckers?" Adam shouted as he and Eric stepped out of the bus.

"I thought we agreed to let Eric drive," I asked.

Eric sent me an apologetic look. "That's what I told him, but you know how he is."

"Whatever, asshole—I just drove here. I'll let Eric take over once we leave for the tour."

"Yeah, good plan. Now help me get this shit in the bus so

we can get out of here. I want to get there before dark," I said as I grabbed a couple of bags and carried them to the side of the bus.

Adam completely ignored me as he walked over to talk to Chloe while Eric and I loaded the rest of the bags and my guitar into the bus. Once we had everything put away, I walked over and smacked him across the back of the head.

"Ouch! What the hell was that for?" he said as he rubbed the back of his head.

"Thanks for helping. Now get out of here—I'll see you guys in a couple of days."

They waved and wished Chloe luck in dealing with the psycho as they left. I had given them the short version of the story, and they were as appalled as I was over the whole mess.

We watched them pull back down the street, and I cringed as Adam nearly took out an oncoming car. I shook my head as we walked to Chloe's car and got in.

"If Adam drives when they come to pick me up, I have a feeling we're going to all be stuck riding in your car with Adam strapped on top," I said as she started the car.

"He can't be that bad," she laughed.

"Oh, trust me, he is. If he keeps a car six months before to-taling it, it's a miracle. I won't even let him ride in mine."

"Wow, I guess you guys better watch your bus, then. How did the band even manage to get that thing, anyway? It had to have cost a fortune."

I squirmed uncomfortably in my seat. "We're only renting it."

"Yeah, but still, even just renting it had to cost a lot."

I figured I might as well just get this out of the way now; I knew she'd be upset when she learned I had kept something like this from her.

"Ipaidforit," I said in a rush.

"What?"

I sighed and ran my hands through my hair. "I said I paid for it. I used my money to rent it for the trip."

She gave me a confused look. "How did you pay for something like that? No offense, but a struggling musician in college doesn't have that kind of cash."

"Well, see, the thing is, my parents left me some money when they died. My dad's best friend was a lawyer at the firm he worked at and invested it for me. My uncle has control over it until I turn twenty-one, but he sent me enough to cover the tour expenses and the bus."

"How much money are we talking about here, Drake?" she asked.

"I don't know the exact dollar amount, but it's right around half a million by now."

Her mouth dropped open. "So basically, we've been a couple for three months and you failed to mention you're loaded? Were you afraid I was going to use you for your money or something?"

I could hear the hurt in her words as she spoke. "No, nothing like that. I know you would never do something like that; it's just not something that I talk about. Besides, I don't even have it yet. When I do, I don't intend on spending it—I'll just leave it where it is and let it grow. I might need it for retirement someday, the way the economy is."

"Wow, I don't even know what to say to that. Who knew I would be dating a rich guy?" She laughed. "I guess that makes you my sugar daddy."

I breathed a sigh of relief as I realized she wasn't mad. "I'll be your sugar daddy any day, babe."

I settled back into my seat to get comfortable for the rest of the six-hour trip in a cramped car. We were silent for a while and I passed the time by watching Chloe as she drove. She seemed nervous, constantly fidgeting and changing the CD in the stereo. I couldn't really blame her; she had a dying aunt to say goodbye to and a crazy-ass mother who would be out for blood in a matter of days.

I didn't really know a lot about Andrea since Chloe hated talking about her, but what I did know was all bad. I don't think she had even one good memory about her mother or her childhood, and that made my heart break for her. How could anyone not love my girl? Sure, she had her issues, we all did, but to completely hate her the way her mother did? It was unacceptable to me. Chloe had to be one of the kindest and sweetest people I had ever known.

If the band hadn't had these tour dates scheduled months in advance, I would have stayed with her the entire time to protect her. I didn't want her to have to face anything on her own, especially not a situation involving her mother. She had mentioned something about her cousin Danny and his friend Jordan being there, and I fully intended to talk to both of them about watching her back. If I couldn't be there, I intended to make sure she was fully protected.

"Will you stop staring at me? You're making me nervous!" Chloe said as she glanced over at me.

"What if I don't want to? Maybe I like looking at you."

She snorted. "Because of my amazing looks? Try again, buddy."

I glared at her. "Don't do that."

"Do what?" she asked, confused.

"Put yourself down like that. You're beautiful, Chloe, the

most beautiful girl I've ever seen. You're always so hard on yourself and I know it's because of your mom, but don't listen to anything she has ever said to you. She has no idea what an amazing person you are."

"Are you hoping to get laid by charming my pants off? Because if so, it's working," she said as she sent a grin my way.

I felt my dick twitch at the thought as I returned her grin. "I'm holding you to that when we get there. Or we can just pull over somewhere and take care of things."

"Drake Allen! I am *not* pulling over someplace to have sex with you! And you're going to have to wait awhile, because I'm certainly not having sex in my dying aunt's house! That's just disrespectful." She glared at me, but I could see her lips twitching.

"I never said it had to be in the house, you know."

She laughed. "You're insatiable—you know that, right? I need to stop and get gas at the next exit unless you want to get out and push us the rest of the way."

"Fine, but you know, since we'll be pulled over . . ."

"Not happening, buddy—keep it in your pants."

. . .

The rest of the trip went smoothly. We stopped in Frederick and a small town called Easton to fill up the car and stretch a bit, but other than that we drove straight through. By the time we started seeing the signs for Ocean City, my ass was completely numb and it was dark outside. I knew Chloe was tired and I had offered to drive part of the way but she declined, saying that the driving took her mind off things.

When she told me we were roughly ten minutes from her aunt's house, we found ourselves weaving in and out of traffic, searching for street signs to direct us. Chloe's aunt didn't actually live in Ocean City; she was on the mainland by the bay, just a few miles away from the Ocean Gateway. Chloe struggled in the darkness to find the right road to turn down, and we accidentally passed it before realizing our mistake and turning back.

As we pulled up a narrow driveway to the house, my mouth dropped. It wasn't a house, it was a freaking mansion. The property was surrounded by a privacy fence and I noticed a guard station next to a locked gate as we got closer. Chloe pulled up next to the guard station and rolled her window down.

A man dressed in black slacks and a button-down shirt came out of the station and approached our car. "Can I help you?"

"Yes, I'm here to see my Aunt Jennifer," Chloe said.

The guard looked down at the clipboard in his hand. "What's your name?"

"Chloe Richards."

The guard checked his list before nodding. "I've got you right here. Go ahead in and I'll let them know that you're here."

With that, he walked to the gate and opened it so that we could enter. As soon as we were through, he closed it and returned to his post.

"Just what does your aunt do? Is she part of the Mafia or something?" I asked as we made our way up the rest of the driveway.

She giggled. "No, definitely not Mafia. My uncle was heavy into real estate and the stock market before he died. He handled his money wisely and left my aunt millions."

"Wow, I'm impressed," I said as we pulled up in front of the mansion. It was a three-story adobe-style home with red Spanish tiles. The driveway looped around in front of it and a fountain sat in the center.

Chloe shut the car off just as two guys stepped out of the front door and made their way over to us. We got out and I grabbed the two suitcases she wanted to take inside, thankful that I wouldn't have to drag in the rest. As I closed the trunk, one of the guys ran to Chloe and picked her up to swing her around. She laughed as he set her back down and pulled her into a tight hug.

"Chloe Bear! You've been away too long, love!" he said as he released her and stepped back to look at her. "You've changed since the last time you were here. I don't see that gangly teenager I used to know anywhere. You look good!"

She smiled up at him. "I missed you too, Jordan. You've grown as well. I don't remember you being so tall, or having so many muscles."

My head shot up to take a closer look at this Jordan guy. From the warm welcome he had given her, I had assumed he was her cousin Danny. He was a big guy, probably around six feet, five inches, and built like a football player. His dark hair was cut short and he had a face I knew most girls would fall for. This was not something I'd expected. She had only mentioned him in passing, but I had pictured him as kind of geeky, not someone girls would be dropping their panties for.

My eyes fell on her cousin Danny as he pulled Chloe into a hug. Now that I looked, I could see the resemblance between him and Chloe. They had the same blond hair and blue eyes, but while Chloe was pale, this guy looked like he lived at the beach, which he probably did. He stood several inches shorter than Jordan and wasn't nearly as built.

Danny pulled back as Jordan caught sight of me. "Who's

your friend over there, Chloe?" he asked, and I didn't miss the emphasis he put on *friend*.

"This is my boyfriend, Drake. Drake, this is my cousin Danny, and that beast of a guy over there is Jordan."

I stepped forward and shook hands with both of them. Jordan seemed to be trying to break my hand when he shook it, but I didn't show any trace of pain. I wasn't about to let this guy get to me.

"Nice to meet you," he said as he dropped my hand. He looked me over before wrinkling his nose and turning to throw his arm over Chloe's shoulders. Yeah, I definitely didn't like this guy.

"Come on, Chloe Bear, Allison has dinner ready," he said as he led her toward the house.

Danny gave me an apologetic smile as we followed them inside.

I was blown away by the extravagance as we walked into the foyer. The floor was black marble, and a large crystal chandelier hung from the ceiling. The walls were covered in art, and a statue stood against the far wall between two staircases. After Chloe and I made a quick stop in the bathroom, we followed Danny and Jordan into the dining area and sat down together. Of course, Jordan took the seat on the other side of her as Danny sat down across from us.

The beautiful handcrafted table was covered with enough food for ten people, and a young woman wearing an apron was walking around the table, filling our glasses with some kind of expensive-looking wine. I felt completely out of place. I'd have rather been sitting at Gold's eating a burger and having a couple of beers.

Chloe gave me an apologetic smile as Jordan set a piece of

chicken on her plate. "Guys, this is way too much. You didn't have to go all dinner party on our behalf."

"It's no big deal. Your mom said you'd told her you would be here today, so I wanted to make sure you had enough to eat after such a long trip," Danny said as he grabbed a roll off the plate across from me.

Chloe's mouth turned down in a frown at the mention of her mother. "Where is she?"

"Out, as usual. She's been out partying almost every night. It's a relief to get her out of here, though. The woman is a nutcase," Jordan said through a mouthful of food.

Since he didn't seem to be worried about manners, I figured I didn't have to worry about them either. I grabbed the first thing I saw, which was some kind of fish, and started eating. I tried to keep my elbows off the table as I shoveled the food in, hoping to look somewhat civilized.

"How bad has she been?" Chloe asked.

Danny frowned. "The same as she always is. She's all rainbows and kittens when my mom is awake, but as soon as she's out of her sight, her inner bitch comes out full force. She tried to bring some guy here the other night, but Paul wouldn't let him past the gate."

"I'm sorry you have to deal with her, Danny. I plan on getting rid of her as soon as possible. How's Aunt Jen doing? Mom said she was bad."

"She is. She sleeps most of the time. I don't think she has much time left, Chloe; there's just no fight left in her. It kills me to see my mother, who was always so full of life, wasting away like this."

I saw tears in his eyes and looked away out of respect. I knew exactly how hard it was to lose your parents, but mine had died suddenly. I didn't have to watch them waste away like he did. Death was a cold-hearted bastard.

We finished dinner as Chloe caught up with Danny and Jordan. Danny wasn't the spoiled rich kid I had expected when I saw this place. Instead of staying home all day and spending his mommy's money, he was enrolled full-time at Baltimore University in pursuit of a teaching degree. Jordan was attending Baltimore as well on a full-ride football scholarship, which explained his bulk.

Danny seemed like a cool guy, but Jordan was another story. I caught him staring at Chloe several times in a way that made my blood boil. This guy was definitely an issue I intended to discuss with Chloe when we were alone. It was like watching Logan chase after her all over again.

When we finished dinner, I grabbed Chloe's bags as they led us up one of the staircases and showed us to our rooms.

Danny asked if we wanted two separate rooms and I smirked at Jordan. "No thanks, I'll keep her in my bed like I always do."

Jordan's nostrils flared, but he remained silent.

Take that, fucker, I thought to myself.

Danny seemed unaware of the staring competition going on between Jordan and me as he continued. "Fair enough, you guys can have this room here. If you need anything, just let me know. Chloe knows where my room is."

"Thanks, Danny. Will I be able to see Aunt Jen tonight or should we wait until morning?" Chloe asked.

"She won't wake up again tonight and she'll probably sleep until later in the day tomorrow, but you can see her as soon as she's up. She'll be glad you're here—she's been asking for you. We can go to the beach tomorrow to pass the time if you want, but we need to go early to avoid most of the tourists."

"That sounds fun, but I didn't bring my swimsuit with me," Chloe said, sounding disappointed.

Jordan spoke up. "No problem—I'll pick one up for you on my way here tomorrow."

I didn't like the sound of that and I started to speak up to tell him so, but Chloe was agreeing before I had the chance. "That would be great, Jordan. Thank you so much."

We told them good night as we stepped into the room and closed the door behind us. I set Chloe's bags by the dresser and she started digging through one to find something to sleep in.

I walked up behind her and wrapped my arms around her, pulling her body tight against mine. "Just sleep naked—it's more fun that way."

She aimed an elbow toward my ribs, but I stepped out of reach. "Not funny. What if someone walked in with me like that!"

I pulled her to me and kissed her. "Good point, but it doesn't change the fact I want to get you naked."

"You always want me naked, but that doesn't mean it's going to happen. Danny is right down the hall and I'm sure Jordan is with him. They could hear us."

I nuzzled her neck. "So, let them. Jordan needs to know you're taken so he'll back off."

She pushed me back gently. "Don't worry about Jordan; that's just how he is. I only have eyes for you, but that doesn't mean I'm going to have wild, crazy monkey sex with you when my cousin is down the hall."

I groaned as I fell onto the bed. "Fine, but I still don't like the way that guy looks at you. You need to tell him to back off. I don't feel comfortable leaving you here with him by yourself."

She rolled her eyes as she climbed on top of me. "Babe, seriously, Jordan won't be a problem, but I'll talk to him if it makes you feel better."

"Yeah, it would. Now get changed so we can go to bed. I'm beat from the drive here."

She kissed me before standing and changing into her pajamas. She stashed her dirty clothes back into her bag before lying down on the bed. How I hated those pajamas of hers: they were long pants and a shirt, which completely ruined my bedroom view. I preferred her naked.

I sighed as I stood and slipped on a pair of shorts from my bag. I threw my shirt and pants into the empty bag I had brought and lay down next to her, wrapping my arms around her as she snuggled into my chest.

"Night, Drake, love you."

"Love you too, babe."

CHAPTER THREE

CHLOE

I woke to the sound of someone beating on the bedroom door. I groaned as I looked at the clock and saw it was barely past five in the morning. Drake's arms and legs were wrapped around me, holding me prisoner, and he grunted as I untangled myself from him and walked to the door. Jordan was standing there when I opened it, a smile on his face.

"It's entirely too early to be up. What do you want?" I croaked out.

He handed me the bag he was holding. "You said you wanted to go to the beach. It's always packed by seven, so we need to get out of here if you want to avoid the crowds."

"Are you serious—right now? The seagulls aren't even up yet!"

"Quit whining and get dressed. We'll meet you guys downstairs in fifteen minutes," he said as he looked me over. "And Chloe? You look even sexier than normal when you wake up in the morning."

With that, he turned and left, leaving me to glare at his back. I turned to see Drake watching me through heavily lidded eyes. "What did *he* want?"

"Apparently we are leaving to go to the beach in fifteen minutes. Get dressed," I said as I reached into the bag and pulled out the bathing suit Jordan had picked up for me. I held it up in front of me as Drake made a hissing noise. I looked up to see him glaring at the bikini in my hands.

"You've got to be kidding me! You're not wearing that out in public, especially not around *him*."

I held the suit out and inspected it closer. It really was kind of skimpy, so I understood where Drake was coming from. It was a bright red string bikini, and I knew I'd be showing more skin than I ever did. But I didn't want to insult Jordan by not wearing it and ruin everyone's beach day.

"I have to wear it, Drake—it'll make Jordan feel bad if I don't. The top isn't that bad, and I'll just wear a pair of shorts unless I'm in the water."

He growled as he grabbed my pillow and pulled it over his head. I could hear him yelling something, but the pillow muffled it too much for me to hear exactly what he was saying. I got the gist of it, though, and I walked over to the bed and jumped on top of him.

I removed the pillow from his face and leaned down to pepper his face with kisses. "Don't be mad, okay? It's fine."

"I'm telling you right now, if he tries something I'm going to beat his ass. I'm giving you fair warning," he grumbled as he rolled away from me.

"Fair enough. Now get dressed."

We dressed quickly and were downstairs waiting when Danny and Jordan appeared at the top of the stairs. Jordan's eyes bulged out of his head when he caught sight of me, and I crossed my arms over my chest, trying to cover myself as much as possible. Maybe Drake had been right about this not being such a good idea. I had a soft spot for Jordan, but I definitely didn't want to give him the wrong idea.

"I take back what I said earlier, Chloe Bear," he said as they reached us.

I gave him a confused look. "What are you talking about?"

"I said you looked sexier in the mornings—well, I take it back. You in a bikini tops it all."

I felt Drake tense beside me and I spoke up before he decided to attack him. "Stop flirting, Jordan—it doesn't work with me. I know you too well."

He glanced at Drake and smirked. "It sure used to."

Drake's eyes narrowed and he opened his mouth to speak, but Danny cut in. "We should probably get going if we want to beat the traffic."

I grabbed Drake's hand and dragged him out the door. "Good idea."

The car ride was tense, to say the least. Drake was glaring holes into the back of Jordan's head as we made our way down the Ocean City Expressway. I squeezed his hand gently and gave him a small smile when he turned to look at me.

"I'll talk to him, Drake. He doesn't mean anything by it," I whispered as Danny parked the car.

We got out and grabbed our towels and a cooler out of the trunk and carried them to a secluded spot next to a cluster of rocks. I spread my towel out in the sand and Drake spread his next to mine. The sun was just starting to peek over the horizon. The sky was that beautiful red color you can only get at sunrise or sunset, and I settled down on my towel to enjoy the spectacular view.

The beach was mostly empty, with only a few groups of people making their way down to stake out their spot for the day. Danny and Jordan had brought folding chairs and set them up next to our towels. I watched Danny as he settled into his chair and grabbed a soda from the cooler. My heart broke as I saw the sorrow in his eyes.

My cousin didn't deserve the pain he had to endure as he watched his mother slowly die right before his eyes. My mother being around certainly wasn't making things any easier for him, either. He had enough to deal with, without having to put up with her, and I intended to take care of that problem quickly. I knew there would be retribution for my actions, but I didn't care. She was a bother to everyone involved and the sooner she left, the better.

I looked at Drake as he tugged on my hand. "Come swim with me?" he asked.

I nodded as I stood and took my shorts off. I left them lying on my towel as he led me down the beach to the water's edge.

I stuck my toes in and shivered. "It's freezing."

"It's not that bad. Come on, get in with me." He gave me a pleading look as I slowly stepped into the cold water.

"You're a nutcase; I'm going to turn blue."

"No, you won't—you'll adjust to the temperature." He grabbed me and pulled me to him as we went deeper. "But until then, I'll keep you warm."

I giggled as he leaned down and kissed me. I felt him pulling me deeper into the water as he prolonged the kiss, but it barely registered in my mind. I moaned as he slipped his tongue past my lips and caressed mine. My hands went around his neck as he grabbed my bottom and lifted me up out of the water so that he had easier access.

I pulled back as I realized he had taken us a good distance from where Danny and Jordan sat. He continued to pull me farther out as we drifted closer to a cluster of jutting rocks. When we reached them, I looked back to see that we were almost completely hidden from Danny and Jordan.

Drake sat me on one of the smaller rocks and pulled my face to his. "I've been waiting to get you alone since I saw you in that bikini. You have no idea how hard you've got me just by wearing that."

I felt heat pool between my legs at his words. I reached down between us and cupped him through his swim trunks. He wasn't kidding; even in the cold water he was as hard as a rock. He moaned as I squeezed him gently. I tugged on the tie of his trunks and slid my hand inside once they were loosened. He was scalding hot compared to the water we were in.

I started stroking him and he groaned.

"Ah, baby, you're killing me." He rested his head against my shoulder as I continued to stroke him, his breathing uneven.

He pulled my hand out and grinned at me. "You're not the only one who gets to play."

With that, he slid my bikini bottom to the side and started rubbing my clit, gently at first, but at each little sound I made he started rubbing harder with his thumb as he slid two fingers inside of me. My head fell back and I clutched his shoulders to keep myself upright. I felt the sensation building as he continued to thrust his fingers, but he stopped before I could climax.

"Drake, don't stop—that's just cruel."

"I'm not letting you get off that easy," he said as he pulled his swim trunks down and grabbed me around the waist to pull me into the water with him.

"What are you doing?"

"You said we couldn't fuck in your aunt's house; you didn't say anything about out here."

"We can't! What if someone sees us?" I asked as I glanced up at Danny and Jordan in the distance.

"No one will see us out here. We're too far away, and the rocks have us hidden for the most part."

Before I could protest any more, he pushed my bottoms to the side and was inside me with one hard thrust. I moaned as I felt him stretch and fill me. He started thrusting, slowly at first, barely moving his hips, but the friction was enough to drive me wild.

"Go faster, Drake!"

He obliged and started thrusting harder as I clung to him. The water hid most of our movements, but the yell I let loose as I came couldn't be denied. I prayed that we were far enough from the beach for anyone to hear us. He groaned as he came, then laid his head on my shoulder again.

We took a minute to control our breathing before either of us spoke. "That never gets old, Chloe. I could have sex with you all day and never get tired of it."

I kissed him briefly as he slipped out of me and set me back on the rock. "Glad to hear it. I don't want you falling for any of those groupies you love so much when I'm not around."

He kissed my nose as he looked up at me. "Those girls have nothing on you, so don't worry about that. No one will ever replace you."

We had never really discussed all the girls he had been with, and I wanted to keep it that way. I was afraid that if we did, all of my insecurities would come to the surface and I wouldn't let him leave me here. I trusted Drake—he had never given me any reason not to—but the thought of hundreds of women far prettier than I was throwing themselves at him scared me. I had found my one true love, I was sure of it, and I didn't want to give him up to anyone.

"Come on, we'd better get back before they start looking for us," he said as he helped me off the rock and back to the beach.

We stepped out of the water hand in hand and made our way back up the beach to Danny and Jordan. I noticed Jordan watching us as we sat down on our towels, but I ignored him. If I looked at Danny or him, I knew I would blush furiously.

The sun had fully risen by now, and I stretched out on my towel to try to get a tan as I closed my eyes. With my pale skin, I knew it was useless, but I was determined to try.

Jordan snorted, and I opened my eyes to look at him. "You guys are so obvious."

I felt my face warm at the knowing look he was giving me. "I have no idea what you're talking about."

"Sure you don't. You and Drake didn't just have sex out by the rocks. I was watching you."

Drake spoke up from beside me. "I don't see how it's any of your business, and I have no idea why you would be watching us if we were."

"What do you mean 'if'? Chloe has that 'I just got laid' look all over her face. I know it well. Tell me, Chloe, what is it about you and sex on this beach?"

I felt the color drain out of my face as he spoke. He was purposely trying to push Drake over the edge.

"What's he talking about, Chloe?" Drake asked in a strained voice.

"You mean she didn't tell you? I took her virginity on this same beach, just past those rocks. I have to say, for her first time, she knew what she was doing."

I scrambled up off my towel and grabbed Drake as he stood and started walking toward Jordan. "Drake, stop! Jordan, that's enough, okay? Stop being an asshole!"

Drake was out for blood, though, and he ignored me as he pushed past me to get to Jordan. Danny, who had been quiet through all of this, jumped out of his chair and grabbed Drake.

"Enough of this bullshit, guys. My mother is fucking dying and you two are out here fighting about something that happened years ago." He pointed at Jordan. "Stop trying to bring stuff up just to get him pissed. And stop hitting on Chloe! I don't know what your problem is, but deal with it."

As Danny finished his rant, Drake stopped struggling and turned to walk down the beach.

I watched him go before turning to Jordan. "What the hell was that, Jordan? I thought you were better than that!" I shouted at him.

"That guy's an asshole, Chloe. I don't know what you see in him."

"He is not an asshole! He's my boyfriend, and he doesn't need to hear that kind of crap. I don't know what's going through that head of yours but you need to stop. I'm with him and it's going to stay that way. If you can't handle it, then just leave me alone."

I turned and started chasing after Drake. He was a good distance away by now, but I ran and caught up with him quickly. As I reached him, I threw my arms around him. "Drake, stop, please! I'm sorry he was such a jerk. It won't happen again."

He stopped and turned to face me. "It drives me nuts to think of you with other guys, Chloe. It nearly killed me with Logan, and now I get to look at that douche bag and know he's been with you too! How many guys have you been with?"

I stepped back as he directed his anger at me. "Just him and Logan, I swear. I didn't want to tell you because I knew you'd be angry. It was a long time ago, and I never thought he would bring it up!"

"Well, he did, didn't he? He obviously still wants you and I'm not going through the same thing that happened with Logan. You tell him to back off or I'm out of here right now!"

My heart seemed to stop beating as I listened to his threats. "Drake, I just told him to back off. I don't want anyone but you. How could you even think that, or give up on us so easily?"

"I'm not giving up, I'm just pissed off, okay?" He pulled me to him and hugged me tightly. "I love you, Chloe, and when I see other guys looking at you, it drives me nuts. You're mine now."

"How do you think I feel watching those girls at the bar trying to get your attention? This doesn't even compare to watching that."

"Chloe, those girls don't even register with me anymore. When I'm up there singing, you're the only girl in the room that I even notice. They can try all they want, but I would never even look at them when I have you."

"That means a lot to me, Drake. I love you so much."

"I love you too. Am I forgiven for being the biggest asshole on Earth?"

"Of course—I'm used to you being that way," I said as he smacked me on my bottom.

"Good to know. Come on, let's head back. I promise not to kill that guy."

We made our way back to Danny and Jordan as they finished packing up our stuff.

Jordan looked up as we approached. "Sorry, Chloe, I don't know what I was thinking, and I'm sorry, Drake. That was a douche move on my part. It won't happen again."

Drake only nodded as he grabbed our things and made his way back to the car. I knew he was still mad, but he was trying to control his anger for me, and I appreciated it. I avoided Jordan as we walked up the beach and barely spoke to him on the drive back to the house. The less time I spent with him, the better off we would all be.

I didn't want Drake leaving tomorrow thinking that he couldn't trust me to be alone while he was gone. I was determined to make up for the mistakes I had made with Logan, for ever putting that doubt in his mind to begin with.

As we pulled up to the house, I spotted my mother outside talking on her phone. I groaned as I stepped out of the car. I really didn't want to deal with her right now.

"I see you finally decided to grace us with your presence," she said as she ended her call and walked over to us.

"Yeah, I'm here. But that doesn't mean you have to speak to me. Actually, it would be great if you just ignored me."

"Not a chance, at least not when we're around Jen. You play the loving daughter and I'll keep my end of the deal. You'll never have to see me again," she said in a low voice so that none of the guys could hear.

"Hey, Chloe, I'm going to see if Mom's awake. If so, I'll come back to get you so she can see you," Danny said as he walked inside the house. Jordan, Drake, and I quickly followed him in hopes of avoiding my mother.

Danny made his way up the stairs as Jordan led us to the living room and sat down in a chair. Drake and I sat down together on the couch across from him as my mother entered the room behind us. I ignored her as she took the only empty seat left and started talking on her phone again.

I tried not to listen in, but with only a few feet separating us, it was hard to avoid overhearing her conversation. She was talking to one of her friends about some party they were going to tonight. My temper flared as I listened to her speak; her only sister was dying upstairs, and she was more worried about partying. My determination to make sure she left with nothing tripled.

Danny entered the room and motioned for me to follow him. I stood and walked to him as my mother ended her call and followed me.

"She's awake now and wants to see you. Try to keep it brief, though—she's tired and needs to rest."

I nodded as he took my hand and led me up the stairs to my aunt's room. He opened the door and we stepped inside. The blinds were drawn tight, leaving the room in almost complete darkness. The only light came from a bedside lamp, and I sucked in my breath as I caught sight of my aunt lying in her bed. It had been years since I had last seen her, and the frail woman lying there didn't even resemble the woman I once knew.

My aunt had always been so bright, radiating her happiness and vibrancy like the sun. The woman before me had none of that; her frail body had deteriorated into almost nothing. Her beautiful blond hair was gone from the chemo treatments; her skin was an ashy gray and hung from her body.

Tears filled my eyes at the sight and I leaned into Danny, barely able to stand. "I know, Chloe, I know. But we have to be strong for her, okay?" he said as he led me closer to the bed.

I glanced back at the door and noticed my mother standing there, watching us. There was no way I could talk to my aunt if she was in the room. I cast another glance at my aunt, unsure if I would even be able to discuss anything with her when she was in such a bad condition. I had to try, though; there was no way I was going to let my mother hurt her.

"Mom," Danny whispered from beside me, "you have a visitor. Chloe is here to see you."

At the sound of his voice, my aunt opened her eyes and gave us a weak smile. "Chloe, I wasn't sure you were going to make it in time. Come here, baby girl, and give me a hug."

I leaned down and gave her a light hug, afraid that I would break her. "Hi, Aunt Jen, I've missed you," I said as the tears I had tried to hold in started flowing freely down my cheeks.

"Danny, can you give us a moment? I want to talk to Chloe."

"Sure, Mom, I'll be back to check on you in a few. Your day nurse should be here shortly as well," he said as he bent down and kissed her on the cheek. His gaze found mine. "Remember, try to keep it short."

I nodded as I pulled a chair up to the bed and sat down. My mother drifted over to stand beside me and wrapped her arm around my shoulders. I cringed at the touch, remembering how many times those very hands had caused me so much harm. If she noticed my reaction, she didn't acknowledge it.

"I'm here too, Jen. How are you feeling today?" she asked in a soft voice I had rarely ever heard her use.

My aunt's eyes fell on her. "Andrea, what I need to say to Chloe needs to be said privately. You can come back and visit me after we're done."

I flinched as my mother's nails dug into my skin. "Are you sure? I don't want her staying too long and bothering you. I'd feel better if I were here."

I knew her game. She was afraid of what I would say if I was left alone with her sister. My mother might be a horrible person, but she wasn't stupid.

"I'll be fine, now go. I'll have her send you in once we're done."

My mother wasn't happy, but she nodded as she turned and left the room.

"Can you close the door for me, Chloe? Wandering ears, you know?" Aunt Jen asked.

"Of course," I said as I walked to the door. I caught sight of my mother standing just a few feet away as I shut the door. I knew she would be standing outside the door trying to listen as long as I was in this room.

"Is she still out there?"

I nodded as I sat back down. "Yes, of course. I don't think she trusts me to be alone with you."

"Of course she doesn't; she knows you'll tell me all the horrible things about her that she is trying so desperately to hide. I might be dying, but I'm not stupid."

"You're right, Aunt Jen; that's why I'm here. I can't let you give her anything. She's a horrible person and doesn't deserve any of it."

"I know what she is, Chloe, and don't you worry. She isn't getting a dime."

CHAPTER FOUR

DRAKE

Chloe was obviously not thinking clearly to leave Jordan and me alone in a room together after our little incident on the beach. I was still pissed over the whole ordeal, but I held my tongue as he grabbed the remote and started flipping through the channels. The television was a nice distraction; he stopped on a wrestling match and I kept my eyes glued to it.

I heard him sigh a couple of times, but I pretended not to notice as I waited for Chloe to reappear. I would leave him alone for Chloe's sake, but that didn't mean I was going to be his best buddy and sit down to have a chat with him.

We sat in silence as we watched the television for a few minutes before Jordan finally spoke. "All right, listen. I know I was an ass earlier, but I only did it to protect Chloe," he said as he turned the television off.

I took my eyes off the now black screen to stare at him. "Exactly how were you helping her by telling her boyfriend you took her virginity?" I asked, dumbfounded by his logic.

"Chloe is a sweet girl, but she's had a rough life and she's been hurt. I don't want to see her hurt anymore. I'm sure you're a nice guy and all, but let's be honest. You're not really the relationship type; even I can tell that after knowing you for less than a day. I see the way she looks at you—she loves you, and you're going to break her heart. I'd rather have you do it while I'm around so I can help her out."

"You have no idea what kind of person I am. No, I wasn't the relationship kind of guy before I met her, but I am now. She's important to me, and I'm not about to hurt her," I said as my temper started to flare.

Who did this guy think he was? I knew he thought he was trying to be the good guy by protecting her from me, but he had it all wrong. I would never hurt her—I'd die first. There was something about her that had drawn me in from the beginning and I knew that I loved her. One look from her and she had thrown my world completely upside down, but I was okay with that. I didn't need the world to be right side up if it meant she wasn't there with me.

"Maybe not, but you will. Guys like us always screw up in the end—we can't help ourselves," he said as he laid his head back against the chair.

"I hate to break it to you, but we're nothing alike."

"That's where you're wrong. Chloe mentioned you're in a band; being a football player has the same effect on women. They constantly throw themselves at you even if you try to ignore them. You and I both know you can only avoid the temptation for so long before you cave and break her heart."

"I have no problem ignoring them when I have Chloe in my bed every night." I felt triumphant as I saw his nostrils flare in anger. "You seem to be a little too interested in her to be sitting here admitting you'd screw up the first chance you had. If you think I'm the one who'd hurt her, maybe you should take a look at yourself."

His eyes narrowed. "That's where we're different: I know I'd screw up. That's why I have no intention of trying anything with her—I care about her too much. You're too blinded by her to realize what kind of person you are."

"Bullshit! You've been after her since the minute she got out of her car," I said.

"Not true. I've been trying to get rid of you from the minute I saw you, but apparently you don't give up that easily, so I thought I'd spell it out for you."

"Well, I'm not going anywhere, so you can forget it; I fought too hard to get her to let her go now. You and I, we're on the same side here—we're both trying to protect Chloe. So just let it go, okay? I'm not going to hurt her."

He seemed to consider my words. I hoped I was getting through to him; I didn't want to leave here worrying about whether or not he was trying something with her.

"I hope you're right, for your sake and hers. You break her heart and I'll break you."

I had to laugh at that. I wasn't a small guy by any means, but I had no doubt Jordan could break me in two if he wanted to. The guy was a beast and I felt no shame in admitting that. I might be cocky, but I wasn't stupid.

"I'll try to remember that. Just stop trying to hit on my girl every chance you get and we'll be cool," I said as I grinned.

I knew where he was coming from now and I truly appreciated it. He was only looking out for Chloe, and if he would back off, I might even like the guy.

"Fair enough," he said as Danny stepped into the room.

Alarms went off in my head when Chloe's mother didn't appear with him. There was no way I was going to leave Chloe alone with her, regardless of whether or not her aunt was with them.

"Where's Chloe's mom? Please tell me you didn't leave them alone together," I said.

He gave me a weak smile. "Nah. My mom kicked me out, but I hung around to make sure nothing went down. Apparently she kicked Andrea out as well, because she came storming out of the room. I have to say, the look on her when Chloe shut the door in her face was priceless. I thought she was going to throw something."

"Well, if she isn't with them, then where is she?" I asked.

"Last I saw, she was standing outside the door with her ear practically pressed up against it, trying to listen. She knows Chloe isn't going to put up with her shit and she's scared of what she might tell my mom."

I smiled as Danny sat down on the couch with me. It was good to know both he and Jordan were aware of what kind of person Andrea really was. If Chloe couldn't talk her aunt out of her decision to leave part of her money to Andrea, maybe they could. That way, Andrea's anger would be directed at them instead of Chloe. They seemed more than capable of handling her. I was still worried about leaving Chloe behind, though; she was obviously the easiest target if her mother decided to go on a rampage.

"I wanted to talk to you guys while Chloe isn't around." I glanced back and forth between them. "Chloe isn't here for the money; I'm sure you two have figured that out. She's planning on trying to convince her aunt to cut her mother out of her will. If she succeeds, we all know Andrea is going to go nuts. I don't want to leave her here by herself, but I have no other choice. I need to know that you two will protect her when her mother figures out what she has done. I'm hoping she'll be with me by then, but I know the chances are unlikely."

"I would think it would be kind of obvious that we'll both protect her," Jordan said.

"I know, but I needed to bring it to your attention. I don't want her left alone," I said as I looked at Danny.

"Of course not. I've known what kind of person my aunt is for a long time. We won't let Chloe out of our sight while Andrea is around. You have my word on that. Besides, I don't think my mom will need much convincing. She can barely stand to look at Andrea; she knows just what kind of person she is, no matter how hard she has tried to hide it."

I nodded. "Good to know. We all know the shit is going to hit the fan before this is all over with."

"I'll take care of Chloe, man, you don't have to worry," Jordan said as he looked at me. "It's good to know you worry about her that much, though."

"You have no idea just how much I worry about her," I said.

It felt like a weight had been lifted from my chest, knowing both of these guys would protect Chloe when I couldn't. I knew I would worry constantly until she was back by my side, but this helped to ease my fear a bit.

I stood and walked to the door. "I need a smoke. If Chloe gets back before I do, let her know where I am."

I stepped outside and shut the door behind me as I pulled a cigarette from my pack and lit it. As I inhaled deeply, I felt my body start to relax. There was too much drama and not enough nicotine in the world, if you asked me. Chloe was constantly on me to quit smoking and I had promised her I would. Which I would, when this whole screwed-up situation was over with . . . maybe. I wasn't sure if I could handle daily life without some nicotine in my system to keep me from ripping someone's head off.

I made my way across the grass and around the side of the house. I had never seen more than the front of the property and I was curious as to what they had hidden away in the back. As I stepped into the backyard, my mouth fell open. Calling this a backyard would be disrespectful; it was more like a massive sports arena.

Directly behind the house was a massive in-ground pool that took up the entire length of the house. It was equipped with two diving boards and a small water slide. Next to it was a hot tub big enough to swim in, and beyond that a full tennis and basketball court stood. I walked to the edge of the pool and stared down into the crystal-clear water as I finished my cigarette.

I decided going for a swim might help calm my mind, so I ran back around to the front of the house and grabbed my still damp swim trunks out of Danny's car. There was a small changing stall next to the pool, so I used it to quickly strip out of my clothes and pulled on my swim trunks. I threw my clothes on a chair by the pool as I walked to the taller of the two ladders and started to climb.

When I reached the top, I stepped onto the board and stood at the edge. Heights were never my thing, and I hesitated for a split second before taking the plunge. I felt the warm water already starting to relax my tense muscles as I kicked my way to the surface. I might not like heights, but swimming was something that I loved, something that I excelled at.

When I was six or seven, my dad bought me one of those generic four-foot-deep pools you saw in almost every yard and had taught me how to swim. He had even built a deck around it so that my mom could lie in the chair and watch us as she read her book.

I smiled at the memory of her yelling at us when we would splash water at her and soak whatever book had her enthralled that day. I remembered laughing as my dad would get out of the pool and grab her, throwing her into the water while she kicked and screamed at us. They were always like that: playful with each other, so full of love. I had spent so many summers with them in that pool or helping Dad as he barbecued for his weekly neighborhood parties.

When they died and I moved in with my uncle, I remember missing our pool and those warm summer nights together. It had taken me years to be able to even stand near a pool, let alone get in one. I finally took the plunge the day after I was released from rehab. I went to the city pool and stayed all day, working up the nerve to face my fears. It was one of the hardest things I had ever done, but I did it. For some reason, stepping into the water that day made me feel free, and I started to wonder if maybe my life wouldn't always hold so much pain if I could just find the courage to let it all go.

Losing my parents at such a young age had completely destroyed me for a long time. Even after I had accepted the fact that they were gone, it hurt so much to think about them that it was hard to breathe at times. But I was learning to live again, thanks to Chloe, even if I was a decade late getting started. She was my newest coping mechanism, and by far the healthiest. With Chloe, I felt alive again for the first time in so long.

I knew using women the way I had was horrible, and I was ashamed as I realized I didn't even know how many there had been. I prayed that Chloe never asked me for the specifics; I didn't think I could stand to see the disappointment in her eyes. I had been angry with her only hours before over being her third, and here I couldn't even give her a number if she asked.

As bad as the women were, the drugs were ten times worse. It had started out innocently enough. My uncle was rarely home to supervise me and I started hanging out with the wrong crowd, as clichéd as that sounds. We would hang around after school, lighting up a bowl and playing video games.

As I got older and started hanging out with a rougher crowd, weed had progressed to pills, and then to harder drugs like cocaine, acid, and heroin. The highs were amazing but always ended too quickly, and I was back to feeling every emotion I was trying to numb. I started using more and selling to pay for my habit so that my uncle wouldn't catch on.

Everything came crashing down around me when I was busted with weed. The fact that I didn't have anything else on me at the time was the only saving grace. Naturally, my uncle was called and went shit-ass crazy on me, not that I could blame him. One week later, I was checking into rehab with orders to get clean or get out. I had hated him at the time, but I knew now that he had saved my life, and I would always be grateful to him for stepping in and caring enough about me to do something. If he hadn't stepped in when he did, I would be dead or in jail by now.

I had been clean for almost four years now, but I still missed the drugs at times. When things got tough in life, my first instinct was to light up and send myself into a peaceful oblivion. Not that I would ever admit to that out loud; if Chloe ever found out that little tidbit of information I knew she'd leave me in a heartbeat. Living with her mother, she had dealt with drugs and alcohol her entire life, and I wasn't about to let it happen again.

It still seemed surreal to me even after three months of being together that she was finally mine. I knew I didn't deserve someone like her, but I sure as hell wasn't giving her up. I was too damn selfish for that. I wasn't sure what I had done in life to find someone like Chloe, but I wasn't about to start asking questions; I just thanked my lucky stars.

I made a few more laps across the pool before making my way to the side and lifting myself out of the water. Swimming really had helped calm me, and I felt relaxed for the first time in days. Sure, we were far from done with her mother and I would be leaving tomorrow, but I knew Jordan and Danny would protect Chloe while we were apart.

I quickly changed back into my clothes and laid my swim trunks out by the pool to dry before making my way back around to the front of the house. Just as I reached the front door, it opened and Andrea came storming out. She completely ignored me as she made her way past me and down the blacktop to her car. She jumped into the car and was gone in the blink of an eye. I shook my head as I watched her speed down the rest of the driveway once she made it past the gate.

I stepped inside to see Danny and Jordan still sitting in the same spots as when I had left them. I took a seat on the couch and turned to Danny. "What was that all about?"

"What? You mean Andrea storming out of here?" he asked.

"Yeah, she almost ran me over trying to get out the door. She looked pissed."

Jordan gave me an easy grin. "That might have been my fault. I kind of got her stirred up. She came in here to complain to us about Jen kicking her out so she could talk to Chloe. Said how unfair it was since she'd brought Chloe here. I kindly told her to go fuck herself."

I laughed. "Nice. It's a shame that I missed that show."

"Yeah, it is. That woman is insane! Wait until I tell Chloe—she'll get a kick out of it!" Jordan said as he continued to grin.

"I'll get a kick out of what, Jordan?" Chloe asked from the doorway.

I jumped at the sound of her voice and turned to look at her. She was grinning from ear to ear, and I took that as a good sign.

"I take it everything went well?" I asked.

She made her way over to me and kissed me on the lips with enough fire to make my dick twitch.

"Oh, it went better than well. I'd say 'perfect' is a better description. Everything is going to be taken care of."

I smiled up at her; it felt like things might finally start falling into place for us after all.

CHAPTER FIVE

CHLOE

I looked down at my aunt in total confusion; if she wasn't planning on sharing any of her wealth with my mom, then why was my mom under the impression that she would be getting her share? I knew my mom wasn't lying to me, because she wouldn't have tracked me down the way she had if she wasn't getting something from it.

"Aunt Jen, I'm confused. My mom told me you were leaving both of us a large amount of money."

She sighed. "Of course she did—that's what I told her. It was the only way I knew she'd look for you. I have so many regrets when it comes to you, and I had to find you before it was too late."

"Wait—I'm confused. If you're not giving us money, then why did you want me here?"

Her words had blown me away; I had this whole speech about why she shouldn't give my mother anything, and here she was telling me it was all a ruse. And what regrets could she possibly be talking about? Sure, I hadn't been around my aunt much, but when I was she had always been kind to me, even letting me stay with her for a while after my mother left that summer.

"Chloe, I've never done right by you. I knew what your mother was like and I never once stepped in to protect you. She would come here from time to time, asking for money to help buy you things, but in my heart I knew you'd never see a dime of it. I just kept hoping that she would change her ways and be the kind of mother you deserved. That summer you came with her I was so excited to see you both together. I thought maybe things were starting to look up for the two of you, but you looked so skinny and I could see the pain hiding behind your eyes. I thought it was strange how you kept yourself covered up all the time, but when you wore shorts that day and I saw the fading bruises you didn't think anyone would notice, I went crazy on your mother. I told her to get out and that I never wanted to see her again. Naturally, she left and didn't bother to take you with her. You seemed so happy to be here with us, and I wanted you to stay, but I knew you missed your home and your friends. I didn't want to take you away from the life you had built for yourself, so I helped you get home, thinking I was doing the right thing."

Tears welled up in my eyes. "Oh, Aunt Jen, don't ever think any of this was your fault. You barely knew me and I'm not your responsibility. I did fine on my own once she was gone, and I'm happy now. I really am."

"It doesn't matter; I still should have taken care of you. Right after you left, my doctor found the cancer and I spent all my time in treatments. After a few months, we thought we had it beat and I went into remission. I had so much to deal with, but I never forgot about you. The only thing I knew for sure was that you were in West Virginia, but your mother would never tell me where exactly. I searched for you for months, but your mom had nothing to her name—no taxes, utilities, insurance—nothing that I could use to track you down with."

I didn't know what to say; knowing that I was living all those years being abused by my mom when I had someone out there who cared enough to search for me was mind-blowing.

My aunt cleared her throat before continuing. "About a year ago, the cancer came back with a vengeance. We tried everything, but nothing helped, and I have accepted my fate. But I knew I had to find you before it was too late. Luck was with me when Andrea showed up on my doorstep a few months ago and started playing the loving sister when I told her I would be leaving part of my fortune to her. When I explained she wouldn't get anything unless I found you, she put all of her time and energy into locating you, not knowing she was sealing her own fate."

I couldn't help but laugh at my aunt's words. "I never would have guessed you were the manipulative type. I'm not sure whether to be proud or ashamed."

She started laughing, but it quickly turned into a coughing fit. I grabbed a cup of water from her bedside table and held it to her while she sipped from the straw. Talking with me was making her weaker, and I felt ashamed.

"Why don't you rest and we can talk about this later?" I asked as I set the cup back on the table for her.

"No, I'm fine. I don't know how much time I have left and I need to say what you came all this way to hear. I've already set up an account with over six hundred thousand dollars in it with your name on it. Your mother thinks she is getting the same amount, and hopefully she won't realize she's been tricked until I've passed and you're long gone. I worry about her reaction to all of this; I want you to disappear for a while once you leave here. I can't stand the thought of her hurting you over me, but I had to do this for you. I had to make up for my wrongs, Chloe."

I shook my head. "I don't want your money, Aunt Jen. I just came here to stop you from giving anything to her. Give mine to Jordan—he deserves it more than I do. He's always been here with you. He's practically your son too."

She frowned. "Nonsense, you're going to take that money if I have to force Danny to make you take it. I don't care what you do with it; pay for your college education, buy a car, a house. It doesn't matter; just never let her have a dime of it."

I leaned down and hugged her frail body. No one had ever shown this degree of kindness and I didn't know what to say, how to thank her. Here she was, on her deathbed, and she was more concerned with my welfare than her own.

"Thank you, thank you so much. I don't even know what to say," I whispered in her ear as I pulled away.

"You don't have to say anything. Just do one favor for me and we'll call it even," she said.

"Of course, I'll do anything you need, anything at all."

"I know you will; you've always been such a good girl. I want you to help Danny when I'm gone. He's taking this so hard and I don't want him to be alone. I know that he has Jordan, but he needs family. The sharks in the water will be circling the minute I'm gone, and I don't want anyone to take advantage of my baby."

"I'll stay with him for a couple of weeks, I promise. Danny has a good heart; I won't let anything happen to him."

"Thank you. You'd better go before your mother tears down the door. Make sure to come back and visit me when you get a chance, but try to keep Danny occupied as much as you can," she said as she was lost to another coughing fit.

"I will. I love you, Aunt Jen."

"Love you too, sweetheart."

I made sure she was comfortable and helped her with another drink before leaving the room. I glanced around the hallway, but my mother was nowhere to be seen. I breathed a sigh of relief, knowing that I wouldn't have to deal with her.

I smiled as I realized that my mother had been duped by not only me, but my aunt as well. Things were going to turn ugly when she found out, but I wasn't worried. I had Drake, Danny, and Jordan to protect me, as well as Logan once we were back at school. I wasn't the type to ask for help from others, but I knew I needed it when it came to her. She would be mad enough to physically hurt me if she got the chance, and if she had any of her friends with her at the time, things would go from bad to worse.

Just as I made it to the top of the stairs, I saw my mother leaving and then Drake coming through the door just seconds later. I stopped and took a minute to look at him. He must have found the pool, because his hair was dripping wet and hanging down into his eyes as he walked from the door to the room I'd left him and Jordan in earlier.

He was absolutely stunning, no doubt about, it and I started to imagine myself running my hands through his wet hair. The mere thought of touching him had me excited, but I quickly pushed it away. If I didn't, I would walk into that room and tackle him while Danny and Jordan watched. While he might enjoy it, I wasn't sure I could say the same for the other two.

I took my time walking down the stairs, trying to calm myself from my previous thoughts. When I reached the doorway, I stopped at the sound of Drake and Jordan laughing. While they had both agreed to try to get along, I had never expected them to be sitting together and laughing just a few hours after their fight.

"Nice. It's a shame that I missed that show," I heard Drake say.

"Yeah, it is. That woman is insane! Wait until I tell Chloe— she'll get a kick out of it!" Jordan said.

"I'll get a kick out of what, Jordan?" I asked as I came around the corner and into the room.

Three pairs of amused eyes fell on me. I was surprised to see just how happy Drake looked.

"I take it everything went well?" he asked.

I made my way over to him and kissed him on the lips, letting all of my desire flow into the kiss.

"Oh, it went better than well. I'd say 'perfect' is a better description. Everything is going to be taken care of," I said as Drake broke out into a grin.

"Glad to hear it, babe," he said as he pulled me into his lap.

"So what was everyone laughing about when I came in?" I asked.

Jordan started laughing again. "Nothing much. I told your mom to fuck off, but she didn't take it very well."

I had to laugh at the expression on his face; he looked like a kid who'd just been told Christmas was coming early. "And why did you do that? Was she bothering you guys again?"

"Nah, just bitching because Jen kicked her out of the room. I think I made her mad, so she took off. The way I see it, it was a two-for-one special. I told her off and she left; can't beat those odds."

"You're horrible, Jordan, but I love it," I said as I settled back against Drake's chest.

We sat and hung out for a while, talking and watching

television. Even though I was heartbroken over my aunt's deteriorating condition, I felt happy, the happiest I had since before my mother found me and offered this ridiculous proposition. Things were far from over, but I felt that they might actually work out in my favor now that I had talked to my aunt.

As Drake and I sat together on the couch, I felt his hands start roaming under my shirt, across my stomach, my ribs, and my hips. I relaxed back into him and let his hands take over, calming me. I hated that he would be leaving tomorrow and since I had agreed to stay with Danny until everything was settled, I knew it would be at least a few weeks until we were together again. That thought dropped my spirits a bit and Drake must have felt my body tense up.

He leaned forward and whispered in my ear as he continued to rub my stomach. "You all right, baby?"

His breath tickled and I shivered. "I'm fine, just thinking about stuff."

He nodded. "Want to go take a walk with me?"

I turned and raised my eyebrows at him. From the expression on my face, he knew what I thought he was hoping for.

"I didn't mean *that* kind of walk, unless you're up for that. If you are, I'm definitely talking about that kind of walk," he said with a devilish smile.

I elbowed him in the ribs as I stood. "I'll take a walk, but that's all you're getting, buddy." I turned my attention to Danny and Jordan. "We're going for a walk. We shouldn't be gone long."

"She's lying—it could be a while, so don't wait up for us," Drake said as he took my hand and led me toward the door.

I saw Jordan frown and roll his eyes, but thankfully, he said nothing.

Once we were outside, Drake pulled me to him and kissed me deeply. His tongue traced my bottom lip and I moaned at the sensation.

I pushed him back and grinned. "I told you it wasn't that kind of walk."

"Can't blame a guy for trying, can you? Let's walk around back; they have a killer pool in the backyard."

I couldn't deny that; my aunt's pool put ordinary pools to shame. As we rounded the corner of the house, I took in just how vast it really was. I still had my bikini on under my clothes, so I stripped off my shirt and shorts and ran to the edge of the pool before glancing back at Drake. "Want to go for a swim?"

He laughed as he started walking to the changing station. "You go ahead. I think I'll just admire the view for a while."

I rolled my eyes as I turned back toward the pool and dove in. The water felt warm yet refreshing, and I relished the sensations as they rippled across my skin. There was something about the water that just calmed and centered me, much like our spot at the Cheat Lake back in West Virginia. My head broke through the surface to see Drake standing by the edge, watching me with an evil glint in his eyes.

"Drake, what are you up to?" I asked with suspicion.

He simply smiled at me as he took a few steps back to get a running start before jumping into the pool next to me. I squealed and tried to get away as the water from his cannonball hit me.

He surfaced quickly and started laughing at me. "What's your problem? You're already wet anyway!"

I splashed water at him as I made my escape. "Still, you didn't have to splash me, you idiot!" I shrieked.

He laughed as he lunged for me. I almost escaped, but he

caught my ankle at the last minute and pulled me back to him. I thrashed around but it was useless; I was no match.

"Just where do you think you're going?" he asked as he fought to hold on to me.

"Nowhere, apparently; you're holding me prisoner," I said as I stopped struggling and let him pull me back.

He pulled me up tight against him and kissed me softly. "I like seeing you happy and smiling. Worried doesn't suit you, baby."

"I'm sorry I've been such a downer. I've been so focused on this whole mess, we haven't even celebrated your tour. Why don't we go out tonight and have dinner somewhere, just the two of us, to celebrate? My treat," I said as he kissed the tip of my nose and let me go.

"That sounds like a plan. I'd like to spend some time with you before I leave tomorrow. I need to call Jade and the guys to make sure they remember to pick me up. My luck, Adam will be driving and completely forget about me."

I giggled as I pictured Adam doing just that. "Jade and Eric will keep him in line. Besides, they won't get very far without their lead singer."

"Good point. I still wish you were going with me tomorrow, though. I hate leaving you here like this—it's my job to protect you," he said as a frown darkened his beautiful features.

I lifted my hand and ran it down his cheek. He caught it and brought it to his lips to kiss. "Don't worry about me—Danny and Jordan will be here with me. They won't let me out of their sight."

"Still doesn't mean I won't worry about you." After a pause, he said, "Jordan and I had a little talk while you were with your aunt. I think we've got things figured out between us."

I raised an eyebrow. "Really? Was all that laughing I heard actually male bonding?"

He laughed. "I wouldn't go that far, but we have an understanding, I guess you could say. And I made sure that he and Danny will be around you all the time. I just hope you only have to spend a few more days here. I'm going to go insane without you around."

I pretended to find the water very interesting so that I didn't have to meet his gaze. I wasn't looking forward to telling him that I wouldn't be with him for a few weeks.

"Uh-oh, it's never good when you do that. What's up?" he asked as he pulled my face up to look at him.

I bit my lip as I debated how to tell him without making him angry. "Well, see, the thing is, I told my aunt I would stay for a few weeks."

"Any particular reason why you did that?" he asked in a too calm voice.

"Don't be mad, please. We were talking about everything and she asked me to stay for a little while to help Danny. She's afraid of how he'll be after she's gone and she wants me to help him any way I can. I told her I would—it's the least I can do."

He groaned as he ran his hands through his hair; his one tell when he was upset. "I don't mean to sound like an ass here, but exactly why do you think you owe her? I mean, you haven't told me anything that was said while you were up there and I'm trying to understand here, I really am, but it doesn't make sense. You were anxious to get out of here."

"I was, but we talked. She isn't leaving my mom anything; she only told her that so she could find me to talk to me before it was too late. I told her I didn't want the money, but she's adamant that I take it and I couldn't refuse her one request. She's dying, Drake—it's the least I could do."

"I just . . . Chloe, I don't want to be away from you that long. You said it would only be a couple of days at most, and now you're telling me weeks. Can you understand why I'm a little upset over all of this?" he asked as he gave me a pleading look.

"I know, and I'm sorry, but I've got to do this. I promise I will leave the first chance I get. I don't want to be away from you any longer than I have to be," I said as I stepped forward and brushed my lips against his.

"This really sucks. You know that, right?"

"I know, but we'll talk every day, I promise. It's going to be hard, but we can do it."

He pulled me into a hug and I rested my head against his chest. It was going to be so hard being apart from each other, but I knew we could handle it, just like we had handled everything else that had been thrown at us. I knew he wouldn't give up on me over something as silly as my staying here for just a few weeks.

He sighed as he rested his chin on the top of my head. "Yeah, we can, but you'd better call me every day and let me know that you're safe, okay?"

"You know I will. I couldn't stand to be away from you that long without annoying you daily. Call me clingy."

"I don't mind clingy; it just means you care." He kissed my hair as he pulled away. "Come on, let's get out of here and go out to dinner like you promised. You're buying, remember?"

"Sounds good to me, but I need to call Amber before we head out. I haven't talked to her since we left and she's going to call and yell at me if I don't."

He pulled himself out of the pool, and I had to close my mouth as I stared at the hard muscles of his arms and abs as they tightened with the effort. He turned to help me out of the water, but he stopped when he saw the desire flash in my eyes. His own eyes turned dark as he watched me, and it took everything I had to control my breathing. He could knock the breath out of me with one look.

"Or maybe you'd rather just stay in tonight? I think I like that idea better," he said as he watched me.

I shook my head to clear the lust-filled thoughts swirling within. "We can't. Now go call the band before I change my mind."

He slipped back into the water and I groaned. "Drake, we can't—now *go*."

He approached me slowly, like a tiger on the prowl, and I prepared myself for his attack. He was on me within seconds and had me pinned to the side of the pool.

"I really like the staying-here idea," he whispered as he traced my jaw with his tongue.

"No, please don't. If you start I'm not going to stop you and I'll feel horrible afterward," I pleaded as he bent his head and ran his tongue across the swell of my breasts.

"You're killing me right now, Chloe. I'm never going to be able to have kids if you keep this up," he groaned.

His words surprised me and I pulled back. "Do you want kids?"

He seemed shocked by my sudden change in subject. "I don't know, I guess. I mean, yeah, I'd love to have kids, especially with you."

My heart warmed as I pictured Drake and me with two little boys who looked just like him. But it was too soon for that; we had too many obstacles to pass before that time came.

"I'd like that too, in a few years from now," I said as I kissed him.

He pulled back and gave me a lopsided grin. "You officially distracted me. Are you happy now?"

"All in a day's work. Now help me out of here."

He exited the pool again and helped me to stand. Once we were both out, we made our way back to the front of the house, then separated to make our phone calls. I stood outside next to Danny's car as I dialed Amber's number.

"Chloe Marie, it's about time you called me! I thought your mom killed you and buried the body somewhere!" Amber said as she picked up.

"No, I'm still kicking. I just wanted to call and tell you that I'm okay. I didn't want you and Logan driving out here to avenge me or anything," I said with a grin.

"Not even remotely funny." I heard someone talking in the background, and Amber say, "It's Chloe—she's fine."

"Who are you talking to?" I asked.

"What? Oh, sorry. Logan. He wanted to make sure you were okay."

"Tell him I said hi and that I miss him."

"Chloe says hi and that she misses you," Amber said, and then I heard Logan say in the background, "Logan says hi and to hurry home."

"Yeah, well, that isn't going to happen anytime soon. I'm going to be at my aunt's for a while."

"Why, what happened?"

I gave her a quick rundown of the last couple of days and she whistled when I was finished.

"So let me get this straight: your aunt is screwing with your mom just like you are? And now you're going to stay at your aunt's instead of going with Drake on tour?"

I heard Logan say something and then the sound of Amber smacking him, followed by an "Ouch!"

I couldn't help but laugh at them. "Yes and no. I'm only

going to stay here for a couple of weeks, then I'll meet up with him wherever he's at by that point."

"Oh, okay, gotcha. Well, I hope everything goes smoothly. God knows your mom is going to flip shit when she figures out what your aunt did to her."

"Tell me about it. I'm just going to stick close to Jordan and Danny after Drake leaves. She won't try anything with both of them around me."

"I hope not. Just watch your back, girlie, and I want you to call me constantly to let me know you're okay!"

"I will, but I need to go. I'm taking Drake out to dinner tonight. I'll talk to you guys later."

I disconnected the call and made my way inside the house and up to my bedroom. Drake was already in there, and my mouth dropped at the sight of him in khaki pants and a nice button-down shirt. I don't think I had ever seen him out of basketball shorts or jeans and a T-shirt.

He looked up and grinned as I entered. "Not a word or I'm changing. I look ridiculous."

I giggled as I stepped closer to inspect him. Even with the change in clothes, there was no way to hide that bad-boy side of him. His tattoos peeked out of both sleeves, and his lip and eyebrow rings were both still in, giving him that "Don't mess with me" look, despite his outfit. He looked the best of both worlds.

"You look great, and I'm impressed—you clean up nice," I said as I ran a hand down his unbuttoned shirt and circled the tattoo over his heart. With our identical tattoos, I felt connected to him, and I loved that feeling.

"Whatever. Just get dressed before I change my mind and go to the closest bar around here," he said as he walked by and smacked me on the butt.

I held up two fingers and gave him a salute. "Yes, sir!"

I decided to take extra care getting ready for our last date in a while. Even once I caught up with him on the road, I knew he would be far too busy to take me out, and I was okay with that. He was living his dream and I fully supported him. I took out a pretty white sundress and a pair of white flats to wear before starting on my hair and makeup. I made a special effort with both, wanting him to remember me like this while we were apart.

When I moved on to my hair, he groaned. "Seriously, woman, how long does it take to get ready?"

I threw my hairbrush at him and he ducked, laughing. "All right, I'll shut up. Just hurry up—I'm starving."

Just to annoy him, I took far longer than was necessary. When I finished, he grabbed my purse off the bed and all but carried me out of the room. I laughed as he led me down the stairs and out to my car. Danny and Jordan were standing by Danny's car and waved as we passed.

"We're going out to dinner. We'll be back later!" I shouted over my shoulder as Drake shoved me to my car.

When we were both settled in, I put the key in the ignition but waited to start it. "Impatient much?" I asked.

"I told you I was starving, now come on!" he said as he reached over and started the car for me.

CHAPTER SIX

DRAKE

Chloe and I spent the entire evening out together. She took me to a restaurant that was far nicer than anyplace I would have wanted, but she seemed so excited and I couldn't deny her anything. When we finished dinner, I convinced her to let me drive her car so that I could take her to the beach as a surprise. I knew how much she loved the beach, and I wanted her to remember this night with me and hold it close to her heart while I was gone.

I had stashed my acoustic guitar in the backseat of her car when we left in case I wanted to practice while I was here, and I decided tonight would be a great night to play for her.

When we passed the turnoff for her aunt's property, she looked at me, confused. "Um, Drake, we missed the turnoff."

I gave her a sly smile. "I know."

"Okay . . . Then where are we going?"

I ignored her question and she fell back into her seat, grumbling. "Fine, be that way."

She was silent as I passed over the Ocean Gateway and made my way through the traffic to the same parking lot where

Danny had left his car earlier. As I parked the car and killed the engine, she turned to me with a questioning look.

I smiled as I opened my door. "Surprise!"

She stepped out of the car and looked over at me. "The beach? We were just here earlier today."

I opened the back door and hauled my guitar case out. "I know, but I wanted to come out here again, just the two of us."

She glanced down at the case in my hand and grinned. "Are you going to serenade me next to the ocean? I think that might be the most romantic thing I've ever heard."

"Something like that," I said as I wrapped my arm around her and led her down the beach. We walked in silence as we listened to our footsteps in the sand and the waves crashing against the shore.

It was late in the evening, but there were still several groups of people milling around the beach. I led her away from them until I found a place where we could sit together and not be disturbed. I released her hand as I sat the guitar case in the sand and pulled my guitar out. She sat down next to me and watched as I tuned it.

When I was happy with the way it sounded, I took a seat beside her in the sand and started strumming softly. I had worked on this song by myself, something just for Chloe, and I felt nervous playing it to her for the first time. The music was similar to Seether's "Plastic Man," and I found myself humming along to get the feel of it. I played a few more chords before I finally found my voice and started singing softly, laying out every emotion I felt for her.

I feel the sun against my skin,
Surrounding me.

The light it brings with it
Sets my world on fire.
Everything feels so clear,
So bright, with it near,
I feel like my life isn't so far off base.
Maybe it was meant to bring me peace,
So that I can discover what's real.
I need to feel you against my skin.
You're my flame,
It burns deep within me,
I think I've finally found it this time.
So sun, promise me,
Even when we're millions of miles apart,
You'll still think of me.

I continued to strum until I had finished the song. I looked up to see Chloe smiling at me with tears in her eyes. I set my guitar carefully back into its case before turning back to her and cupping her face.

"You mean the world to me, baby—I hope you know that. I feel like I'm complete when I have you around and I don't want this time apart to change anything about us. I don't think I'd survive without you, now that I've found you," I said as I leaned down and kissed her softly on the lips.

I loved this woman and I wanted to show her how much. I was never good with expressing my emotions, but I could do it through music. It had always been my outlet, and I hoped she would understand just how important she was to me. I wanted to give her everything on this Earth, and I knew that one day I wanted to give her my last name as well. I knew asking her right now would be wrong; neither of us was ready for that, but someday I would.

Tears slid down her face as she looked up at me, and I felt like I was watching a crying angel.

"I'm going to miss you so much, Drake, you have no idea. This is going to be so hard," she whispered as I wiped her tears away.

"Don't cry, baby. I'll call you every day until you're with me again. You'll be sick of me and throw your phone into the ocean before it's all over with."

She grinned. "I don't think you have to worry about that happening. I don't think I could get sick of you even if I tried."

"I'm holding you to that, just so you know," I said as my lips found hers. The kiss said everything that I couldn't. I threw myself into it, telling her just how much I loved and wanted her, how much I was going to miss her.

I laid her down on the sand and covered her body with mine as I continued to kiss her. There was no feeling in the world like having her skin pressed against mine. I moaned as she slowly undid the buttons on my shirt and ran her hand across my bare skin. Lightning shot through my body as she tugged on one of my nipple rings, and I pressed myself harder into her.

I glanced around to make sure there were no eyes on us, but we were by ourselves; the other people had made their way farther down the beach and we were completely alone. I kissed a trail from her lips down her neck, to her rapidly rising and falling chest, before scooting farther down her body. I eased up the hem of her dress as I kissed from her ankles to her thighs.

Her legs fell apart slightly when I reached her thighs and I smiled. Chloe was always ready and wanting when it came to me, and I felt a sense of pride over that. I wanted to satisfy her, body and mind, and her body told me I was doing everything right. I tugged her panties down her legs as my tongue found her clit and started making small circles around it.

She moaned as her hands found my hair and tugged gently, urging me on. I was more than happy to meet her demands as I flicked my tongue ring over her most sensitive spot before sucking. Her body convulsed as her hips rose, trying to pull me closer. I pulled away and kissed my way back up her still covered body to her lips, moaning as her tongue darted out and ran across my bottom lip.

It killed me to leave the dress on her, but I didn't want to take the chance of someone walking up to us with her naked, regardless of how far down the beach we were. I pulled away enough to find the buttons on my shorts and released them. I sprang free as soon as they were undone, and I positioned myself over her and was inside with one thrust.

I felt my body grow tight as we worked in unison, fulfilling each other in a way only the two of us together could. This wasn't sex to me; it was gentle and loving as I tried to tell her just how much I loved her without those damn words that always got in the way.

We went slow, both of us wanting to prolong this moment, knowing it would be our last for a while. I held back, refusing to come without her. When I felt that I couldn't take it any longer, her body tightened around me as she cried out. All it took was that one small sound from her to push me over the edge and I exploded inside her.

I let my forehead fall against hers as I tried to catch my breath. I would never get tired of the feelings she provoked in me, both mentally and physically. When I felt like I could move again, I slowly pulled out, already missing the feel of her. I buttoned my shorts back up and helped pull her dress back down before lying down next to her. She snuggled in against me.

"I'm really going to miss that, but I think I'll miss this more," she said.

"I think I'll miss the sex more," I said as I tried to keep a straight face.

She turned in my arms and glared at me. "You really know how to ruin a moment, don't you?"

"You know it, but you still love me."

"For reasons I'll never know," she said as she continued to glare at me, but I could see the effort it was taking her not to smile.

We spent the next hour curled up together on the beach. She fell asleep, and I took the time to watch her as she slept. She was always so tightly wound when she was awake, and it was nice to see her relaxed and peaceful. I hated to wake her up, but the night air was growing chilly and I didn't want her getting cold.

I nudged her a couple of times, but all I received in return was a smack across the face and some groaning. I smiled as I picked her up and carried her to the car. She was obviously exhausted since she didn't wake up as I carried her, or when I put her in the car. I kept the radio low on the drive home, afraid I would wake her.

Once I was through the gate, I pulled up to the house and parked as close to the front door as I could. The lights were still on downstairs, so I knew Jordan and Danny were both still up even this late at night. I got out and made my way around to Chloe's door, opening it softly. I cringed when it squeaked, but she never stirred.

I picked her up and carried her to the house, trying not to jostle her. Just as I reached the door, Jordan opened it.

"It's about damn time," he said as he looked out at us.

"Shhh, she's asleep. Move so I can carry her upstairs."

He held the door open for me and I passed through it and up the stairs to our room. I laid Chloe down gently on the bed and pulled her shoes off. After tucking her in, I stripped down to my boxers and crawled in next to her, holding her tightly in my arms, not wanting to fall asleep and miss a minute of this. I finally gave up and let my heavy eyelids slide shut.

I awoke the next morning to Chloe crawling back into bed with me. I peeked up at her through sleep-filled eyes to see her watching me with a sad expression on her face. She had obviously just come from the shower; her hair was still wet and I caught the scent of her shampoo as she moved around on the bed.

When she noticed that I was awake, she gave me a tiny smile, but I could still see the sadness in her eyes. She was dreading today as much as I was.

"Morning, baby," I whispered.

"I didn't mean to wake you; I was just watching you sleep."

"You didn't, but stop watching me sleep. That's stalker tendencies and I might have been drooling," I said as she poked me in the ribs.

"I'll be your stalker any day, even though you do have a massive pile of drool under your head."

I rose far enough to check the pillow. She was lying, of course, and I laughed. "You're so full of shit—I don't drool."

I propped myself up on my elbows and pulled her down to me, kissing her hard on the mouth.

She pulled away, breathless, and looked down at me. "You don't play fair, you know that, right?"

"Never said I did," I said as I threw the covers off and stood up. I walked over to my bag and grabbed clean clothes before heading to the bathroom attached to our room. I glanced back at the bed to see her watching my every move.

"See something you like?" I asked.

She threw a pillow at me as I laughed and ran into the bathroom, closing the door behind me. After stripping out of my boxers, I stepped into the shower, letting the hot water engulf me. I took extra-long in the shower, knowing it would be the last one I would be able to enjoy for a while. Showers in the cramped bathroom of the bus wouldn't exactly be luxurious, but at least we had one.

I quickly toweled off before dressing and making my way back to our room. Chloe was still sitting in the exact same spot on the bed, looking depressed as she played with the rings on her hands. I picked up the pillow from earlier and threw it at her.

It smacked off her head and she turned to glare at me. "Hey! What was that for?"

I gave her a pointed look. "Quit moping—you're only making us both feel bad. It seems like a long time right now, but a few weeks will pass in a blur. Before you know it, we'll be back together again."

"I know; I'm just going to miss you so much. What time will Jade and the guys be here to pick you up?"

I glanced at the clock and my eyes widened. It was almost one in the afternoon; I couldn't remember the last time I'd slept in that long. I'd practically slipped into a coma. "Shit, they'll be here in about an hour! I need to get my stuff packed up."

I started grabbing my personal items and clothes from around the room and threw them into my bag. Chloe stood up from the bed as she slipped her shirt over her head and threw it at me. It hit me in the face and fell to the floor as I stared at her almost naked body. While she had a pair of boy shorts on, she had skipped the bra this morning, and I felt myself standing at attention at the sight.

She laughed as she walked to the dresser and pulled a tank top and shorts out of one of the drawers. "Close your mouth— you're going to catch flies."

I groaned as I bent down and picked the shirt up off the floor. I noticed it was one of my shirts that I wore constantly. "You know it's cruel to do that to me when I have to leave. I'm going to have that image stuck in my head all the way to the show. Try explaining a raging hard-on while I'm standing onstage thinking of you."

She threw the tank top on, but was still bra-less and I could see her nipples through the thin material. "Good, that way you won't forget about me."

"Please, for the love of all things holy, put a bra on, woman. You're going to kill me if you don't."

She grumbled as she pulled the tank top off and slid a bra on. "There, happy now?"

"Not really, but it'll do," I said as I carried the shirt over to her. "Here, keep this to remind you of me while I'm gone. You can sleep in it every night."

"Deal, but I feel like I should give you something of mine," she said as she looked around the room, searching for something to give me. She looked down at the rubber bracelets on her wrists and smiled as she pulled one off. "Here, you can wear this. I'd give you a shirt, but I don't think it'd fit all that well."

I took the bracelet from her and slipped it onto my own wrist. "I'll wear it all the time, promise."

I grabbed my two bags and walked to the door. "Come on,

I want to grab something to eat before we leave. I'm not looking forward to fast food and bar food for the next couple of months, so I'd better enjoy real food while I can."

"I'm sure Allison has something ready for lunch by now," she said as she stood and followed me.

We made our way down the stairs to the entrance, and I set my bags by the door before following Chloe into the kitchen. The woman who had served us the first night was standing by the stove, working on something. Whatever it was, it smelled amazing, and my empty stomach growled loudly.

Chloe giggled as the woman looked up and smiled. "I'll have this ready in just a minute if you two want to join Danny and Jordan in the dining room."

"Sure, thanks, Allison," Chloe said as she took my hand and led me into the dining room.

Sure enough, Jordan and Danny were already sitting there waiting on their food.

"Don't you guys feel weird sitting here waiting for someone else to cook for you?" Chloe asked as we took the seats across from them.

"You've tried Allison's cooking. Any guilt I felt was squashed long ago by my need to eat more of it," Jordan said, unashamed.

I watched Chloe roll her eyes as Allison entered the room carrying a massive pan of lasagna. She gave us a small smile as she disappeared back into the kitchen, only to return with a plate full of garlic bread. My stomach growled again and Jordan laughed as I dug in. He had a point; the woman's cooking was a gift from above. If I ever made it in the music business, I was so stealing her from Danny to cook for Chloe and me.

Allison drifted back into the kitchen as everyone else grabbed their plate and filled it up. Danny, Jordan, and I made small talk as we ate, but Chloe remained mostly silent. I knew she was upset over me leaving, but there was nothing I could do to avoid it. I debated kidnapping her, but I knew she'd probably beat me in my sleep for that. She had obligations to her family, just like I had obligations to my band.

Just as we were finishing up, my phone rang and I saw it was Jade calling.

"Hello?"

"Drake, hey listen, we're outside by the gates, but the nice gentleman in the guard station won't let us in," Jade said.

"Oh yeah, I forgot to let him know you were coming. Give me a minute and I'll have Danny call him." I hung up and turned to Danny. "Can you let your guard know it's okay to let my band in?"

"No problem," Danny said as he pulled his phone from his pocket.

I stood and walked to the door as Danny made the call. Chloe caught up with me and wrapped her arms around my waist as I grabbed my bag. Danny and Jordan followed close behind as I stepped outside. The bus was pulling up the driveway, and I breathed a sigh of relief when I saw Eric behind the wheel. As soon as he parked next to us, Jade and Adam were out of the bus. I smiled as Jade came over and hugged Chloe; the two of them had grown a lot closer over the last couple of months, and I knew having Chloe go on tour with us would help keep Jade from getting lonely. You can stand to be on a bus with three guys for only so long before you lost your mind.

Eric stepped off the bus and smiled at me. "Tight security around here?"

"Yeah, just a little," I said.

"I almost had him convinced until this asshole"—he

motioned over his shoulder at Adam—"stuck his head out the window and started yelling. Nothing screws your chances like a guy with a purple Mohawk yelling obscenities at people."

I laughed as Adam walked over and fist-pumped me. "Let's get this show on the road!"

I grabbed my bags and threw them on the bus before stepping back out to make introductions. "Danny, Jordan, this is Jade, Eric, and Adam."

Danny and Jordan shook hands with everyone, giving Adam strange looks. I had to admit, he was a lot to take in at first glance. Then when he opened his mouth, he always made it worse.

Jordan and Danny approached me as Jade and the guys hugged Chloe and waved goodbye before stepping back into the bus. Jordan shook my hand as he leaned into me and whispered, "I'll take care of her—you've got nothing to worry about. You have my word."

"Mine too," Danny said as he clapped me on the back. "Good luck to you guys."

As Chloe approached me, they stepped back to give us a moment. I gave her a smile as I wrapped my arms around her and picked her up off the ground. She laughed as I swung her in circles around me.

"I'm going to miss you so much, baby," I said as I set her back down.

"I know, me too. It's only a couple of weeks, though—we can handle that."

"Damn straight," I said as I kissed her. I drew the kiss out as long as I could.

I groaned and pulled away as Adam started beeping the horn on the bus and stuck his head out the window.

"Come on, lover boy! We've got places to be!" he shouted.

I sent a glare his way as I flipped him off.

"You'd better go before he comes out here after you," Chloe whispered as tears filled her eyes.

"Don't cry, or I'll never be able to leave."

She grinned as she pulled me in for one last kiss. "If I'd known that earlier I would have cried more."

I stepped away from her and turned to the bus. "I love you, Chloe."

I felt like my shoes were filled with lead as I crossed the driveway and stepped onto the bus. Adam and Jade were sitting around a small table, so I took the seat across from them. The space was cramped, but I barely noticed as Eric put the bus in gear. My stomach clenched as I saw Jordan walk over to Chloe and wrap his arms around her. She waved as she watched us pull away.

CHAPTER SEVEN

DRAKE

When we passed through the gates, I groaned. Chloe's mother was pulling up the driveway toward the house. I hadn't been gone for more than a minute and Chloe would already have to deal with her without me. I fell back into my seat, fuming, as Eric pulled out onto the main road. Jade and Adam caught me up on anything they thought I needed to know from the past two days, which wasn't much.

There was a nervous energy around all of them, and I quickly caught it. Shows didn't make me nervous, but the fact we would be traveling up to New York and a few other big places did. There was a chance, however small, that we might get enough attention that someone important might notice us. We had recorded a demo a few weeks ago and sent it in to a few record labels, but so far nothing had come of it. Not that I expected them to call us or even listen to it right away.

Adam stood and went to the restroom in the back as my phone dinged with an incoming text. I smiled when I saw it was from Chloe.

Chloe: **You alone?**

Me: **Yeah, why?**

Chloe: **I'm going to send you something, hold on.**

Me: **Ok . . .**

I raised my eyebrows, wondering what on Earth my girl was thinking. I was starting to grow impatient after a few minutes of staring at my phone with no reply. Finally, my phone beeped and I unlocked it as fast as my fingers would let me. My mouth hung open as I looked at the picture Chloe had sent me.

"Holy fuck!" Adam shouted from behind me.

I spun around in my seat to see him standing behind me, his eyes glued to the naked picture of Chloe on my screen. I threw my phone on the seat beside me and lunged for him.

"You tell her you saw that and I'll fucking kill you, asshole!" I shouted as I knocked him into the seat behind me.

"Jesus! I won't say a word, but damn, buddy. How the fuck did you get so lucky? My dick's going to be hard for hours after seeing her like that!"

"Did you really just say that about my girlfriend?"

He grinned. "Sorry, Chloe just puts off an innocent vibe. I never expected her to send something like that; it makes her ten times hotter."

I groaned as I collapsed back into my seat. "Dude, stop talking. *Now.*"

Jade laughed as Adam and I bickered. "Chloe is going to kill you if she finds out he saw that."

"Don't tell her, Jade—I mean it. She'll never show her face around any of you again if she knows," I said.

"Don't worry, my lips are sealed. But I have to admit, that was kind of funny," she said.

I glared at both of them as my phone dinged again. I realized that in all the chaos of the last two minutes, I had never replied. She was probably freaking out.

"Shit," I mumbled as I unlocked my phone to see another text.

> *Chloe:* I'm sorry if you didn't like it. I don't know what I was thinking.
>
> *Me:* I loved, it baby. Sorry it took me so long to reply, I was speechless.
>
> *Chloe:* Oh, ok. I thought you were mad or something.
>
> *Me:* Never, you can send me as many of those as you want. It'll keep me preoccupied when I'm on the road. ;)
>
> *Chloe:* I'll keep that in mind. I'm going to the beach with Jordan, I'll talk to you later.

I hated the fact that I had left her alone with him, but I knew I could trust her even if I wasn't completely sure about him. Still, it didn't mean I wouldn't get pissed off every time she mentioned him, not that I'd ever tell her that.

> *Me:* Have fun, wear pants.
>
> *Chloe:* Not a chance, buddy. Think of that while you're stuck on a bus with the guys. Love you.

I groaned as I pictured her almost naked on the beach without me around. This was going to be a very long couple of weeks.

. . .

Our first show was a couple of hours north of Ocean City in Caroline County. It was at a small bar, much like Gold's, and I instantly relaxed at the familiarity of it. We had a couple of hours to kill before we had to set our stuff up, so we walked a few blocks away to grab something to eat. We wasted time and annoyed our waitress at a small diner before heading back to the bus to start dragging out our gear and setting everything up.

We had everything ready to go and were sitting at a table near the stage when the owner stepped onstage and introduced us. A few people clapped for us as we stood and took our places, but the response was nothing to brag about. Apparently they weren't into new bands showing up.

Jade started into the first song, quickly followed by Adam and Eric. The room grew quiet as they realized we might actually have talent. I started singing a few seconds later, and it was as if the world exploded around us. I knew we were good, but their reaction completely blew me away; several people stood and made their way to the front of the stage, screaming up at us.

The longer we played, the more people showed up, and the bar was soon at max capacity. I was grinning like an idiot by the time we finished the last song and people were shouting for more. If every show went like this, we'd be set. I told everyone good night as we packed up our instruments, Adam helping Jade tear down her drum set.

I walked over to help them when Adam glanced over my shoulder and frowned. "Oh shit."

His words caught Jade's attention, and she let out a string of curses that would have made a sailor proud as she caught sight of whatever it was over my shoulder. I was about to turn and see for myself when a pair of female arms wrapped themselves around my waist.

"Drake, baby, it's been a while."

I mentally groaned as I turned to face my visitor; I knew that voice anywhere. "Kadi, it's been a while."

"Not long enough," Adam coughed out from behind me.

Kadi smirked at him before running her fingers across my chest. "Imagine my surprise when my cousin and I get a text about this awesome band down at the bar that we just have to check out, and I walk in to see you."

I removed her hand and took a step away from her. The band had nicknamed Kadi "Drake's Stalker." I met her not long after joining the band, at one of my first shows with them. She was a gorgeous girl, with long blond hair and green eyes, and had a body to kill for despite her barely reaching five feet tall. Her personality was what had drawn me to her at first, though; she was a little spitfire, and I loved a girl with attitude.

I got a little more attitude than I'd bargained for. I made the mistake of taking her to bed not only once, but multiple times, and she decided that in her book, it was the equivalent of dating. It had taken me weeks to get her to back off, but even then I'd catch her sitting outside my house when I came home in the middle of the night, or she'd come to my shows and try to get me to take her home.

She was a couple of years older than I was and had moved to Morgantown to attend W.V.U. I had practically thrown a party when she had to transfer from W.V.U. back to her home state of Maryland my senior year in high school.

"It's good to see you, Kadi," I lied. "We were just leaving."

She pouted as I wondered what I had ever seen in her besides her appearance. Sure, she was pretty, but definitely not worth all the baggage that came along with her.

"Aww, come on, Drake. Come have a few drinks with me for old times' sake," she said.

"Can't—we've got a show tomorrow that I have to stay sober to get us to."

She glanced at the band standing behind me. "Surely you could take an hour or two out of your schedule for me. We can go hang out in your bus I saw outside while the band stays in here."

The meaning in her words was clear. After all the times I had told her to stay away from me, she still didn't get it.

"Not gonna happen, Kadi. Might as well go find someone else to sink your claws into," I said, getting truly irritated now.

"But I only want to sink my claws into *you*."

Jade stepped around me to glare at her. "Listen, Drake just told you to get lost, so take the hint and leave. He's not interested in you; he's got someone a little more permanent now."

I had to smile as I watched the two women face off. Jade usually kept out of everyone's business, but she obviously liked Chloe enough to defend her, or maybe she just couldn't stand Kadi. Either way, I wasn't going to complain. Jade could punch her, whereas I was stuck with the dude card.

"If she's so permanent, why isn't she here by his side?" Kadi made a grand gesture of looking around the club. "I don't see any girl coming over to fight for him, so that makes him mine."

"Hate to break it to you, but I have a say in that and I've already told you I'm not interested. Besides, Chloe would be here if she could," I said.

She frowned. "What could be more important than being here to support you?"

I eyed her suspiciously, not wanting to give her any more information on Chloe than she needed. My luck was bad enough for her to start terrorizing Chloe.

"She's staying with her cousin to help with her sick aunt in Ocean City," I said.

Her eyes widened. "What a coincidence! I live in Ocean City when school isn't going on. I'm just here visiting my cousin for the weekend. What's her cousin's name?"

This couldn't go well at all. There was no way I was practically drawing her a map right to Chloe's front door. I thought for a minute, trying to come up with some generic name. Of course, my mind froze and I couldn't think of a single name besides Danny or Jordan. I decided to go with the lesser of the two evils.

"His name's Jordan, but I'm sure you don't know him. He's younger than you are."

"Jordan Wiles, the guy who hangs out with Danny? I love that guy, but I thought Danny's mom was the sick one."

Shit. Shit. Shit.

I was digging myself in a deeper hole every time I opened my mouth. "I'm not sure. I only met the guy once."

She smiled in a way that made me want to run home and grab Chloe. "I'm sure that's who you're talking about. Anyway, since your girlfriend is so far away, she'll never have to know if you want to go to your bus with me."

I grabbed my guitar case off the floor and started walking to the door. "Not a chance, Kadi, so just back off. You're definitely not worth ruining what I have with her. I'm out. Later."

There was no way I was hanging around to help the guys pack up Jade's drum set if Kadi was anywhere around. I made sure to lock the bus door as I shut it behind me and threw my guitar on the table. The band would understand why they had to knock; if not, they'd get over it. No way was I letting Kadi in here with me when no one else was around.

I sat down at the table and pulled out my phone to check for any new messages from Chloe. She had sent me one about an hour earlier, telling me she and Jordan had made it back to the house and wishing me luck at my first show. I smiled as I texted her back and let her know everything had gone well, but I made sure to leave out the part where Kadi showed up.

We had never really talked about all the girls at the shows, but I knew they bothered her. There was no way I would ever cheat on Chloe and I think she knew that down deep inside, but her insecurities often got in the way of rational thought. Mentioning Kadi showing up would only send her into hyperdrive and she would start freaking out.

I felt my temper flare as I realized just how much her mother had screwed her up over the years. She was a beautiful girl with a heart of gold, but her mother had literally beat it into her head that she was garbage and a waste of time.

I was pulled away from my thoughts as a knock came at the door. I peeked out cautiously, making sure that it wasn't Kadi trying to get in. Adam stood there, looking impatient. I unlocked the door and stepped back as he and Jade climbed onto the bus.

"That was fucking awesome!" he shouted, crashing into one of the seats.

Jade rolled her eyes as she grabbed clean clothes from her bunk and went into the bathroom to change.

"Where's Eric?" I asked.

"Collecting our cut. I wanted to hang around for a while and see if I could get lucky, but Eric threatened bodily harm since that crazy bitch is in there. He wanted to leave as soon as possible so she doesn't try to follow us. You really know how to pick them, don't you?"

I threw the guitar pick I had just pulled out of my pocket at him. "Shut up, asshole. That was a long time ago; I've learned from my mistakes."

He laughed as he caught the pick and slipped it into his own pocket. "Damn straight. Chloe is way hotter than that thing in there. I can vouch for that after seeing that picture earlier."

I punched him in the shoulder. "Quit bringing up the fact you've seen her naked or you're going to have to learn to play your guitar with your toes."

He laughed as Eric entered the bus, looking frazzled.

"What the hell happened to you?" I asked.

"Being the only band member left in a bar full of women is not nearly as exciting as it sounds. I seriously almost got mauled. Jesus!" he said, shaking his head.

"Lucky bastard," Adam grumbled as Jade exited the bathroom and took the seat next to me.

Eric grabbed a wad of money out of his pocket and divided it into four separate piles. There wasn't much there, but it would pay for gas and food for a couple of days.

"You guys ready to head to our next stop? I talked to the manager earlier; he said it was cool to crash in his parking lot," Eric said as he took the driver's seat.

"Sounds good to me. I'm going to call Chloe and then crash for the night," I said as I made my way back to the bunks.

The bunks weren't much, especially considering that I'd just spent the last two nights sleeping on a king-sized bed next to Chloe. It had been weeks since I'd had to sleep without her beside me and I missed her already. *God*, I thought, *I sound like a chick sometimes!* I stripped down to my boxers and folded my body into the too-small bunk. After several minutes of shifting to get comfortable, I gave up, knowing there was no position that could help me.

I dialed Chloe's number and waited as it rang, but her voicemail picked up.

"Hey! You've reached Chloe. I can't come to the phone right now, but if you leave me your number I'll call you back. Eventually. If I remember."

I smiled at her stupid message as the phone beeped. "Hey, baby, just got finished with my show. I guess you're already asleep, so just call me in the morning. Love you."

I was disappointed that I couldn't talk to her before I went to sleep, but I knew she had probably stayed up as late as she could, waiting on me. She was worn out and needed to rest so she could deal with her mom.

I unlocked my phone and took one last look at the picture she sent me earlier before closing my eyes and drifting off to sleep with a smile on my face.

CHAPTER EIGHT

CHLOE

The first week without Drake was the worst. I knew I had turned into one of those clingy girls I despised, but I missed him so much that it hurt. On top of that, my aunt was getting worse every day. I would visit her once or twice a day, depending on how she felt, and I could literally see her withering away right before my eyes. Each day she would eat less, drink less, and sleep more. Her nurses told us to be prepared, that she could pass at any time.

I hated how helpless I felt as I watched it all play out before my eyes. Danny was trying to stay strong for her, but I knew that his mother's death was eating him alive inside. On more than one occasion, I caught him sitting in the hallway outside her door with tears streaming silently down his face, and it broke my heart.

Jordan and I tried to keep him busy as much as possible, but it was hard since he refused to leave the house. He was afraid the minute he left that she would die and he wouldn't be there with her. The overall feeling of the entire house was dismal to say the least, and Drake seemed to catch on to this whenever we talked on the phone. He was worried about me, but I assured him that I was fine. I think he felt as helpless as I did, being so far away while all of this was happening around me.

The band was a huge success at every stop on their tour so far, and I was happy for all of them. They had worked really hard to pull all of this together, and they deserved to reap the rewards.

Jordan had stuck to his word about watching out for me and stayed with me almost constantly, especially when my mom was around. Thankfully, he had stopped trying to use his charms on me and we quickly fell back into our old friendship. My mother must have finally realized that she was about to lose her sister and started staying around the house more.

It made me miserable at times, but it also gave me hope that maybe she actually had a soul in there somewhere, that maybe she cared about someone on this Earth other than just herself. Even if that person wasn't me, I was okay with that. I had accepted long ago that we would never have any kind of relationship, but the daughter in me didn't want her to be the horrible person she portrayed most of the time.

I had just hung up with Drake and was making my way down the stairs and into the living room when I was caught off guard by a pretty girl sitting next to Danny on the couch. He never had visitors besides Jordan, who pretty much lived here, and I was surprised at how close he was sitting to her. They seemed to know each other well, even to the point of being involved.

I sifted through my brain, trying to remember if he had mentioned having a girlfriend since I arrived here. Nothing came to mind as I took a seat in the chair next to Jordan and glanced at him. By the look on his face, he was less than thrilled with the arrival of our new guest. Jordan was the type of guy who liked just about everyone, but he had disdain clearly written all over his face.

I turned my attention back to the girl and noticed her watching me closely. I shifted slightly in my seat, uncomfortable with her scrutiny.

"Who's your friend, Danny?" she asked.

Danny looked up, slightly confused. "What? Oh, sorry, I didn't see you come in, Chloe. This is my cousin Chloe. Chloe, this is my friend Kadi."

"Nice to meet you, Chloe. I'd say I've heard wonderful things about you, but since I didn't know you existed until just now, I'd be lying," she said with a small laugh.

Her voice surprised me, but it really shouldn't have. She was tiny and her voice matched her perfectly. It had a musical quality to it that reminded me of a small child and I instantly felt drawn to her, almost as if I needed to protect her.

"It's nice to meet you as well. Danny didn't tell me we'd have a guest today," I said as I smiled at her.

"Oh, well he didn't know I was coming. We're old friends and I heard about his mom when I got back into town, and I wanted to see if there was anything I could do."

"That's very kind of you. Danny could use all the support he can get," I said.

Danny rose from the couch and pulled Kadi up with him. "We're going to go for a walk. I won't be far, so call me if you need anything."

"Of course, take your time, Danny. You need time outside this house," I said.

I waited until the door clicked behind them before I turned to Jordan. "All right, what was the grumpy face for?"

He glared at the door behind me. "I can't stand that girl. She's used Danny more times than I can count and yet here he is, welcoming her back with open arms the minute she decides to come back around."

"The girl who was just here? Are you sure? She doesn't exactly seem like that type. She seems kind of sweet, actually."

"Trust me, she's a manipulative little slut. She was a couple of years older than us in high school, but she went after Danny as soon as she heard about him. She just uses him for money and then dumps him when she's bored. Mark my words, she's here to see what she can get out of him while his mom is in there suffering," he said.

I just couldn't picture her doing something like that; she seemed so sweet to me. But I knew Jordan had a lot more experience with her than I did, and if he said not to trust her, I would listen. I thought about my aunt telling me the sharks would start circling, and it seemed one had already arrived.

"What are we going to do about her? Maybe we should talk to Danny?" I asked.

"Danny has always had a soft spot for that chick. He'll just ignore anything we say about her, especially given how things are with his mom. We just need to make sure they aren't alone together very much."

"How exactly are we going to do that? You've already got your hands full babysitting me when my mom's around."

"I'm still planning on sticking close to you, but you're going to have to be buddies with Kadi. Just talk to her about clothes and shoes or something like that," he said as he grinned.

"Jordan, seriously? Do I look like the type of girl who

knows anything about clothes or shoes? If I didn't have Amber breathing down my neck most of the time, I'd have two pairs of jeans and my skater shoes. I suck at being a girl."

"You have no problem being a girl, trust me. Just keep her busy—I don't care what you have to talk about," he said.

"Ugh! This is going to suck!" I groaned.

"Oh suck it up, it won't be that bad. Hopefully we can get rid of her before too long; that way you won't have to deal with her very much."

"I have the worst luck ever. If we plan on getting her out of here quickly, she'll end up being a bridesmaid when Drake and I get married!"

His eyes narrowed. "Are you really talking about having a wedding with Drake? Please tell me you aren't in that deep with him."

I fidgeted on the couch. Neither Drake nor I had ever mentioned getting married, but it had crossed my mind. I knew it was stupid to think about marriage since I couldn't even legally drink yet, but I couldn't help myself around him. It wasn't as if I were waiting around for him to drop to one knee or anything, though; I knew it would be a long time before either one of us was ready for that step. We were still in the honeymoon stage of our relationship.

"Of course not. I was just trying to explain how bad my luck is. Wait—I thought you liked Drake now that you two did your whole male bonding thing."

"We didn't bond; we just both agreed that you're more important than the two of us fighting over you. He seems like an okay guy, he really does, but I just don't see you guys together in a year," he said quietly.

My heart dropped to my stomach. Did he see something in Drake that I had missed? "Why do you say that?"

"Come on, Chloe, you're smarter than that. Guys like him never stick around for long, and all they do is leave broken hearts behind them," he said as he gazed at me with pity.

"Drake isn't like that. Yeah, he screwed around before we got together, but he hasn't even looked at another girl since we decided to give the whole relationship thing a try. I won't judge him for his past mistakes; God knows I've made enough of them."

"I didn't mean to upset you, Chloe, I just worry about you. I'm sure he really does care for you, but he's in a band, covered in ink and piercings—his whole persona fits the womanizer vibe. He might not intend to stray, but those girls are going to be drawn to him, and a guy can only hold out so long."

"I have to trust him," I whispered, "otherwise I'll go crazy worrying about where he is every second of every day."

Jordan stood and pulled me out of my chair and into a hug. "I'm sorry, Chloe Bear, I didn't mean to make you worry. I'm sure you're right about him; he wouldn't give up someone like you for one of those girls."

"Oh, I'm sorry. Am I interrupting?" a voice asked from behind me.

I pulled away to see Kadi standing in the doorway, holding her phone. "No, you're fine. I was actually just about to go out to the pool and try to tan for a while. Care to join me?"

"Sure, I could use some girl time. Let me grab my bikini out of my car and I'll meet you out back," she said as she turned to leave.

As soon as she was outside, Jordan smirked at me. "Girl time, huh? This should be good."

"Shut up. You're going to be stuck with us too, since you won't leave my side," I said as I elbowed him.

"Nope, you're mom left earlier while you were upstairs. I'm going to watch some television and chill out while you two go bond."

I flipped him off as I walked to the door. "Jackass!"

"Have fun!"

I sighed as I walked to the pool and pulled my shorts and shirt off. I wasn't looking forward to spending time with someone who was only here to use my cousin. Besides, my people skills weren't exactly top-notch.

I slipped into the shallow end of the pool as Kadi walked over to me, her suit already on. She took a seat on one of the chairs as she watched me swimming laps.

"So Chloe, tell me about yourself," she said when I passed close to her.

"Not much to tell, really. I'm pretty boring," I said as I grabbed the side of the pool and pulled myself out.

She motioned for me to take the chair beside her. "I doubt that—you hang out with Jordan and Danny; that's more excitement than most girls ever see."

I laughed as I sat down next to her. "Yeah, I spent the summer with them a couple of years ago. They can get pretty wild, but obviously not with everything that's been going on."

"I came as soon as I heard. Danny has always been a good friend of mine and I didn't want him to deal with this alone," she said as she looked out across the water.

"He's not alone. He has Jordan to take care of him, and I'm here too," I said.

"Well, I know that now, silly. I had no idea he even had a cousin; they never mentioned you before. Do you live nearby?"

I shook my head. "No, I live in West Virginia. I grew up in Charleston, but now I'm in Morgantown attending W.V.U."

Her smiled brightened. "What a small world! I went there for a couple of years before transferring back here. I didn't want to leave, but my mom needed me here."

"I guess it is, isn't it? Are you still in school?"

"Nah, I graduated earlier this year, but I'm taking a year off before I start job hunting."

"I see," I said, unable to think of anything else to say.

We were silent for several minutes before she spoke again. "I hope you don't mind me asking, but are you and Jordan together?"

My eyes widened. "No, why would you think that?"

"I thought I was walking in on some kind of private moment in there earlier. I was just curious," she said.

"No, Jordan and I are just friends. I have a boyfriend," I said as I thought of Drake and smiled.

"Oh, you've got that lovestruck look written all over your face. He must be something special! Tell me about him," she said excitedly.

I felt like a fourteen-year-old telling her friend about her first real boyfriend, but I couldn't help myself. Kadi was surprisingly easy to talk to, and it felt nice to talk about Drake.

"I don't even know where to start; Drake is just . . . Drake. He's moody and bossy at times and he tries to act all badass, but he's really not. He is so sweet when we're together and tries his hardest to take care of me. He just makes me feel . . . I don't know, I guess he makes me feel alive. And he has to be the hottest guy I have ever seen in my life. Dark hair, dark eyes, tattoos, piercings—dear Lord, I could go on forever." I smiled sheepishly as I finished my speech. "Sorry, I think I got a little carried away there."

She laughed. "Not at all—I think I just fell for him after that description. He sounds like the perfect guy."

"He is," I sighed happily.

"Then why isn't he here with you?" she asked.

"He's in a band and they've had shows scheduled for months in advance. I couldn't let him give that up just for me. Once everything is settled here, I'm going to catch up with him on the road."

"I don't blame you, but doesn't it make you nervous to have him out on the road all by himself?"

"No, I trust him. He wouldn't cheat on me," I said.

"I'm glad you guys are so tight. I bet it makes it a lot easier to be around Jordan all day."

I had no idea what she was trying to say with that comment, but it bothered me. "What do you mean by that?" I asked.

"Oh, come on, Jordan is to die for. Being stuck in a house alone with him day after day has to be a big temptation, no matter how good this Drake guy is. You're only human."

"It's not like that at all," I said calmly, even though my temper was starting to rise. "Jordan is just my friend. Are you asking this because you think I'm cheating on my boyfriend with him or because you're interested in Jordan and are trying to find out if he's available?"

She bit her lip. "Am I really that obvious?"

"Depends on which option you're talking about."

"I do have a bit of a thing for Jordan, but I don't think he's interested. I was with Danny for a while and I think that threw him off," she said as she smiled timidly.

"I don't really talk girls with Jordan, so I can't help you out there. All I can tell you is that there is nothing going on between the two of us."

I actually felt kind of sorry for her. I knew she had no chance with Jordan; he couldn't stand her, yet here she was, trying to get information out of me about him. Maybe he was overreacting about her going after Danny; maybe she really was here just to help him. I decided to pass no judgment on her until I got to know her better.

"Well, that's good to know. I'm sorry if I came off kind of as rude; that wasn't my intention."

I smiled as I stood. "No problem, I get it now. I'm going to head back inside to check on my aunt. Were you planning on staying for dinner?"

"No, but I want to tell Danny bye before I leave. I'll swing by tomorrow for a little while to hang out if that's okay with you."

"That's fine with me. Danny could use some company—he never leaves this place anymore," I said as I walked to the patio doors and slid them open. I'd made it no farther than the stairs when Jordan came running down them and almost knocked me over.

"Whoa! What's wrong?" I shouted as I grabbed him to keep from falling.

"Chloe! I was just coming to get you. It's Jen," he said in a near panic.

In that moment, I knew. Seeing Jordan like this told me everything; Aunt Jen had died, but I had to ask.

"What? What about her?" I asked as tears filled my eyes.

"She's gone. Her nurse came to get us, but by the time we made it back up to her room it was too late," he whispered.

I felt my legs give out as he supported me. I knew it was coming, but now that it had happened, I realized I hadn't prepared myself at all. I hadn't known my aunt that well, but I knew enough to realize the world had just lost someone very special. I let my tears fall as he held me close and tried to comfort me.

"It's all right, Chloe Bear, don't cry. She isn't suffering anymore," he whispered into my ear as he sat down on the stairs and pulled me onto his lap.

"I should go. I'm sure you guys want to be alone right now. Just let Danny know I'm here if he needs me," Kadi said from the doorway.

In my shock, I had completely forgotten about her being here. I felt horrible for her seeing me with Jordan like this when I knew she had feelings for him. I pulled away slightly, but he kept his arms around me.

"Thanks, I'll let him know," he mumbled as he focused his attention on me.

I heard the door click and knew that we were alone again. "I'm all right, but I need to see Danny. Where is he?"

"He was still with her when I came to find you. Just give him a little while; he needs time to process it."

I pulled away from him and stood. "I'm going to go wait in his room. I don't . . ." I took a deep breath. "I can't be around her. I just can't."

I had never dealt with death before this, and I wasn't sure how to feel. I'd never had so much as a goldfish to mourn, and here I was trying to find a way to accept the death of a family member.

My mother decided to walk in at that moment. She took one look at my tear-stained face and dropped her purse to the floor as she ran to me. She grabbed my shoulders and pulled me closer to her. "What?! What's wrong? Is it Jen?" she asked as she shook me slightly.

Unable to find my voice, I simply nodded.

She released me and ran past Jordan up the stairs.

I looked at Jordan, unsure what to do. "Should we try to stop her? I don't want Danny dealing with her right now."

He shook his head. "There's no point. It's her sister, and she's going to be in there no matter what we do. I don't want to fight with her around him right now."

I nodded as I started up the stairs. "I just want to be alone right now."

"I understand. Just come find me if you need someone."

I stopped at my room long enough to change out of my bikini before continuing down the hall to Danny's room. I knew he wouldn't be in there, but I wanted to be there for him when he entered. The door opened easily when I pushed, and I looked around. Everything was tidy in his room—no clothes on the floor or anything out of place, which surprised me since most guys were total slobs; even Drake could be if I didn't remind him to pick up after himself.

I sat down on the neatly made bed and pulled my legs up to my chest. I had no clue how to comfort Danny when he came in here; I wasn't even sure how to handle my aunt's death myself. All I could do was keep my promise to her and be there for him when he needed me.

I debated calling Drake, but I decided against it. I knew he would know how upset I was and he'd want to come back to be here with me. I needed to calm down before I spoke with him so that he wouldn't feel guilty. I wished he could be here for me; he always knew what to do, and I felt lost without his comfort.

I looked up as the door opened and Danny stepped inside. His face was red and splotchy from crying and he looked completely broken. We simply stared at each other, neither knowing exactly what to say. He finally walked over and wrapped his arms around me. I held him tight as he broke down in my arms. I'm not sure how long we sat there together, both trying to take comfort in the other.

CHAPTER NINE

CHLOE

The next few days passed in a blur as people I had never met before drifted in and out of the house, several of them bringing us tons of food we would never eat as they gave their condolences. Danny was still struggling with it all, but he put on a brave face as he greeted every guest with the polite and collected disposition befitting his status within the community. I, on the other hand, hid in my room like a six-year-old as much as possible until everyone left for the night.

Jordan drifted between Danny and me, trying to make sure we were both all right. He was obviously hurting as well; he had practically grown up here with Danny, and Jennifer was like a second mom to him, but he pushed the pain back to make sure we were taken care of. My mom stayed here most of the time, but she kept her distance from me. I could tell she was hurting, but I knew better than to try to comfort her.

I had finally pulled myself together enough to call Drake the day after Aunt Jen passed away. My voice shook as I explained what had happened, but I managed to keep myself from completely falling apart. Drake had immediately offered to come back, saying that the tour could wait if I needed him. I refused, explaining that Jordan was helping me and that there was no need for him to cancel shows and cause the band to lose money. He hadn't been happy with the situation, but he finally agreed.

Kadi surprised me by showing up the next day as she'd said she would. She had been back every day since then and was doing her best to help Danny. He seemed to truly appreciate her being there, and I was thankful that she had stuck around. She had even come with Jordan a couple of times when he would check on me in my room. I felt as if he might have misjudged her intentions; she seemed to be trying her hardest to help all of us.

The day of the funeral was the hardest by far. In my daze, I hadn't even thought about what to wear, and I quickly realized I had nothing that was suitable for a funeral, so Jordan and I ran to the local shopping plaza to find a dress and a pair of heels. I finally found a plain black dress and a pair of shoes in the third store we tried. I paid quickly and Jordan rushed us out of the store and back home, trying to make sure that we wouldn't be late.

We made it back just minutes before the limo arrived at the house. I rode next to Jordan on the way to the funeral home while Kadi sat with Danny and tried to comfort him. My mother came with us as well, but she sat on the opposite side of the limo from the rest of us. When we arrived, they gave us a few minutes to say our final goodbyes before they started letting the mourners in.

This was the first time I had seen my aunt since she died, and I wasn't sure what to expect. I knew everyone said that once people were gone, they didn't look anything like how they did in life. As I followed Jordan to stand in front of her casket, I realized they were right.

This thin, pale woman was not my aunt, and I refused to remember her like this; I would picture her the way she was that summer so long ago. Her hair shining in the sunlight, her eyes sparkling with mischief, her skin glowing and tanned from the hours she spent in the sun—that's how I wanted to remember her.

I felt my breaths grow shallow and I ran to the nearest exit to avoid the panic attack that seemed to be drawing near. I flung the doors open and breathed in the fresh air, a welcome reprieve from the stale, flowery air inside. My body started to relax as I stood there, and I could finally breathe freely again.

I jumped when warm hands wrapped around my shoulders.

"You all right, Chloe Bear?" Jordan asked.

"Yeah, I just had to get out of there for a minute."

"I can understand that. I know this is rough on you," he said as he massaged my shoulders.

"It is, but it's harder on you and Danny. I appreciate you watching out for me, but you need to mourn too. You've barely said anything since it happened," I said as I turned to face him.

His hands dropped to his sides as he turned to look across the street. "I'll be fine—don't worry about me. I deal with things in my own way."

"By suffering in silence? I don't think so, Jordan; you need to talk about it. You know I'm here if you need me."

"I know that, Chloe, and I appreciate it, I really do, but I don't talk about stuff like this," he said.

I reached up and cupped his cheek. "Well, if you change your mind, come find me."

He pulled away, looking uncomfortable, and I dropped my hand to my side.

"We'd better get back inside before someone comes looking for us," he said as he cleared his throat.

I nodded as he took my hand and led me back inside.

The funeral services were beautiful. So many people showed up that there weren't enough chairs for everyone, and several of them were forced to stand in the back of the room. It brought tears to my eyes as person after person asked to speak about my aunt. She had touched so many lives during her time on this Earth, and I felt a sense of pride just being related to such an outstanding woman.

After the services were over, we followed in the limo directly behind the hearse to the cemetery. Danny finally lost it when they lowered his mother's casket, and Jordan had to help him back to the car. Most people held a banquet in honor of the deceased, but Danny had requested that no events be scheduled for her. I knew it was because he was reaching the end of his rope stress-wise and I respected that. I had never seen the point in throwing a party over someone dying anyway.

When we arrived back at the house, Kadi and Jordan made sure Danny got to his room while I changed back into comfortable clothes. As soon as I had my dress off, I threw it in the garbage can. I know it seems childish, but I never wanted to look at it again; all it would do was remind me of this day.

My mother hadn't come back with us after the services, and I hoped that she would stay away, at least for a few more hours. I didn't have it in me to put up with her, and I knew Danny wouldn't be able to watch out for me. That left Jordan to play babysitter again, and I didn't want to put any more stress on him; he had enough to deal with today.

I spent the rest of the day sitting by the pool with Jordan and Kadi as Jordan shared stories about Aunt Jen from his childhood. I laughed as he told story after story about him and Danny getting in trouble for anything from playing simple pranks to coming home drunk one night and Aunt Jen grounding both of them. Danny appeared a couple of hours later and started to tell his own stories. He was still hurting, but it was good to see him smile at the memories of his childhood.

I told everyone good night and made my way up to my room. The day had been tiring, and Aunt Jen's lawyer would be here tomorrow to discuss her will. I needed all the sleep I could get for that fiasco, because my mother would be there and she would find out exactly what my aunt had left her: nothing. I debated buying full body armor to wear to the reading tomorrow; I would probably need it by the time she got done with me.

It was late, but I decided to try calling Drake. I knew he was probably still working and sure enough, I was sent straight to his voicemail. I left him a message letting him know that everything had gone okay and I would talk to him tomorrow so he wouldn't worry about me. This was the first day that we hadn't talked at all. It worried me, but I pushed it aside. It was only one day, not a week, and we were both busy.

I closed my eyes and imagined Drake with me, bringing me the warmth and comfort I desperately needed after today. Just the thought brought a smile to my face.

I woke the next morning to Jordan gently shaking me.

"Whatdayawant?" I mumbled, trying to pull the covers back over my head as he ripped them off.

He laughed as he grabbed them again and pulled them to the bottom of the bed. "Wake up, sunshine. Lunch is ready and that lawyer guy will be here in an hour."

"Ugh, what time is it?" I asked.

"Just after one, so get your butt up and get dressed."

I sat up on one elbow and glared at him. "You know, I could have been naked under the covers. Might want to think about that next time."

"Do you usually make a habit of sleeping naked?" he asked with a smirk.

"Only when Drake's around," I said, then stuck my tongue out at him.

"Well, a guy can dream anyway; now get up before I make you get up," he said as he walked to my bedroom door. "If you're not downstairs in twenty, I'll be back for you. Naked or not."

He closed the door as I stood up and crossed the room to my dresser. I had no idea what you were supposed to wear to a will reading, so I settled on a simple knee-length skirt and one of the few dressy shirts I had thought to bring with me. I applied a small amount of makeup and managed to pull my hair into a semi-neat bun to keep it out of my face.

Despite the purple streaks that I had running through my hair, I felt like I looked presentable enough. Not that it mattered anyway; my aunt's lawyer wouldn't care what I looked like as long as I was there so he could do his job.

Just as I was about to walk out the door, my phone rang. I smiled when I saw Drake's face pop up on the screen.

"Hello?"

"Hey, baby, I was just calling to see how everything was going. I got your message last night, but it was too late to call you," he said.

"It's all right, I know you're busy. We're all hanging in there. Danny is pretty messed up, but he's trying to keep it together."

"Yeah, I figured. Let him know I'm thinking about him."

"I will. Where are you guys at now?" I asked. He had given me his schedule before he left, but in all the chaos, I had no idea where I had put it.

"We're back in West Virginia at the moment, down in Huntington. Once we finish up here we have a show in Fairmont, and then it's on to Pennsylvania."

"It sucks having you so far away. I miss you."

"I know, babe, me too. Hopefully you'll be with me soon," he hinted.

"I'm probably going to stick around here for another week and then I'll meet you, unless something happens. We're doing the reading today; I'm sure that's going to end well." I was sure he could read the sarcasm in that remark.

"Stick close to Jordan and Danny; she won't mess with you while they're around. If something happens, call me. I'll be there in a matter of hours to take you away."

I sighed. "I know you would, but I'm sure it'll be fine. I'll stick close to them until I leave."

"Just be careful, babe. I don't want anything to happen to you."

"I will. I'd better get downstairs before Jordan comes back up here after me. I'll call you later."

"All right, but just one more thing?" he asked as I started to hang up.

"What?"

"You know, I haven't had any more pictures from you since the one you sent the day I left. I'm feeling a little neglected over here. Think you can help me out?"

I could hear the laughter in his voice as my face turned red. I'd sent him that picture when I was thinking about all the bar skanks he would be around. I wanted to give him something to remember me by when he was gone.

"I have no idea what picture you're talking about." I decided to play dumb just to torture him.

He laughed. "You know exactly what I'm talking about. I'd love to see some more skin."

Jordan decided to open my door at that moment. "Come on! I'm going to throw you over my shoulder and haul your ass downstairs if you don't hurry up!" he shouted.

"Hold on a minute, I'm talking to Drake!" I turned my attention back to Drake. "I'll see what I can do, but I've really got to go."

"Fine, call me when you get a chance. I'll be checking my texts."

I hung up just as Jordan walked over and threw me over his shoulder. I squealed and kicked as he turned and started carrying me down the stairs and into the dining room.

"Put me down, asshole!" I shouted.

He sat me down in one of the chairs as he laughed. "I *told* you to hurry up."

I glared at him as I grabbed a grilled cheese sandwich off the plate in front of me and started eating. "I *was* hurrying. You didn't have to manhandle me."

I noticed Kadi and Danny sitting across the table from us. Kadi gave me a small smile, but Danny looked like he hadn't slept at all and I instantly felt bad for joking around with Jordan.

"You doing all right, Danny?" I asked quietly.

He shrugged his shoulders as he glanced up at me. "Not really, but I'll survive. I just want to get this day over with."

I nodded, unsure of what to say.

My mother entered the room and sat down at the opposite end of the table from the rest of us. She looked tired as well, but no one asked her if she was all right; we all knew better than to try talking to her. All conversation ceased, and the quiet felt awkward as I finished my sandwich.

The doorbell rang and cut through the silence like a knife. I jumped at the sound. Danny stood and walked to the door. A few minutes later, he walked back into the dining room with a tall, dark-haired man following him.

"This is Mr. Evans, my mother's . . . I mean my attorney. Kadi, if you don't mind, can you wait here? The rest of you follow me; we'll discuss everything in my mother's office."

"Of course not. I'll be by the pool when you guys are done," Kadi said as Jordan, my mother, and I followed Danny out of the room.

My aunt's office was located on the third floor, or to be more specific, it took up the entire third floor. The stairs that led up to it were just past my aunt's room, and I couldn't help but glance at her closed door as we walked past. It seemed as though if I walked over and opened it, she would still be there. Death was a hard thing for me to process, and my mind wasn't quite ready to realize she would never be in there anymore, that I'd never be able to walk in and visit with her again.

I felt a tear slide down my cheek as we walked up the steps leading to her office.

Jordan noticed and wrapped an arm around me. "It's all right, Chloe Bear, just hang in there for Danny," he whispered as we entered the office.

Mr. Evans sat behind my aunt's desk as the rest of us took a seat in the chairs across from him. I ended up in between Danny and Jordan, with my mother on Jordan's other side. I breathed a sigh of relief that it wasn't Danny between us. I wasn't sure he had it in him to fight with her.

"For those of you who don't know me, I am Jim Evans, Jennifer's attorney and close personal friend. I am saddened by the news of her death; there are very few people out there as good as she was and she will be missed by many. Before she was too ill to handle her affairs, she left me specific instructions on how she wanted her estate settled. I am here today on her behalf to distribute her assets."

I fidgeted nervously in my seat as he pulled a folder out of his briefcase and set it on the desk in front of him. Jordan pressed his hand down on my jumping leg and gave me a look as Mr. Evans started pulling documents out of the folder. I smiled apologetically and tried to still my body, but it was useless. I was too hyped up over what my mother would do when she found out what my aunt had done to her.

"Here we go. First is to a Mr. Jordan Wiles. Jennifer has set up an account for you with six hundred thousand dollars in it."

Jordan's mouth fell open as he looked over me to Danny. "Did you know about this?"

Danny glanced down at his hands as he spoke. "She might have mentioned it," he mumbled.

Jordan fell back into his chair, looking shocked. "I don't even know what to say."

Mr. Evans smiled at him. "No need to say anything. Here is the information on the account, as well as a letter Jennifer left for you." He handed the papers to Jordan before continuing. "If you have any questions, please let me know and I will be glad to assist you. Next is Chloe Richards; Jennifer has left the same amount for you, six hundred thousand dollars in an account under your name."

I took the papers he offered to me with a small smile. It didn't feel right taking her money, but I had promised her I would. I had no intentions of spending it; I would donate some to various charities and the rest would sit where it was. Call it my rainy-day fund.

"Next is for Ms. Andrea Richards," he said as my breath stilled. This was the moment I had been dreading.

He pulled an envelope out of the file and handed it to her. "Jennifer requested that I give you this."

She gave him a questioning look as she took the envelope and opened it.

Mr. Evans didn't waste any time moving on. "And finally, Danny. Your mother has left you her remaining assets, as well as complete control over her stocks and any businesses that she owns. When you are ready, just give me a call and I will explain everything to you. Until then, I will watch over everything for you. I understand that you need time to grieve."

Before Danny could reply, my mother was out of her chair and trying to pounce on me. "You stupid little bitch! You did this, didn't you? You'll pay, I fucking swear you will!" she screamed as Jordan grabbed her and pulled her away from me.

I flinched as she threw the envelope at me. "You just wait, Chloe. You've done nothing but fuck up my life since you were born! I'll get you back."

She jerked free from Jordan's grasp and stormed out the door. I could hear her screaming my name and a string of profanities as she went.

Mr. Evans was staring at me with a look of shock on his face. It would have been comical if the situation hadn't been so dire.

Danny cleared his throat and we all turned to him. "Thank you for your help, Jim. I'll be in contact with you soon. But right now I think you should probably go before Andrea does something stupid."

He nodded as he pushed papers back into his briefcase and

stood. "Yes, I'll just be going now." He glanced at the door my mother had just left through before settling his eyes back on me. "If you have any . . . trouble, please don't hesitate to contact me. I'll help you any way I can."

We all thanked him as he left the room. I fell back into my chair and started looking through the papers in the envelope my mother had thrown at me. There were several brochures for rehab clinics in the area that dealt with alcohol and drug addiction, along with a handwritten letter addressed to her. I unfolded it slowly and started reading.

> *My Dearest Andrea,*
>
> *I know I will be gone by the time you read this, but I had to make one final attempt to reach out to you. I love you so much, little sister, and I can't stand to watch as you self-destruct from the inside. I have enclosed several brochures with this letter for rehabilitation clinics in this area and I beg of you to consider going to one. I have already spoken with my lawyer, and if you are willing, he will make sure that your treatment is paid for.*
>
> *I've watched you waste your life for years and I can't stand to do it any longer. It pains me to do this, but I have no choice. You will receive nothing from my estate until you check into one of these programs and complete it in full. For the year following your completion, you will be required to take a drug test weekly. Again, contact Jim and he will set everything up for you. If you manage to pass all of the tests, there is an account containing ten thousand dollars that will be placed in your name. I'm sorry that I led you on, but I cannot stand the thought of you taking any money I give you and using it on drugs.*

Please do not blame Chloe for any of this; she had no idea of my plans for you. I know that will be your first thought, but I made this decision long before I spoke to her. You have put that poor girl through enough already. Just let her go her own way until you get your act together, and if afterward you want to make amends with her, do so. She needs a mother, Andrea, and you are the only one who can give her that.

Again, I'm sorry that it came to this, but just know I do this out of love for you.

Love always,
Jennifer

I wiped a tear from my eye as I finished reading my aunt's final plea for my mother to get help.

I looked up at Danny as he laid a hand on my shoulder. "You okay?"

"Yeah, I will be. I just hope she listens to your mom," I said as I handed the letter to him.

He read it quickly before placing it and the brochures back in the envelope. "I'm going to make sure this gets to her room; hopefully she will take my mom's advice and get straightened up. Until she does, I don't want you out of Jordan's or my sight."

"Damn straight, she's freaking nuts," Jordan growled.

I smiled as I stood up and walked out the door behind them. "Thanks, guys."

We were quiet as we went down the stairs to the second floor. Danny stopped at my mom's room and left the letter on her dresser before continuing on to his own room.

"I'll catch up with you guys in a bit. I just want to be alone for a little while."

"You sure, man? I hate for you to be alone right now," Jordan asked.

"Yeah, I'm sure. You guys go hang out or whatever. I'll find you later," Danny said as he closed the door.

I glanced up at Jordan as we walked to my room. "What do you want to do? Since you have to babysit me, I'll let you pick."

"Kadi said she was going to be by the pool and I still don't trust her. Let's go down there to keep an eye on her until Danny decides to come out."

"Sounds good to me. Just let me change and I'll meet you down there," I said as I started to close my door.

Jordan caught it and smiled. "I'm not leaving you alone that long; I'll wait out here until you're ready."

CHAPTER TEN

CHLOE

I changed quickly, not wanting to make Jordan wait, and was back out in the hallway in record time. Jordan and I were making our way down the stairs and toward the patio door when I noticed Allison standing in the kitchen doorway.

"Your mother just tore out of here like she was on fire."

"That's probably for the best—give her some time to cool down," Jordan said as we walked by her.

Allison gave me a sympathetic smile. "It went that bad, huh?"

"Pretty much."

I smiled as Jordan and I walked to the pool; Kadi was sitting in one of the chairs, sound asleep. I moved quietly to a chair next to her, afraid I would wake her. Jordan laughed as I tripped over one of her shoes and nearly fell on top of her. I turned to glare at him and held a finger up to my lips. I glanced back at her to see that she was still sleeping, despite the racket I had just made.

"You're a klutz, Chloe," Jordan mock whispered.

"Shut up! She looks so peaceful and I don't want to disturb her."

"Whatever," he muttered as he flopped down into the chair

next to me. I sighed at the creaking sound it made and he shot me a grin.

He tried to talk to me several times, but I cut him off with a look as I relaxed back into my chair and let the sun warm my skin. Within minutes, I felt myself growing drowsy. I finally stopped fighting it and let sleep overtake me.

Somebody was poking me on the cheek. I groaned and swatted my attacker away, refusing to open my eyes. I heard someone giggling close by.

"Man, she's really out of it."

"Knock her out of the chair."

That was Jordan. And I had no doubt he really would push me out of my chair. I opened my eyes to see both him and Kadi standing over me.

"She's alive!" Kadi shouted.

"I can't even take a nap around here!" I grumbled.

"Well, you've been out here for over two hours. If you don't roll over you're going to burn," Kadi pointed out.

I glanced down to see that I *was* starting to burn, and I was sweaty. "Ugh, I'm all sweaty and gross."

Jordan gave me a wicked smile. "I can fix that."

My eyes widened as he bent down and scooped me out of my chair. "Wait! What are you doing?" I shrieked as he threw me into the pool.

The cool water was a shock to my overheated body. I came to the surface, coughing and sputtering. "You asshole!"

He was sitting next to the pool, laughing like an idiot. I swam over to the side and pretended to get out before falling back in.

"Need some help? he asked.

"Not from you!"

He stood and held out his hand for me. "Oh, come on, I'm sorry."

"I bet you are," I said as I took his hand.

Just as he started to lift me from the water, I tugged with all my strength and pulled him in with me, clothes and all. The look of shock on his face before he went under was priceless, and I had to grip the side of the pool because I was laughing too hard to stay afloat. He surfaced beside me and pulled me away from the side to dunk me.

Kadi was laughing hysterically and grabbed her phone to record us. We spent the next several minutes taking turns chasing each other around the pool and dunking each other. Or more like, I spent the next few minutes trying to get away from him as he dunked me over and over again. When I'd had enough, I launched myself at him when he turned away from me for a split second. It was all the time I needed, though; I landed on his back and he slipped under.

He resurfaced with me somehow still clinging to his back and walked over to the edge of the pool. I hopped off him and stood beside Kadi as he pulled himself out. She shut off the video on her phone and fell into her seat laughing.

"You two are like two little kids together, you know that, right?" she asked.

"Yeah, and she does a hell of a job playing the annoying little sister," Jordan said, pulling his soaked shirt off.

I stuck my tongue out at him as I sat down beside Kadi.

"See what I mean?" he asked.

"Oh, whatever. You love me and you know it," I said as I looked at his bare chest. A thought struck me and I smiled. "Hey, Jordan, can you do me a favor?"

He eyed me suspiciously. "Depends on what it is."

"Nothing major. Drake asked me to send him a picture with some skin in it. He didn't specify if it had to be *my* skin."

He glanced down at himself before grinning. "You know you're going to piss him off."

"Nah, he'll laugh. Hopefully," I said as I grabbed my phone and held it up to take the picture.

"Should I strike a pose or something?"

"You're taking a picture, not modeling," I said as I snapped a couple of shots.

"You ruin all the fun."

I sent a few of the pictures as I smiled to myself. Drake was on the road right now, so I was sure he would see them soon. Sure enough, he texted back a minute later.

Drake: **Not. Even. Funny.**

Me: **Hey, you said you wanted to see some skin. I was only doing what you told me.**

Drake: **I'm not sure what bothers me more—the fact that you're taking pictures of Jordan shirtless and wet or that you thought I would enjoy them.**

Me: **LOL. Sorry, I had to.**

Drake: **I'm sure you did. At least Jade got some enjoyment from them. What are you doing?**

Me: **Sitting by the pool. Everything went ok at the reading today, mom stormed out.**

I decided it would be better if I left out the part about her threatening me. He would freak out, and I didn't want to add any more stress to his life.

Drake: **I'm glad. We're about to stop for some food so I'll talk to you later.**

Me: **Ok, love you.**

Drake: **Love you too.**

I set my phone back down and smiled at my own joke. I glanced up to see Jordan and Kadi watching me closely. "What?"

"Was he mad?" Kadi asked.

"Nope. He didn't appreciate them, but Jade certainly did."

Jordan gave me a smug smile. "Who wouldn't? I mean, look at me. My abs have abs."

Kadi and I started giggling like idiots. "I still don't think that's enough to make Drake bat for the other team. Sorry about your luck," I wheezed out between giggles.

"Whatever," Jordan mumbled. "I need to run inside and make a quick call to my coach. Will you be okay here by yourself for a couple minutes? You're mom still isn't home."

I waved him away. "I'll be fine—go do what you need to do."

He walked to the patio doors and slid them open. "I'll only be gone a few minutes."

I rolled my eyes as he closed the doors behind him. "He worries too much. I think I can survive sitting by the pool for five minutes."

"He just worries about you," Kadi said as she stood. "I need to head home, so I'll see you later."

"Okay, later." I waved goodbye as she grabbed her clothes and left.

I decided to go for a quick swim while I had some alone time. It was nice to have Jordan around, but I wasn't much of a people person and I enjoyed being by myself more often than not. I climbed the ladder to the diving board and did a cool little spin dive into the water. After I surfaced, I started leisurely swimming back and forth from one end of the pool to the other. I felt the muscles in my arms and legs start burning as I killed some of the pent-up nervous energy inside me.

I did a few more laps until my arms felt too heavy to move. Deciding I had pushed myself enough, I swam to the steps and climbed out of the pool. The swim had the intended effect; I was worn out, but my mind was calmer.

I walked over to grab my phone, but before I reached it, I felt a pair of hands circle my neck. I shrieked as I was thrown to the ground and someone kicked me in the ribs. I groaned as I tried to roll over, pain slicing through my ribs.

My mother was standing above me with a look of pure rage on her face. "You little bitch, you're going to pay."

Before I could utter a word, she kicked me in the ribs again and bent down to grab me by my hair. I tried to free myself, but she must have been on something because my strength was nothing compared to hers. She lifted my head and slammed it down onto the ground in front of me repeatedly. I felt blood running from my nose and I could taste it in my mouth. The taste alone made me gag.

She pulled me to the edge of the pool and held my head an inch from the surface of the water. "Maybe next time you'll think about crossing me. If there *is* a next time."

With that, she pushed my head under the water. I struggled to free myself as she held me there. I don't know how long she kept me submerged, but I knew it was longer than I could hold my breath. Without thinking, I opened my mouth to take a breath and the water flooded my mouth. My lungs instantly started to burn as it filled them.

I felt myself losing consciousness, when suddenly I was free. Strong hands grabbed me and pulled me from the water. I rolled onto my stomach and started coughing, trying to get all of the water out of my lungs. I felt it leaving my mouth and nose in streams, and I panicked because I still couldn't breathe.

"Jesus Christ, breathe, Chloe! Breathe!" Jordan shouted as he hit me on the back.

I laid my head on the ground when I was finally able to take a breath. My lungs and throat felt like they were on fire.

"Jordan," I croaked, "Mom."

"Shhh, you're safe. She ran when I pulled her off of you," he said as he gathered me into his arms and cradled me there. The movement caused pain to shoot through my ribs and I cried out.

"What is it, Chloe?" he asked, sounding frantic.

"My ribs."

"Holy shit!" he shouted as he finally took a good look at me. I knew I had to look a mess from the beating she had given me. "You're face is fucking bleeding from everywhere! We need to get you help!"

He started shouting at the top of his lungs, trying to get someone to hear him and get help. Within a few seconds, Allison came running out of the house with Danny right behind her.

"Oh my God!" Allison shrieked as she saw me.

"What happened?" Danny demanded.

"I left her alone for a couple of minutes because I thought her mom wasn't home. Call 911—it looks like she's going to need an ambulance as well as the cops."

Allison was gone in a flash as Danny leaned down in front of us to inspect me closer. "Where does it hurt, Chloe?"

Sobs were overtaking my body, causing my ribs to hurt even worse, and I couldn't bring myself to speak through the pain.

"She cried out and said her ribs hurt when I picked her up. It looks like the bitch kicked the shit out of her before she tried to drown her."

I felt cool fingers gently press against my ribs and I cried out again.

"I'm going to bet they're broken, or at least cracked. Jesus!" Danny growled.

"This is all my fucking fault!" Jordan shouted. "I shouldn't have left her alone."

"Don't beat yourself up—you said you left for just a couple of minutes. Even with the way Andrea reacted earlier, I never thought she would do something like this," Danny said quietly.

"How can I not beat myself up? Look at her! If I had been there this wouldn't have happened. She nearly killed her, all because I needed to make a fucking call!"

"Not your fault," I wheezed.

"Don't try to talk, Chloe Bear—just stay still."

I heard the patio door slide open and then footsteps approaching. I tensed, afraid my mother was coming after me again.

"I called 911. They said not to move her until they get here in case her back is injured," Allison said as she approached.

Danny and Allison sat with us as Jordan continued to hold me until we heard sirens in the distance. I felt myself drifting in and out of consciousness as the pain increased. My eyes flew open when someone started to pull me from Jordan's grasp.

"No!" I managed to get out as I clung to him for dear life.

"It's all right—my name is Aaron and I'm a paramedic. I'm not going to hurt you, but I need to take a closer look at your injuries."

I looked up to see a middle-aged man crouching in front of us. He gave me a small smile as his eyes went down my body, searching for injuries.

"It's all right, Chloe. You need to let him check you over," Jordan said as he looked down at me.

I was lifted from Jordan's arms and placed on a stretcher. My body screamed in protest at the pain as everything went black.

CHAPTER ELEVEN

CHLOE

I awoke to an annoying beeping sound. I tried to open my eyes to see where it was coming from, but I failed miserably; it felt like they had been glued shut. I lay there and listened to the never-ending beeps for several minutes before trying to open my eyes again. I made a little more progress this time, as I managed to open them enough to see my surroundings. I was in a plain white room with bright lights beating down on me. The light hurt my eyes and I blinked several times, trying to adjust to the brightness of the room.

After my eyes adjusted, I glanced around the room and realized I was in a hospital bed. The annoying beeping sound was coming from some kind of machine sitting next to me. I looked around, confused, as I tried to figure out why I was here. I shifted slightly and a searing pain shot through my ribs. I sucked in a deep breath at both the pain and the memories that started flooding my mind. *My mother.* She had beaten me, apparently bad enough that I was in a hospital room.

Tears stung my eyes as I remembered every blow she had given me. I knew she hated me, but to do this? *If there* is *a next time.* She hadn't just meant to hurt me; she had tried to drown me. In all the years of abuse I had suffered at her hands, I had never feared for my life the way I had by the pool.

I caught movement from the corner of my eye and turned my head. Jordan was sitting in a chair by the window, sound asleep. He looked as bad as I felt; even in sleep his face was drawn tight with worry, and his normally clean-shaven face had scruff covering it.

Danny entered the room with a steaming coffee cup in each hand. He smiled at me when he noticed me watching him.

"I see that you're finally awake."

I nodded, not trusting my voice at the moment.

"You scared us when you blacked out. We thought she did damage internally," he said as my eyes widened. "Don't worry—they checked you over when the paramedics brought you in. You've got a couple of cracked ribs and you're beat up, but that's it."

"How long have I been here?" I croaked out. My throat felt raw, but at least I could speak.

"Almost twenty-four hours. Jordan hasn't left your side since they put you in this room. I had to get him something to eat because he wouldn't even leave for that. He's been beating himself up, thinking he's responsible."

I shook my head. "He's not."

"I know, but he thinks you're going to hate him. I'm surprised he even went to sleep; I guess he couldn't handle it any longer." He sat both cups on the table next to Jordan. "I need to go get one of the nurses—I'm sure they'll want to know you're awake."

"Wait! Where's Drake?" I called out as he turned to leave.

"I didn't call him. I wasn't sure how much you wanted

to tell him, and I wanted to wait until you were awake so he wouldn't freak out."

"Thank you."

He nodded as he left the room. A few minutes later, he returned with a nurse following him.

"Good to see that you're awake, Chloe! My name is Audrey and I'm your nurse tonight. How are you feeling?" she asked loudly.

At the sound of her voice, Jordan jerked awake in his seat. His eyes instantly found mine and he jumped out of his chair and ran over to me. "You're awake! Oh, thank God, I've been freaking out! Are you okay?"

"I'm fine," I said to both him and the nurse.

Neither looked convinced as Audrey pushed Jordan out of the way and started checking me over. She prodded my ribs, and I stifled a scream at the pain it caused.

"Tender?"

Well, no shit. "A little."

"Let me get the doctor and he can talk to you about everything. I need to contact the police and let them know you're awake as well. I'm sure they'll want your statement."

I turned to Jordan and Danny as she left the room. "The police?"

"Yeah, they showed up right before the paramedics. Your mom was gone by then, of course, but they've been searching for her. Jordan and I both gave statements, but I missed all of what happened and he only caught the end, so you'll need to fill in the rest."

Even though I knew I shouldn't, I felt guilty about the police being involved. "Do I have to file charges against her?"

I nearly flinched at the rage that crossed Jordan's face. "I'm going to pretend you didn't just ask us that, Chloe. She nearly killed you!"

"I know, I just feel guilty. She's still my mom."

"Chloe, think about this. She obviously isn't worried about herself, so you shouldn't worry about her. Even if you refuse, I'm still filing charges on her; it happened on my property," Danny said.

I looked down at my hands and saw the tattoo on my wrist that I had gotten with Drake. Now more than ever, the words *Nunquam Amavit* seemed like the perfect choice.

"You're right; she deserves to be locked up for this. I won't let her hurt me again."

Jordan nodded, looking satisfied. "That's my girl."

A couple of minutes later, a doctor and two police officers entered my room. The doctor glanced down at the chart in his hand before smiling at me.

"Evening, Miss Richards, I'm Dr. Browing. How are you feeling?"

"I'm all right, just a little sore."

He nodded. "Yes, I bet. You took quite the beating, but the good news is that there isn't any permanent damage. We've tended to the cuts on your face and taped your ribs. I want you to stay one more night just for observation, but if everything stays the same you will be released tomorrow morning."

I smiled. "That sounds great. Thank you."

"Not a problem. I'm going to prescribe you something for the pain to help with your ribs and overall soreness. If you need more, just contact me and I can write another prescription for you."

He waved as he left, and the two officers stepped forward. Neither one of them looked happy as they stared down at my bruised and battered body.

The younger of the two stepped forward and shook my hand. "Hello, Chloe, I'm Officer Daniels and this is Officer Bradley. If you're feeling up to it, we have a couple of questions for you about last night."

"Sure, go ahead," I answered.

He pulled out a small notebook and flipped it open. "All right, we have the end of the story, but can you tell us what happened from the beginning?"

I nodded. "Sure. I decided to go for a swim. When I got out I started to walk over to get my phone, but my mother came up behind me and grabbed me around my neck. She threw me to the ground and started kicking me, and then she grabbed my hair and started hitting my head against the concrete."

I looked at Jordan as I spoke, and I saw him tensing up more and more with every word I said. I immediately felt guilty for telling the officers all of this with him in the room.

The officer noticed me watching Jordan. "Would you rather we did this without anyone in the room?"

I nodded, but Jordan shook his head. "No, Chloe, I want to hear it too."

The officer raised an eyebrow but said nothing.

"I don't want to upset you, Jordan."

"I'm already upset. Nothing you say will make it worse."

I sighed before turning my attention back to the officer. "It's fine. Where was I? Oh yeah, after that she pulled me over to the pool and held my face right above the water. She said something like, 'Maybe next time you'll think about crossing me, if there *is* a next time.' And then she shoved me under the water."

My throat closed off as I thought about how much venom she had put into those words.

"And then what happened?" the officer asked.

"I don't really know for sure. I think Jordan pulled her off of me and then pulled me out of the water. Danny and Allison came running out right after that, and then Allison called you guys."

He nodded as he continued to scribble in his notebook. "Got it, but just one question. What was she talking about when she said you had crossed her?"

Danny spoke up from the corner of the room. "My mother just passed away and left Chloe a substantial amount of money. My aunt thought she would be getting some of that money as well, but she was sadly mistaken. She is severely addicted to drugs, and my mother refused to leave her anything unless she sought treatment. Andrea has it in her head that Chloe is to blame for my mother's decision, but that's not the case. My aunt has abused Chloe for years."

The officer looked at me sympathetically. "Is that true?"

A simple yes was all I could manage to get out.

"All right, then, we've got everything we need here. We are already searching for her, but so far she's disappeared without a trace. As soon as we know something we'll be in touch, but in the meantime if you can think of anything else, just give me a call." He handed me his card and I smiled.

"I will, thank you."

After the officers left, Audrey brought in a tray with some soup and Jell-O. "Here you go, honey. If you need anything else, just push the call button and I'll be right in."

The soup felt like nails as it slid down my tender throat, but I forced myself to finish it. I didn't want to give them any reason to keep me here longer than necessary. Jordan helped by feeding it to me, and I couldn't help but giggle.

He cocked an eyebrow. "What?"

"Nothing, it's just some big bad football player is spoon-feeding me soup. If this gets out, it's going to ruin your macho football player reputation."

He snorted. "Like I give a damn about my reputation. I'd quit football right now if it meant you weren't lying in this hospital bed nearly beaten to death. It's because of my football shit that you're here anyway."

"Don't say that, Jordan—she was after me and it would have happened eventually. You can't blame yourself for another person's actions."

"It was my fault. Drake trusted me to take care of you and I let both of you down."

I sighed as I gave up arguing with him. There was no changing his mind, and I was too tired to fight about it. Jordan could be just as stubborn as Drake when he wanted to be.

I forced Danny and Jordan to both go home for the night. I thought I was literally going to have to get up and push Jordan out the door, not that I would have been able to do so, even on a good day.

He finally gave in when I told him he looked like crap and was starting to smell funny. As they walked out the door, he told me that he would be back bright and early the next morning. I had no doubt that he'd stick to his word.

Once they finally left and the night nurse came in to check on me, I grabbed my phone off the cart beside me and unlocked it. Danny had been thoughtful enough to bring it with him the night before.

My stomach dropped as I noticed several missed calls and texts from Drake. I read through all of his texts quickly, each one growing more and more concerned. The last one had been sent only an hour before.

Drake: **Chloe, I'm seriously freaking out over here. I can't reach you, Danny, OR Jordan. If you don't answer me soon I'm coming back to check on you!**

Me: **I'm fine, I've been sleeping all day. I caught some kind of stomach bug.**

As I hit send, I instantly felt guilty about lying to him yet again. But if I told him what happened, he would cancel all of his shows and coming running back to me. I got a reply almost instantly.

Drake: **Good God, Chloe, you scared the shit out of me. Why the hell wouldn't Danny and Jordan answer their phones?**

Me: **I have no idea. I haven't talked to either of them much today. I'm fine so you can stop worrying, but I am tired so I'm going back to bed.**

Drake: **OK. Sorry I pretty much blew up your phone, I just worry about you with your mom being there. I'll talk to you later. Love you.**

. . .

I was released the next morning, just as the doctor had said. After a quick stop at the pharmacy to pick up my pain medication, Jordan drove me straight to Danny's home and helped me up to my room. I decided that if his football career ever ended, he would make an excellent nurse. He fussed over every little thing, constantly asking me if I was comfortable.

After the fourth time he fluffed my pillows, I pointed to the door. "Enough! You're going to drive me nuts, Jordan. Go fluff Danny's pillows or something!"

He smiled sheepishly. "Sorry, Chloe Bear, I just want to make sure you're comfortable. Do you need another pain pill? Or I can have Allison make you some soup."

I groaned and threw a pillow over my face. "Just smother me with the damn pillow—it'll save us both some time."

He ripped the pillow away and glared at me. "Not funny."

"Sorry, but seriously, I'm fine. Just grab my iPod off the dresser and hand it to me. I'll just lie here and listen to some music and you can go do something else."

He walked to my dresser and grabbed my iPod for me. "I'm not leaving you alone again, so you might as well get used to me."

"She's not going to come back here, Jordan—she's not that stupid. I'm officially relieving you of your babysitting duties."

"I'm not taking any chances, so you're stuck with me."

I snatched the iPod out of his hand. "You have to sleep sometime, you know."

"I will, but I'll be sleeping in here. If you won't let me sleep in the bed with you, I'll just sleep on the floor."

"You're going to drive me to drink—I hope you know that."

He scooted me over and settled down on the bed beside me as he took one of the earbuds from me. "I intend to. Now play us some music."

We spent the next couple of hours listening to some of my favorite artists, including Three Days Grace, Seether, Disturbed, Papa Roach, and Avenged Sevenfold. Jordan didn't know half of the songs I played, and I spent most of the time telling him about each of the bands while playing what I considered must-haves.

By the time evening rolled around, I had him addicted to several new bands and I felt proud of myself. If there was one thing I valued above all else, it was music. When I played some of Drake's songs, he was as blown away by them as I was.

There was a soft knock on the door and Kadi stuck her head in. "Can I come in?"

I pulled the headphones from our ears and motioned for her to enter. "Sure, I was just educating Jordan on real music."

She smiled as she stepped inside the room and closed the door. "I heard what happened. How are you feeling?"

"I'm fine, just a little sore."

Her phone dinged and she held it up to read the text. She texted back and held the phone up in the air. "Ugh, I have like no service in this room!" She finally managed to get it to send and slipped the phone back into her pocket. "Anyway, I feel terrible. If I hadn't left you alone she never would have had the chance to hurt you."

"Don't worry about it—you had no idea she would show up." I glanced at Jordan. "No one did."

He frowned but kept his mouth shut.

Kadi gave me a small smile. "That still doesn't make me feel any better."

"Everyone needs to stop beating themselves up over it. My mother is the one at fault, no one else."

I was getting so sick of everyone blaming themselves for something that was completely out of their control.

"All right, well, I just wanted to see how you were doing. I'm going to be out of town for a couple of weeks, so I probably won't see you for a while," she said as she walked to the door.

"Okay. Where are you going?" I asked.

She paused for a moment before answering. "Uh, I'm going to go stay with my cousin."

She seemed uncomfortable with my question, but I couldn't figure out why. I decided to let it go as we said our goodbyes.

Jordan hopped out of bed and grabbed some clothes off the chair beside my dresser. "I'm going to go shower."

"Have fun. I'll try to stay out of trouble while you're gone," I said, then stuck my tongue out at his back.

He laughed as he walked into the bathroom. "I saw that."

. . .

I spent the next week holed up in my room with only Jordan for company. Danny would stop in from time to time, but I knew he was busy trying to work with Jim to handle his mother's companies. We spent most of the time watching television, and I would call Drake when he wasn't busy. I promised that I would try to meet up with him the following week. Jordan didn't seem happy about me leaving, but he wouldn't say anything about it. I was worried too; when Drake saw my bruises I knew he would flip.

By the end of the week, I was able to get up and move around the house a bit. I was still sore, but the exercise was helping to loosen my body. I even convinced Jordan to take me across the Ocean Gateway so that we could walk around the boardwalk for a while. I tried to ignore the looks people gave us when they saw the bruises on my face. They had turned a nasty yellow color, and I knew I looked horrible.

I laughed out loud when Jordan forced me to stop at a place called The Fractured Prune. "Are you serious?" I asked.

"Trust me, they have the best doughnuts ever!" he said as he ordered us two doughnuts.

After my first bite, I had to agree. They put all doughnuts that I had ever had to shame, and I made him get me another one before we left.

As we were walking back up the boardwalk to the car, my phone rang. I pulled it from my pocket and looked at the screen. I was surprised to see that it was Jade calling me.

"Hello?"

"Chloe? Hey it's Jade. I'm sorry to bother you, but I was wondering if you had talked to Drake lately."

I could tell that she was worried. "No, it's been a couple of days. Why?"

"I don't want you to freak out, but I haven't been able to find him."

"What do you mean you can't find him?" I asked frantically.

"He split after a show the other night and no one has heard from him since. He sent me a text telling me that he was going to a party, and now he won't answer his phone."

"Oh God, what if he's hurt? Where are you guys at? I'll be there as soon as I can."

She gave me the address of the bar where they'd last played. "We've had to cancel two shows, Chloe—this isn't like him at all."

"I'm on my way—just call me if you find him."

I hung up with her and turned to Jordan. "We have to go to Pennsylvania. Drake is missing!"

"All right, calm down. Let's go back to Danny's and pack a few things, then we'll go."

Every bad thing possible flashed through my mind as I ran to Jordan's car. I couldn't lose Drake, I just couldn't.

CHAPTER TWELVE

DRAKE

I smiled as the crowd screamed out our name, feeding off their energy. We had done well at every show so far, but this crowd was absolutely wild for us. I had no doubt we had secured some new fans, especially from some of the women standing in front of the stage. As I sang the last few verses of our last song and told everyone good night, the screaming turned into a roar.

Adam slapped me on the back as we packed up our instruments while Eric went to find the owner to collect our pay. "You were on fire tonight, buddy."

"Thanks. I guess I'm excited that Chloe will be with me in the next couple of days."

"Somebody is going to get laid," he said in a singsong voice, waggling his eyebrows at me.

I punched him in the arm as I grabbed my guitar and headed for the back door. There was no way I was going to go through the massive crowd of people to reach the front exit. I stepped out into the warm evening air and lit a cigarette, inhaling deeply to calm my after-show nerves.

The quietness outside the bar was a welcome reprieve from

the madness that I had just left behind. I walked slowly across the lot toward the bus, giving myself time to finish my cigarette before I boarded. Just as I reached the bus door, a figure stepped out of the darkness and blocked it.

"Hey, Drake, miss me?"

I groaned as I realized it was Kadi standing in front of me. "What do you want? How did you even find me?"

She held up one of the fliers we handed out at every bar we played in. They had our entire schedule on them. I mentally smacked myself as I realized I had pretty much given her step-by-step instructions on how to find me.

"I thought you'd be happy to see me," she whined.

"If I wasn't excited in Maryland, what makes you think I'd be excited in Pennsylvania?"

"Oh, come on, baby, you know you've missed me. We were always great together."

"Can't say that I have. And like I told you before, I'm with someone now, so you need to back off. You're starting to act like a stalker." I tried to push past her, but she held her ground.

"You mean someone who cheats on you when you're not around."

I rolled my eyes. "What are you talking about? You don't even know Chloe."

She gave me a smug smile. "Oh, but I do. I've spent some quality time with her and Jordan since the last time I saw you."

I felt a burning rage take over. "You stay the fuck away from her, Kadi—I mean it."

"Don't worry, I don't normally associate with cheaters, but I needed proof."

"Proof of what exactly?"

She huffed as she handed me an envelope. "Haven't you

heard a word that I've said? I needed proof that she wasn't good enough for you and I have it. She's been cheating on you while you've been away."

I snatched the envelope out of her hand and opened it. There were several pictures inside, and my breath caught as I looked through them. Picture after picture showed Jordan and Chloe together: hugging in the living room, Chloe holding Jordan's cheek and staring into his eyes, walking down a street hand in hand, Jordan with Chloe thrown over his shoulder, Jordan carrying Chloe in his arms by the pool, Chloe sitting on his shoulders in the pool. But the last one was the worst. It was a picture of the two of them cuddled up in Chloe's bed.

I had no idea how Kadi had managed to get all of these pictures and I didn't want to know. I threw them on the ground and pushed her aside to step onto the bus.

She followed me up the steps but stopped at the top of them. "Do you see now? No one will ever be as good to you as I was."

I barely contained my temper as I pointed outside. "*Get. Out.*"

She looked at me, shocked. "You can't be serious! I was only watching out for you. Drake, I love you!"

I shook my head, disgusted. "You don't love me, you're obsessed with me. I don't want anything to do with you even if Chloe *is* cheating on me. Now get the fuck out or I'll remove you myself."

She glared at me. "You'll be sorry, Drake Allen!"

"Yeah, yeah, whatever. Just go!" I shouted.

She turned and stomped off the bus as I collapsed into one of the seats. How could Chloe do this to me? She hadn't seemed interested in Jordan at all and that dirt bag had said he was only looking out for her, that he would never be with her. I was a fool, just like Logan had been. Only it sucked a lot more to be on this side of it.

I obviously meant nothing to her or she wouldn't be off screwing some other guy while I was away, and doing it in the house of her aunt who had just died. I looked around for something to throw before I punched one of the windows. Seeing nothing close, I stormed off the bus and walked back to the rear entrance of the bar. I was going to get drunk off my ass; being sober hurt too damn much.

When I reached the entrance, I noticed a guy standing a few feet away in the shadows. I caught the smell of weed as the wind blew in my direction. Without a second thought, I walked over to him. He looked surprised but said nothing as I stopped in front of him.

"You have any more of that?" I asked.

He nodded. "Yeah, I've got this and a lot more if you're interested."

"I am."

I needed a release and I knew just how to find it. I had managed to stay clean for years, yet here I was, throwing it all away for Chloe. I guess it showed just how stupid I really was.

He motioned for me to follow him. "I don't have anything on me, but if you want we can go back to my place. It's not far from here and I can hook you up."

I nodded as I sent a quick text to Jade, letting her know I was going to a party and that I would be back on the bus in the morning, before shutting my phone off. I knew it would throw us behind schedule if we didn't leave tonight, but I didn't care.

We walked to a beat-up car parked in the corner of the lot and the guy unlocked it. "I'm Jack, by the way."

"Drake."

"You don't say much, do you?"

"Nope."

He lived only a couple of minutes away, in the run-down part of town. I exited the car and followed him up the stairs to a small, dirty apartment. The air was thick with smoke, and several people looked up as we entered. Jack raised a hand to all of them but continued through the apartment until we reached a bedroom. There were two girls and a guy having sex on the bed when we entered, but he quickly tossed them out, still naked, into the hallway before shutting the door behind them.

"I've got just about anything you want."

"Coke?"

He smiled as he pulled a lockbox out from under the bed. "I'll take care of you."

He unlocked the box and pulled out a small bag of cocaine. I held out my hand but he shook his head. "Money first, buddy, or no deal."

I took my wallet from my jeans and pulled some cash out. "Here's everything I have on me. Give me whatever you've got."

"I like you, kid. Here you go."

I took the bag from him and grabbed a small mirror off the bedside table. It had obviously been used recently; it was cloudy from the leftover powder that covered its surface. I dumped a small amount out and made a line with one of the credit cards from my wallet. Then I grabbed a dollar from my wallet as well, before rolling it and snorting the line.

Within minutes, I started to feel the effects. I smiled up at Jack as my body relaxed and I fell back onto the bed, grinning. Why had I ever given this up? There was no feeling in the world like this high; all my worries disappeared and I felt as if I could conquer anything.

I had no idea why I had gotten so crazy over Chloe. What the fuck did she matter, anyway? No need to go all crazy over some chick who didn't care about me. I could get any woman I wanted, and there were always several lined up and waiting with no strings attached. I had my music, money, my band, and a bag full of coke. What else could a guy ask for?

I stood and followed Jack back out into the living room, the cocaine and mirror still in my hand. I spent the next several hours sitting around and joking with my new friends, snorting another line when I felt my high start to dwindle. By the time morning rolled around, I was out of coke and out of money. Jack drove me to the nearest ATM and I withdrew a couple hundred dollars to make sure I had enough.

When we made it back to his place, I paid him for twice the amount of coke I'd bought last night, as well as enough "hydros" to knock out a horse. I spent the rest of the day high as a fucking kite off both the coke and pain pills. I hadn't felt this good in a long time and I savored every moment. I crashed at his house that night and stayed late into the afternoon the following day. I finally decided I needed to get back to the bus before Jade or one of the guys beat the shit out of me.

Jack drove me back to the bar parking lot, and I was relieved to see the bus still sitting where it was the other night. Before I got out, I bought enough to hold me over until I could find someone else to supply me.

"If you're ever back in the area and need more, you just let me know, kid."

"Thanks, I will."

I stepped out of the car and waved as he pulled back out. I walked across the lot to the bus and headed up the stairs. Eric and Adam were sitting around our small table, and both their heads snapped up as they caught sight of me.

"What the fuck?" Adam roared.

"Thank God—where have you been?" Eric asked with concern.

"Sorry, I met some guy after our show the other night and lost track of the time," I said as I sat down beside Adam.

"You lost track of time? You've been gone two days, not two hours," he said as he leaned over and sniffed me, "and you fucking smell. Did you forget to take a bath?"

I grinned. "Sorry, I'll go shower."

I smacked him across the back of the head as I walked to my bunk and grabbed some clean clothes before stepping into the small bathroom. The cocaine I had snorted before I left Jack's place was already starting to wear off, so I grabbed one of Jade's mirrors and did a couple of lines before getting in the shower.

Once I'd finished, I dried off and dressed before walking back up front to join the guys. Jade came up the steps just as I sat down and launched herself at me.

"You asshole! Do you know how worried I've been?"

I grabbed her wrists and pushed her off me. "Sorry, like I told the guys, I lost track of time."

She stared at me with her mouth gaping. "Lost track of time? *Lost track of time?* I get a text saying you're going to some party and then no one can get ahold of you for two days! I thought you were dead, Drake!"

"I said I was sorry, what else do you want?" I shouted back at her.

"I don't want you to say anything! We had to cancel two shows because of your stupid ass!"

Eric slid out of his seat and stepped between us. "Both of you, calm down. Shouting at each other isn't going to help anything, all right?"

"Tell *her* that!" I growled.

"Oh, shut up. I want answers, Drake. Where the hell have you been?"

Jade was a tiny little thing, and I almost laughed at the sight of her so wound up. She rarely yelled at us, with the exception of Adam, and it was comical. It was like being yelled at by a baby kitten.

"I told you, I went to a party. I made a couple of new friends and decided to stay for a while."

She raised her eyes to the ceiling and mumbled something about needing patience. "Drake, as long as I've known you, you have never done anything like this. Why didn't you at least answer your phone to let us know you were okay?"

I pulled my phone out of my pocket and held it up for her to see. "I turned it off and then forgot about it."

"Drake, can I talk to you outside for a minute?" Eric asked as he stood.

I nodded and followed him off the bus. He walked halfway across the lot before he stopped and turned back to me. "Why don't you tell me what's really going on? I already have an idea."

I raised an eyebrow but said nothing.

He sighed as he pulled the envelope Kadi had given me out of his pocket and held it up. "I saw Kadi inside the bar and then found these lying on the ground by the bus, so I put two and two together. Have you talked to Chloe?"

My eyes were glued to the pictures as I shook my head. "I have nothing to say to her. A picture is worth a thousand words, and there are several in there."

"I might be overstepping my boundaries here, but I think you need to talk to her before you jump to any conclusions. Kadi is a nasty piece of work, and she could have taken innocent moments and turned them into something ugly."

"I don't see how Chloe and Jordan in bed together could be innocent."

"She was obviously in the room with them and it's not like they're naked. I mean, Chloe is looking right at the camera."

I ran my hands through my hair as I thought about what he said. He did have a point, I had to give him that, but it still didn't explain everything. I had barely been able to get Chloe to answer my calls lately, yet she seemed to have no trouble spending all of her time with Jordan.

"I don't know what the fuck to think."

"That's why you need to talk to her before you do something stupid." He looked at me closely. "You haven't already done something stupid, have you?"

No, nothing at all except buying enough coke to put a small dent in my bank account.

"If you're talking about girls, then no, I haven't."

He looked relieved. "Glad to hear it. Chloe is a good girl, Drake, and I've grown to like her over the last few months. I've seen the way she looks at you; there's no way she's cheating."

I motioned toward the bus. "Did you show those to Jade or Adam?"

"No, I figured they were the reason you bolted. I wanted to give you time to cool off."

"Thanks, man. I don't want them involved in this if they don't have to be."

We both looked up as a familiar red car pulled into the parking lot. My mouth hung open as Eric cursed under his breath.

"I might have forgotten to mention that Jade called Chloe this morning freaking out, and Chloe left to come find you."

I glared at him. "You think that might have been important?"

The car stopped next to the bus and Chloe was out and running toward me. I saw red as Jordan climbed out of the driver's seat. Before I even realized what I was doing, I was crossing the lot. I bypassed Chloe and went straight for Jordan. When I reached him, I pulled back and punched him in the face with enough force to send him flying backward.

CHAPTER THIRTEEN

CHLOE

The elation I felt at seeing Drake standing in the parking lot quickly turned to confusion as he weaved around me and headed for Jordan. I watched in horror as he pulled back and punched Jordan with enough force to break his nose. Jordan, taken by complete surprise, flew backward and landed on the ground with his hand up to his nose.

"What the hell?" he roared as he tried to stand back up.

Drake was on him in a flash and started punching any part of him that he could reach. Jordan, who was almost twice Drake's size, instantly started fighting back. He rolled and pinned Drake under him. After getting in a few good punches, he managed to grab both of Drake's arms and pin them to the ground.

Jade and Adam came running out of the bus just as Eric reached them and tried to pull Jordan away, with no luck. Eric was smaller than Drake, and there was no doubt in my mind that Jordan could take both of them if he had to.

I ran to their side and started pulling on his arm. "Jordan, let go of him."

He shook his head. "Not until he tells me what the hell that was for."

Drake struggled underneath him, his eyes full of rage. "Get off of me!"

"So you can try to beat the shit out of me again? I don't think so," Jordan growled as blood dripped from his nose.

"Holy shit, Chloe! What happened to *you*?" Adam asked.

All eyes instantly went to me and I let my hair fall forward to cover most of the bruises. "That's not important right now."

Eric walked over and held an envelope in front of me. "I think it has something to do with these."

I took the envelope from him and opened it. My mouth dropped open as I flipped through the pictures inside. "Where on Earth did he get these?" I asked.

"From some stalker named Kadi who has been following him around. She showed up here the other night and gave them to him."

"Kadi? *Danny's friend* Kadi?" I asked, completely confused. "How does she even know who Drake is, and why would she take these and then give them to him?"

Eric glanced at Drake, who was still struggling on the ground. "I think that's something you need to discuss with him."

"Jordan, let him up."

He looked at me like I was crazy. "Are you serious? He'll just start hitting me again!"

"No, he won't, will you, Drake?" I asked calmly.

"As long as he stays the fuck away from me, then no."

Jordan released Drake and stepped out of his range as I walked over to him and started inspecting his face. His nose was still bleeding and his left eye was starting to swell, but other than that, he looked fine.

"Are you okay? Is your nose broken?"

He wiped the blood away and gave me a small grin. "Nah, I'm fine. I get hit harder than that on the field."

I nodded as Drake stood and glared at us. "Go ahead, make sure I didn't hurt your little boyfriend."

Jordan glared at him, but I put my hand on his chest to keep him back. "Don't. He has good reason to think that."

I held the pictures out to him and he grabbed them, flipping through the pile quickly. "You've got to be kidding me! I knew that bitch was up to something."

"Yeah, you were right. Only she wasn't after Danny like you thought, she was after us," I said as he handed the pictures back to me.

I glanced up at Drake to see him watching us closely. "Why don't you go hang out on the bus for a while. I think Drake and I need to have a talk."

Jordan didn't seem to like the idea of leaving us alone together, and he made that obvious as he walked away. "You lay a finger on her and I'll break your neck. As far as I'm concerned, you fucked up our truce the minute you disappeared on everyone and scared her to death. The fact you hit me just adds to it."

Drake flipped him off as he walked away. "Asshole."

"Real mature, Drake. Seriously. He's only looking out for me."

"That's the problem. He watches out for you just a little bit too much."

I looked back at the bus to see Adam and Jordan both staring out the window at us. There was no way that we could have a private conversation with those two around.

"Want to take a walk?" I asked.

He shrugged his shoulders. "Sure, just let me grab my phone out of the bus first."

"Not like you were worried about it before," I grumbled as he walked away.

I had no idea what I was supposed to say to make those pictures look better. Kadi had caught the most innocent moments and turned them into something ugly and dirty. I had to admit that she had completely fooled me; the girl I was starting to consider a friend would never do something like that.

The fact that she had used my grieving cousin to get to me infuriated me more than anything, though. Only a truly sick individual would pull something like that. I hoped that either Drake or Jordan was with me next time I saw her or there would be some major bloodshed. Growing up with my mother, I was a strong advocate against violence, but Kadi had crossed too many lines in my book: using Danny, taking those pictures, and stalking Drake. The girl had a bad case of the crazies.

I was starting to wonder if Drake had decided to just hide in the bus when he finally emerged. He still looked pissed, but he seemed to have calmed down a bit.

"You ready?" he asked as he walked up to me.

"Yeah. You know this area better than I do, so lead the way."

We walked side by side down the street, but he kept at least a foot between us at all times. I noticed that he kept wiping his nose as we walked.

"Are you getting sick?" I asked.

He glanced up at me. "What?"

"You keep wiping your nose—I thought maybe you were sick."

He shook his head. "No, just allergies or something."

We walked in silence until the bus was out of view. I was uncomfortable with the silence and the awkwardness of the entire situation. With the exception of when I was with Logan, we had always had an easy relationship with each other, even when we were just friends. With one small envelope, I felt as if all of that had disappeared right before my eyes.

We turned the corner and walked into a small park. There were several children playing on the swings, but I continued past them to a more isolated location. What we needed to say wasn't for small children to hear.

"I don't even know where to start," I said as I sat down on a picnic table.

Drake moved to stand a few feet away from me. He leaned against a wooden beam that supported the roof of the shelter above us as he looked down at me. "Neither do I. I just never thought you'd do that to me."

"I didn't do anything, Drake. You know me better than that!"

"I saw the pictures myself, Chloe—you can't deny them."

I grabbed my face in aggravation and winced as I put pressure on my bruises. "She took those pictures during innocent moments and twisted them, Drake. I would never cheat on you—I love you too much."

"Like you loved Logan?"

That stung. He was throwing our past back in my face and I wanted to slap him for it. I did love Logan, but I knew now that it wasn't the same kind of love that I felt for Drake. If I had figured that out a little sooner, it would have saved all three of us a lot of pain.

"You're an asshole."

"No, I'm honest. It just sucks being on this side of it. I always felt guilty about Logan, but now that I'm in his shoes, I pity him. Getting burnt by you hurts like a bitch."

"I know I screwed up with Logan, and I came clean. But

you have to believe me, I never did anything to hurt you. Jordan is my friend, that's it." I pulled the pictures out of the envelope and held them up. "Every single one of these can be explained."

"By all means, explain them to me then." His tone was sarcastic, but I ignored it as I held the first one up.

"This one, he was hugging me because I was upset. There was nothing romantic about it, just two friends dealing with a lot of shit. These two were taken at my aunt's funeral. He closed up and I was trying to get him to talk to me. He held my hand because he needed comfort. The one where I'm thrown over his shoulder, that was the day I was talking to you when he threatened to drag me downstairs if I didn't hurry up. The one by the pool was taken just before he threw me in the water—we were just playing around. The one in the pool was when I was trying to dunk him. They're all completely innocent."

"You forgot my favorite one, though: the one with the two of you in bed together."

I didn't want to explain the fact that I was stuck in bed because my mother had beaten me, but I didn't see how I was going to make him believe me if I didn't tell him the absolute truth. I stared down at the picture for several seconds, trying to figure out just where to start with that horror story.

"Your silence says it all, Chloe." He turned and started to walk away.

"My mother beat me," I blurted out.

He stopped dead in his tracks and turned to glare at me. "That was a long time ago, so that won't work as an excuse now."

I shook my head. "No, I mean that's why we were in my bed. My mother beat me a couple of days before that picture was taken and I was stuck in bed with a couple of cracked ribs and a bruised body. Jordan refused to leave me—he was afraid she would come back to finish it."

I pushed my hair back so that he could see my face clearly. I knew the bruises covering my face would speak much louder than words. I felt vulnerable showing him my wounds, but I couldn't lose him.

He walked back over to me and raised his hand to trace one of the darker bruises on my cheekbone. I winced at the touch and he pulled back, looking pained.

"Jesus, Chloe, I didn't even fucking notice," he whispered.

"It's all right, I was trying to keep them covered. I didn't want to have to tell you this way."

"Your lip is busted and your face is practically green it's so bruised. How the hell did I not notice that? I really am an asshole. I was too worried about myself to even look at you. Why didn't you call me when it happened?"

"I didn't want you to worry and I knew you'd come right back to me. I wouldn't do that to the band—they depend on you far too much for me to constantly pull you away from them."

He ran his hands through his hair as he sat down beside me. "I really fucked up, didn't I? I should have known better than to believe anything that came from Kadi."

I shook my head. "No, I would have believed it too. But you've got to believe me now, Drake—nothing happened with Jordan, I swear."

"I believe you. I'm the stupidest idiot who ever lived for doubting you. I just saw those pictures and thought that I'd lost you." He cupped my face gently, trying not to touch any of the bruises. "I thought I lost the one person that I truly loved and I couldn't deal with it."

He leaned forward and kissed me. I felt my body sag in relief as I realized he truly believed me; I wasn't going to lose him.

"I love you too, Drake. When Jade called and said you'd just disappeared, I lost it. I'm in so deep with you, I don't think I'll ever surface. But I'm okay with that. If I'm going to drown, I want it to be with you."

He smiled. "Do you know how corny we sound? I think I just threw up a little."

I elbowed him in the ribs. "I don't care. I don't want you to ever doubt how I feel about you again."

"I won't, I promise. If there is ever anything that bothers me, I'll ask you before I assume anything."

"Good, I'm glad we cleared that up. But there's still one thing that's bothering me," I said nervously.

He raised an eyebrow. "What?"

"When you wouldn't answer your phone, where were you? Did you . . . Were you with someone?"

He instantly looked guilty and my heart almost stopped. He thought I'd cheated and went to some other woman to forget about me. I turned away as tears stung my eyes.

He grabbed my arm and turned me back to him. "I didn't cheat, if that's what you're thinking. I met some guy outside the bar and partied with him and his friends for a couple of days."

I raised my eyes to meet his. He sounded sincere, but the look of guilt was still there. "If you did, just tell me."

"I didn't, I swear. I was too . . . drunk to do anything. I spent most of my time lying on his couch."

His eyes pleaded with me to believe him, but I felt like he was keeping something from me. If it wasn't another woman, there was something else he was hiding; I just couldn't put my finger on it. I just hoped he would come clean with me. I didn't want anything to keep us apart.

"All right. If you say you didn't, then I believe you."

He seemed relieved as he pulled me to him and hugged me gingerly. "Thank you. I don't deserve it after how I reacted to the pictures."

"Of course you do. I know you would never keep anything from me," I said, trying to gauge his reaction.

There it was: a small flash of guilt crossed his face. He quickly hid it, but it confirmed that there was something he wasn't telling me.

He pulled away and I winced as he brushed against my ribs. His eyes dropped to my shirt as he lifted it slowly, revealing the wrap.

"How bad are you hurting?"

I shrugged. "I'm fine, just a little sore."

"With cracked ribs, I'd say 'a little sore' is an understatement. Want to tell me what happened?"

I tugged my shirt back down. I really didn't want to talk about my mom right now; I'd had enough stress for one day. Bringing up the fact that my own mother had tried to drown me was not going to help the situation any.

"Not really; it's not a big deal anyway. The cops are looking for her, so hopefully I won't have to deal with the drama anymore."

"It's a big deal to me. Please?" he asked as he brushed the hair that had fallen back around my face away.

I sighed. "She got really mad and threatened me when she found out that she wasn't getting anything from Aunt Jen. Jordan stuck close to me, but she'd left and he needed to make a phone call. I was with Kadi, but she had to leave too, so it was just me by the pool." I stopped as I realized what I had just said. "You know what? Kadi left right before my mom showed up. I would bet every dime my aunt left me that she passed her when she was leaving and didn't even warn me!"

As I realized just how much of a manipulative bitch Kadi really was, my temper flared all over again. There was no way I was letting her get away with all of this. And then she'd had the nerve to come up to my room and pretend to feel guilty, while taking pictures of me and Jordan in bed to show Drake. She just kept digging that hole of hers deeper.

"That doesn't surprise me; Kadi is twisted and always has been. I was young and stupid when I met her, and I regret ever getting involved with her. I was still in high school and blown away that some college girl was interested in me. She hid the crazy side of herself well at first, though, in my defense."

I cringed at the thought of Drake with Kadi. She was a perfect example of the type of girl I always worried about when it came to Drake doing shows without me around. Knowing he had been with someone like her didn't help my self-esteem one bit.

"Why are you so quiet over there? What'd I say?" he asked with a confused look on his face.

I couldn't help but smile at his obliviousness. "Knowing you've been with girls like her hurts a little bit; I won't lie. You have all those girls at shows fighting for your attention, and I always feel like I don't add up."

He looked at me as if I'd lost my mind. "Are you kidding me? I noticed you the minute you walked into the room that first day. I'd never seen anyone as beautiful as you were. I can't change my past or the things I did, but I don't want that to hold us back." He frowned. "You know, you're really good at distracting me."

"Huh?"

"You never told me what happened with your mom. Don't think I didn't notice that, so start talking."

I groaned. "I thought I had you. She got me when I got out of the pool; she snuck up behind me and threw me to the ground. She kicked the shit out of me, beat my head against the concrete, and then tried to drown me. Jordan showed up around then and got her off of me. Allison called the police and paramedics, and I spent a couple of days in the hospital. No one has seen her since."

I thought that was a good summary of what happened. I didn't want to get into the details with him; I knew it would only make him angrier, and I didn't need him chasing after my mother. If I had any luck at all, she'd just disappear and leave me alone.

"I shouldn't have left you there alone. I put my stupid band before you."

I shook my head. "It's not your fault. Jordan was watching me like a hawk and it still happened. Even if you had been there, she would have found a way to get to me. Your band is important to you. I would never expect you to give it up for me."

"Nothing is more important than you."

"Seriously, stop beating yourself up. Regrets will get you nowhere; we're together now and that's all that matters."

He kissed me again and I shivered at the sensations that it caused. "I've missed you."

"I've missed you too. I feel like we have a lot of time to make up for." I gave him a devious grin.

He laughed as he shook his head. "Not happening; at least not until you're healed. Besides, it's kind of hard to do any of the things I want to do to you in a small bunk on a bus filled with people."

"I'm not made of glass, and I'm sure they wouldn't mind if we went to a hotel for the night."

He brushed his hand against my ribs and I grimaced. "Not made of glass, huh? While I'm not opposed to getting a room with you, we've got to get back on the road. Jade already had to cancel two shows because of my dumb ass. If we miss any more, she'll be out for blood."

"Fine," I pouted, "we should probably get back then. I need to take Jordan home, then I'll meet back up with you."

He frowned. "Stay with me overnight, then you can take him home. I just got you back; I'm not ready to give you up just yet."

"Sounds like a plan to me as long as he's okay with it."

He pulled me to my feet and started leading me through the park, but stopped at one of the pits that were used to build fires in.

"Give me those pictures."

I handed him the envelope and watched as he placed it in the pit and pulled his lighter out. Without a second thought, he lit the envelope on fire and watched as it, and the pictures inside, started to burn.

When there was nothing left but ashes, he turned to me. "There. Now I'm ready."

I smiled up at him as he took my hand and led me out of the park and back to the bus. Jordan exited as soon as he saw us, worry etched into his face.

"Everything okay?" he asked as he eyed Drake suspiciously.

"Yeah, we're good. You up for a small road trip?" I asked as I walked back to my car.

"Um, sure?" It came out as a question more than a statement.

"Just one more night and then I'll take you home."

"Fair enough. You want me to drive?" he asked.

I pulled my keys out and handed them to him. "Sure."

Drake pulled me to him, careful not to touch my ribs. "She's on the bus with me, or I'll just ride in the car with her. Your choice."

Jordan rolled his eyes as he tossed the keys to Drake. "By all means, princess. I'll just hang out on the bus."

I gave him an apologetic smile as he shook his head and boarded the bus.

Drake helped me into the car before taking a seat behind the wheel. "He's had you long enough; it's my turn."

Shortly after Jade came out and Drake explained the driving situation, we were on the road. I smiled as I rolled my window down and let the warm summer air blow through my hair. Drake was safe and we were going to be okay; things were finally starting to look up for us.

CHAPTER FOURTEEN

DRAKE

I laughed as I watched Chloe stick her head out of the car window. "What are you doing?"

"Pretending to be a dog," she deadpanned. "What do you think? I'm letting the wind blow my hair!"

"The dog excuse sounded better," I said as she smacked me.

"Shut up! This is the first time I've felt free in a long time."

"Go right ahead, but when you eat a bug don't come crying to me."

She stuck her tongue out as I gunned the engine and flew down the interstate, passing the tour bus. She flew backward into her seat, cursing and clutching her side. "Damn it, watch the ribs!"

I instantly felt guilty. "Sorry, babe."

She grinned as she leaned back out the window. "Just kidding!"

I frowned. "Not funny."

I took the next exit to fill up on gas and make a pit stop. As I drove down the exit ramp, she stuck her body farther out the window. Her ass was the only part of her I could see, and I grinned to myself before smacking it. She squealed and sat back down in her seat.

"Stop it!"

"What? You had it right there in front of me—what did you expect me to do?"

She rolled her eyes as I pulled in next to the gas pumps. I sent a quick text to Jade, letting her know that we would be right behind them once we filled up. As I stuck my card in the machine, Chloe got out and walked into the store. I watched her go, smiling to myself. It was good to have her back with me, especially now that I knew everything Kadi told me had been a lie.

I finished filling up and walked into the store to find the bathroom. Chloe was standing in the checkout line and I pointed to the restroom in the back of the store, letting her know I'd be just a minute. As I walked in and locked the door, I was relieved to see that it was a single-stall bathroom so I knew I wouldn't be interrupted.

The bag in my pocket felt like a lead weight as I pulled it out and stared at the white powder inside. What the hell was I doing? Everything was fine between us now and I didn't need to do this. I debated on dumping it down the toilet, but I quickly shoved the thought aside. There was no reason to just throw my money away; I would finish this bag and then be done with it all.

I pulled the mirror and dollar bill out of my pocket and set them on the sink. I dumped a small amount out and made a line, snorting it quickly. Just as I finished, someone started beating on the bathroom door.

"Hold on!" I shouted as I stashed everything back in my pocket. My heart was beating out of my chest as I looked around, making sure that I had left no evidence behind. I threw the door open to see Chloe standing there waiting for me.

She smiled brightly as she handed me a soda. "You take longer than a girl. Hurry up or we'll never catch up with the bus!"

I wiped my nose to make sure there were no traces of powder as I followed her out of the store. I started to feel the effects as we walked back to the car; it had been a couple of hours since my last fix, and I instantly started to relax as I felt the rush running through my veins. I stopped Chloe just as she started to open her door and kissed her hard on the mouth. She sighed, and her lips parted as I ran my tongue along her bottom lip.

I pulled away and she stared up at me, breathless. "What was that for?"

"Because I felt like it. Do I need a reason?"

"Nope, you can kiss me like that anytime you want," she said as she slid into her seat.

I closed her door and walked around the car to get in. As I sat down, I noticed her sifting through the massive bag she called a purse. I refused to ever stick my hand in that thing; I had seen her pull her hand out cursing from some kind of injury far too many times to feel safe sticking my own hand in. How would I play guitar if I lost a hand to some unknown purse beast?

"What are you doing?" I asked as she continued to dig.

"Ha! Found them!" She pulled out a pill bottle with a triumphant look on her face. "My ribs are starting to hurt, so I was trying to find my pain pills."

I watched her wearily as she popped the top and pulled out a small white pill. I didn't want that temptation around me as well. "Do you really need those?"

"Um, yeah. If I don't take one every few hours my ribs and face start throbbing. What's the big deal?"

"Nothing, I just don't want you stoned and trying to seduce me while I'm driving," I joked, hoping she wouldn't notice my discomfort.

"Pretty sure I'd have to take more than one to make me do that while you're on the interstate." She smiled at me playfully. "Although, we're not on the interstate just yet."

She reached across the console and ran her hand across my leg. I bit back a groan as I pushed her hand away. I was trying to be the good guy and she wasn't helping me any.

"Don't even think about it," I said as I pulled out of the parking lot and up the ramp to merge into three lanes of traffic.

She pushed my hand aside as she cupped me through my pants. I bit my lip as I tried to focus my attention on the road in front of me. I wasn't doing a very good job paying attention.

"If you keep that up, you'll be sorry," I groaned.

"That was the plan."

"Not happening. I don't want to hurt you, Chloe."

She pouted. "You're not going to hurt me. I'm starting to feel like I'm not wanted."

I grabbed her hand and pressed it against my hard-on. "Now tell me you're not wanted. All you did was touch me through my pants and I'm about to bust my zipper. Wanting you isn't the problem."

"Well, I don't see the issue then. I bet I can change your mind tonight."

I sighed as I pushed the gas harder when I noticed the bus in the distance. "You're not going to make this easy, are you?"

"Nope. I know you'll cave eventually."

We spent the next two hours catching each other up on

everything that we'd missed by being apart and fighting over what CD to listen to. As the miles crept by, I started feeling restless and debated pulling over again, but I couldn't think of a good excuse. I smacked the steering wheel in aggravation, feeling weak.

Chloe looked up at me in surprise. "What was that for?"

I took a deep breath to control my temper. "Nothing, just tired of driving."

"We can switch if you want."

I shook my head. "Nah, I just want out of this car."

I was not going to let this get to me. I had spent years staying away from drugs and I wasn't about to relapse after only a few days of using again. I controlled my own actions, not some fucking powder.

Chloe helped to distract me by singing along to the songs she had blaring from the speakers. I laughed as she did as much of a car dance as her ribs would allow. My laughter soon died as I noticed two guys driving next to us, watching her. Chloe was oblivious to the attention as I flipped them off and sped up. I had never been the jealous type—not that I had ever cared enough about anyone to get jealous—but with Chloe, anytime a guy looked her direction, I wanted to rip his head off. It made life difficult when she was around, since she always seemed to catch men's eyes without even trying. Her innocence when it came to the opposite sex was cute, but sometimes it became annoying when she acted like I was blowing things out of proportion.

Before I knew it, we were following the bus down an exit ramp. We drove through a small town before stopping at a bar just past the city limits. The bar looked small from the outside, but it was a lot better-looking than some of the ones we had played in recently. The parking lot was free of any litter, and the bar itself looked like it had just recently been painted. I hoped the inside was just as nice; it would be nice to leave a gig without needing to shower right after we finished.

I parked the car next to the bus and got out to stretch my legs. The long ride had made Chloe stiff and I had to help her out of the car. As I pulled her out and shut the door, Jordan and the band stepped off the bus and walked over to us.

Jordan was instantly by her side. "Are you okay? Did you take your pill?"

I felt my temper flare again as I watched him look her over. She didn't need him to take care of her anymore; I was back around to do that.

"I'm fine, and yes, I took my pill. Stop acting like you're my mom."

He snorted. "Gee, thanks—that's who I was trying to be."

"Oh, you know what I meant."

I wrapped my arm around her shoulders as I glared up at Jordan. "You can back off now; I can handle her from here on out."

I knew I was being an ass, but I couldn't seem to help myself. Whatever truce I'd had with Jordan had disappeared when I looked at those pictures. I knew now that they were innocent, but I didn't like that he had curled up in bed with her while I was away. It was taking the whole friendship thing a little too far.

"Drake, don't," Chloe pleaded.

I ignored her as I continued to glare at Jordan. "Chloe explained the pictures to me, but I still don't appreciate the fact you had your hands on her more than once when I was gone. She's mine, and I'm making that clear right now. If you don't like it, I'll be glad to go another round with you."

Jordan laughed, which only infuriated me further. "It's not

like that with us, but she *is* still my friend and I'll take care of her if I need to. You need to tone down the jealous boyfriend thing; you're making yourself look like an idiot."

I stepped forward and shoved him. My body was tight with anticipation as I waited for him to shove me back. That was all I needed to start punching him again. I willed him to hit me, but he shook his head and stepped back.

"You need to get your shit together or she's going to dump your sorry ass," he growled.

Chloe stepped in between us and put her hands out. "Enough! What's wrong with you, Drake?"

"Nothing," I spat as I turned away from them to look at the band. "Let's carry our stuff in and start setting up."

Eric watched me closely as we unloaded the instruments and carried them inside. I tried to ignore him, but I could feel him staring at me as I helped Jade set her drums up. Out of everyone, Eric was the one who I was most worried about. He was always so quiet, but I knew he spent that time observing people. He had an uncanny ability to see things that others missed, and if anyone caught me, I knew it would be him.

We finished setting up and started walking back out to the bus. Jade had forced us to stop a couple of towns back to pick up real food from the supermarket because the constant fast food was starting to get to her. I knew there had to be something microwavable in there, and I was dreaming of macaroni and cheese as we entered the bus. All thoughts of food left me as soon as I saw Chloe sitting at the table with Jordan, leaning against him with her head on his shoulder as he ran his hands through her hair.

I saw red as I stomped over to stand in front of them. "What the fuck?" I shouted.

Jordan held a finger up to his lips and pointed to Chloe. I looked down at her and noticed that she was asleep. I felt like an ass as I watched her stir in her sleep before slowly opening her eyes. They landed on me and she smiled, until she noticed the look on my face.

"What's wrong?"

I motioned between her and Jordan. "Sorry, I just came in and saw you two all cuddled up together. Again."

She must have realized that she was still leaning on him and pulled away instantly. "I must have fallen asleep. I didn't mean to make you mad, Drake."

I ran my hands through my hair and turned to start digging through the cabinets for food. "It's all right; I jumped to conclusions again."

Unable to find any macaroni and cheese, I settled for the next best thing: Pop-Tarts. I pulled a pack from the box and ripped them open. Chloe stood and walked over to me, wrapping her hands around my waist.

"I'm sorry, I really am. But you promised to always ask before you jumped to conclusions again, remember?"

I nodded as I stuffed food in my mouth so that I didn't have to reply.

She sighed and walked back to the bunks. Either she was good at guessing or she noticed the picture of us I had hanging against the wall, because she lay down in my bunk.

"I'm going to sleep until it's time for you to go on. Just wake me up when you're ready."

I pushed away from the small counter and walked into the bathroom. After double-checking that the door was locked, I pulled my stash out of my pocket. If I didn't do something, I was going to rip Jordan in two. Or at least I would try; I didn't see myself coming out on top in that fight.

After snorting a couple of lines, I put everything away and sat down on the toilet with my head in my hands. I had no idea what I was doing, but I did know that if Chloe ever found out she would freak and possibly leave me. I sat up and punched the wall beside my head, trying to release some of the anger that was radiating from me. I jumped as someone started beating on the door.

"Dude, hurry the fuck up or I'm going to come in there and piss on you!" Adam shouted.

I grinned as I stood up; leave it to Adam to lighten the mood. I threw the door open, still grinning.

"I don't want to see that little dick of yours, so have at it."

Adam started unbuttoning his pants as he blocked my exit. "Want to compare them? I'm sure mine is bigger."

I busted out laughing as I pushed him out of the way. "I think I'll pass. I don't have a magnifying glass with me anyway."

He punched me in the stomach as I walked by, and I grunted. "Whatever. Not my fault you can't handle all of this."

With that, he shut the door in my face. I was still laughing as I walked to the front of the bus, and Eric raised an eyebrow at me.

"Should I even ask?"

I shook my head. "Adam was trying to get naked with me in the bathroom. He was kind of upset when I turned him down." I said it loud enough to carry back to the bathroom, hoping Adam would hear me.

I heard a muffled "Fuck you" and started laughing all over again.

Eric shook his head as he motioned toward the door. "You got a minute?"

I felt uneasy, but I nodded and followed him off the bus. If he wanted to talk to me alone, it couldn't be anything good. I leaned against the side of the bus and waited for him to speak. Instead, he just stood there and studied me as I fidgeted nervously under his watchful eye.

"You said you wanted to talk?" I asked when I couldn't stand it any longer.

"Yeah. I just don't know how to say this without being a dick."

I snorted. "Adam is the one who's a dick, not you."

"Fine, I'll just say it. I don't know what's going on with you, but you haven't been acting right all day. I understood when you were pissed about Chloe, but since you guys rode here together, I'm assuming that was cleared up. Is something else bothering you?"

I knew Eric would be a problem; he was too smart for his own good sometimes. I looked around the parking lot, trying to figure out what to say. My eyes fell on Jordan, who was standing across the lot, talking on his phone.

"I don't like Jordan around Chloe. I know I've been an asshole all day, but once he's gone I'll calm down."

Eric nodded. "I figured it was something like that. Listen, though: I really don't think you have anything to worry about with him, so stop stressing. All you're going to do is drive Chloe nuts and tick her off. She's taking him home tomorrow, isn't she?"

"Yeah, and I'm not too happy about that either."

"Don't worry about it. She'll drop him off and come right back here with you. Problem solved."

"Yeah, I know. I'll try to get my shit together."

He clapped me on the back as he walked past me. "I know you will."

We spent the next hour killing time by playing cards. I laughed as Jade repeatedly beat all of us. The woman was a damn card shark and we all knew it, yet we still played her like the idiots we were. After I all but gift-wrapped and handed her a hundred bucks, I walked back to my bunk and started poking Chloe on the shoulder, trying to wake her up.

She groaned in her sleep and rolled away from me. I smiled as I reached down and picked her up, careful not to touch her ribs. The movement woke her up and she jumped in my arms as her eyes flew open.

"What are you doing?" she asked, still groggy.

"Waking you up." I sat her down and leaned in, peppering her face with kisses.

She smiled and tried to squirm away, but I held her tight against me. "You're not going anywhere."

"Quit it—I probably have drool all over the side of my face!"

"I like drool; it's sexy," I said as I pulled away.

"Drool is sexy on no one, not even you. What time is it?" she asked as she stretched and winced.

"We go on in twenty. Go wipe the drool from your face so we can go in."

I waited by my bunk as she walked into the bathroom to retie her hair and wash her face. I loved the fact that it didn't take her an hour to get ready like most girls. With Chloe, what you saw was what you got, and I found it refreshing. Sure, she dressed up from time to time, but most of the time she was in a pair of jeans and a T-shirt. Instead of it bothering me, I found it incredibly sexy.

She exited the bathroom and walked up to me, throwing her arms around me as she pulled my mouth down to meet hers in a hungry kiss. As her tongue slipped into my mouth, I groaned and grabbed her ass. If she kept this up, there was no way I could keep my vow to wait until she was healed. We hadn't been together in weeks, and a guy can take only so much.

"You're going to kill me, you know that?" I asked as she pulled away. I took a deep breath, trying to distract myself from the raging hard-on she had given me.

"I'm trying. Are we getting a hotel room tonight?" she asked breathlessly.

And there went any hopes of calming down before I had to go onstage.

I leaned down and brushed my lips against the corner of her mouth. "Yeah, we are, but if you try anything on me, I'm tying you to the bed."

Her eyes lit up and she grinned at me. "Is that supposed to make me behave? If so, you need to think of a better threat."

I wasn't a bondage type of guy, but damn! Picturing Chloe tied to my bed naked was enough to make me come in my pants. I groaned as I grabbed her hand and led her off the bus.

"I have to be onstage in ten minutes—please don't do that to me."

She laughed as we walked across the now full lot and into the bar. Jade and the guys were already sitting at a table close to the stage, and I pushed through the crowd to them. I kept Chloe close to me, trying to protect her from anyone who might bump into her. We took the two empty seats left at the table, with Chloe ending up between Jordan and me. That grated on my nerves, but I took a deep breath and let it go. Eric was right; if I kept acting like a jealous freak, all I would do was drive her away.

I relaxed back into my seat as a waitress brought me a beer and waited for the owner to introduce us. The crowd around us was already hyped up, and I let their excitement flow into me. I had no doubt that they would keep us going throughout the night with no problem. There was nothing I despised more than a crowd with no energy; it made it twice as hard to play and sing well, and we weren't nearly as good when that happened. We might supply the music, but it was the crowd itself who set the mood for the entire set.

I gave Chloe a quick kiss before walking to the stage with the rest of the band as the waitress who had brought me a beer introduced us. Several people crowded around the stage as I spoke into the mic. "Evening, guys. I'm Drake, and we're Breaking the Hunger!"

With that, Jade started us into our first song as the crowd shouted their approval. As I sang into the mic, I watched Chloe and Jordan out of the corner of my eye. Jordan was whispering something in her ear, but she was ignoring him as she stared at the crowd in front of me. I glanced down to see several women all trying to catch my attention.

This was where things got tricky for me. If I ignored them and pissed them off, we'd lose fans; if I smiled and flirted with them, Chloe would be angry with me. As far as I was concerned, it was a no-win situation. I had been angry with Chloe for paying attention to Jordan when here I was, surrounded by women with lust-filled eyes. Sometimes karma is a bitch.

I glanced over at Chloe and grinned as an idea struck me. For the rest of the song, I smiled and flirted with the women with my eyes. I caught Chloe throwing death glares my way and I hoped that my plan wouldn't backfire on me.

When the song ended, I waited for the crowd to settle down

before I spoke into the mic. "Thanks to everyone who's out here tonight. You guys rock!" The crowd started shouting again, and I had to wait for them to calm down so that they could hear me. "Tonight is kind of a special show for me. There's this girl that I happen to be crazy about, and this is the first show she's been able to make it to. Now earlier today, she told me that I could kiss her anywhere I wanted, and I feel like kissing her right now. Why don't you come up here with me, Chloe?"

I looked at her expectantly, but she was hiding her face in her hands. I laughed as I pointed her out to the crowd; I knew she was going to kill me for this later. "She doesn't seem to want to come up. Think you guys can convince her?"

Jordan was laughing as the crowd started chanting her name and she smacked him. I couldn't keep the stupid grin off my face as she rose slowly and walked up the steps and onto the stage. She stopped beside me and tried to glare at me, but the small smile she was trying to hide gave her away.

I slid the mic back into its stand and pulled her close against me. "Am I embarrassing you?" I whispered into her ear.

"Just a little."

I laughed as her cheeks flushed and turned my attention back to the audience staring at us. "Do you think I should kiss her now?" I asked them.

The wolf whistles and cheering from the crowd gave me the answer I was looking for. I turned back to Chloe with a huge grin on my face. "We can't disappoint them, now, can we?"

"I'm going to tie *you* to the bed tonight for this, Drake Allen!" she yelled as I pulled her close and slammed my mouth against hers.

As soon as our lips touched, the fight in her evaporated and she wrapped her arms around my neck. Maybe it was because we were standing onstage in front of so many people and my body was feeding off the energy that was pouring off them in waves, or maybe it was because I had the added bonus of co-caine in my system, but for some reason the kiss was crazy hot. At least it was to me, anyway, and I was pretty sure Chloe felt it too from the way she was clinging to me.

I let myself be taken over by the kiss; as she moved her lips against mine, the screaming crowd and the band behind us faded away. I probed her lips with my tongue until she opened them to allow me access. A moan came from deep in her throat as she flicked my tongue ring with her own tongue. I pulled away before I did something we'd both regret later. Chloe opened her eyes and my resolve nearly caved as I saw the lust in them.

I forced myself to turn back to the crowd with an easy smile plastered on my face. "Now that we've got that out of the way, who's ready for some more music?" I shouted.

Chloe walked offstage as we started into the next song, and I noticed several of the women in the front glaring at her. I was glad when I noticed Jordan watching them as well; I knew he would keep her safe until I was finished. I kept a close eye on her as we played a few more songs, just to make sure.

It seemed as though I had looked away from her table for only a minute as we played our last song, but when I glanced up, both of them were nowhere to be seen. We finished the song and before the last note stopped, I was off the stage and looking for Chloe.

CHAPTER FIFTEEN

CHLOE

s I walked offstage and took my seat next to Jordan, I felt
the eyes of several people in the crowd on me. I followed
Jordan's glare and noticed that most of the eyes were attached
to several women standing in front of the stage, glaring at me.
I smirked at them before turning my attention to Jordan, who
was watching me curiously.

"You okay?" he asked.

"Yeah, why?"

"I just assumed that he embarrassed you to death up there."

"Oh, he did, but the glares of death I'm getting from over
there"—I pointed to the women standing by the stage—"made
it totally worth it."

He shook his head. "I worry about your self-preservation
skills sometimes."

I patted him on the shoulder and grinned. No one would
be stupid enough to approach me with Drake a few feet away
onstage and if that didn't scare them, Jordan the Hulk sitting
beside me would.

I jumped as my back pocket started vibrating. It took me a

minute to realize that it was my phone. By the time I got it out, it had stopped vibrating. I had called Amber a few times since my accident, but I had left out what had happened and used the stomach bug excuse with her as well. She called me daily to check on me, and I assumed it was her calling.

I was surprised to see an unknown Maryland number pop up on my screen. Before I had time to consider who it was, the phone started vibrating again. I pushed through the crowd, trying to get outside; it was far too loud inside the bar to hear anything. I finally made it to the door and hurried outside, worried that it might be someone calling for Danny.

"Hello?" I asked breathlessly.

"Chloe?"

I froze as I heard my mother's voice. I hadn't considered the possibility that it might be her. I'd just assumed that with the cops looking for her, she wouldn't be stupid enough to contact me.

"Yeah, Mom, it's me. What do you want?"

"You know you ruined everything for me, don't you?" she slurred.

Great. Not only did I have to deal with her, but I had to do it while she was drunk.

I sighed. "I had nothing to do with what Aunt Jen did, but if you want the truth, I did go there planning to convince her to change her mind. But I didn't have to say anything; she told me that you wouldn't be getting anything the first day that I talked to her. You did this to yourself, Mother, so don't try to blame me."

"You're lying. You always lie to me, Chloe. I'm so tired of having to put up with you. You're a disgrace."

"If all you did was call me to yell at me, I'm hanging up. You've really screwed up this time, you know that? The police are looking for you as we speak for what you did to me. You nearly killed me, Mom. Doesn't that bother you in the least?"

I wanted her to tell me she was sorry, or that she at least felt some regret for what she had done to me. I knew I was being ridiculous, but the little girl inside of me hoped that somewhere in that blackened heart of hers she loved me.

"No, it doesn't. The world would be better off without you; without both of us."

That surprised me; in all the years I had put up with her verbal abuse, never had she once said anything bad about herself.

"That's not true. You've made some really bad decisions in your life, Mom, but you can change all of that. I wish you would consider one of the treatment programs Aunt Jen left for you."

She started to reply, but a train's whistle in the background cut her off.

"Mom, are you at a train station? Are you leaving?"

The train's whistle blew again as I waited for her to speak.

"Fuck those programs and fuck you," she growled. "And yeah, you could say I'm catching the train. I just wanted to call and tell you exactly what I thought of you."

The train's whistle was loud enough now that I actually pulled my phone away from my ear. It ended suddenly as my mother ended the call, and I sighed. I should have known she'd call before she left just to make my life hell.

"You all right, Chloe Bear?" Jordan asked from behind me.

I screamed like a twelve-year-old and nearly jumped a foot

off the ground at the sound of his voice. I was in a dimly lit parking lot by myself, or so I had thought, and hearing a voice that close to me nearly gave me a heart attack.

"Holy shit, Jordan! Don't do that to me!" I shouted.

Instead of laughing, he frowned and looked down at the phone in my hand.

"How long have you been out here?" I asked.

"I followed you outside; I heard everything, at least on your side."

I groaned as I crammed my phone back into my pocket. "I don't even know what to do anymore when it comes to her. She said she was calling to tell me goodbye and I hope she meant it. I don't think I can deal with her anymore."

He walked over to me and wrapped me up in his arms. "Don't worry about her; if she calls again we'll just have your number changed."

I hugged him back, glad that I had someone besides myself to depend on who had seen her craziness firsthand.

"I never really thanked you for saving me. I was too busy trying to convince you that it wasn't your fault. So thanks for, you know, not letting me die in the pool."

He gripped me harder and kissed my forehead. "Never thank me for that; I put you there in the first place. I don't know what I'd do if something happened to you."

I looked up as someone cleared their throat. Drake was standing behind Jordan with a pissed-off look on his face. Were the fates plotting against me lately or what? Every time Jordan touched me, Drake appeared out of thin air at the worst possible moment.

I pulled away from Jordan and gave Drake a weak smile. Jordan tensed beside me as he turned to face Drake.

"Before you get all pissy and jump to conclusions again, let her explain," Jordan said.

"No need to—I trust Chloe."

I raised my eyebrows in surprise; from the look on Drake's face I had assumed he and Jordan were going to get into it again.

"Good to know. Chloe said you two are spending the night in a hotel room, so I'm stealing your bunk for the night if you're okay with it," Jordan said coolly.

"Have at it. I'll be too busy to worry about who's in my bunk."

I felt my cheeks warm at his words. I wasn't a prude, but it still felt awkward to have Drake say something like that to one of my friends.

"Will you please shut up?" I pleaded.

"Sorry. Why don't you wait in the car while I help the guys carry everything out?" Drake asked.

"Sure."

Jordan stepped forward as Drake turned to walk back inside. "Go to the car and lock the doors. I'll go help them once I know you're safe."

I rolled my eyes and saluted him before turning and walking across the lot to my car. After getting in and locking the doors, I watched Jordan walk inside.

A few minutes later, the band and Jordan appeared as they carried their instruments back to the bus. With Jordan helping, they had everything put away in record time. I watched as Drake talked with Eric for a minute, both their heads bent together. He waved good night to them and made his way to my car. I unlocked the door for him and he sat down beside me, grinning.

"Ready?"

He nodded. "Yeah. I saw a decent-looking place when we came through earlier. Let's check it out and see if they have anything available."

I pulled out of the lot and drove in the direction we had come from earlier. Drake fidgeted nervously as I drove. I assumed it was from the high the show had given him; he was always hyped after they performed and I tended to reap the rewards. Sometimes several times in a row.

The hotel lot was quiet as we pulled in and parked next to the entrance. Drake got out of the car and grabbed the bag he'd stashed in my car earlier, as well as mine. We walked into the reception area and approached the counter to see a pretty woman in her late thirties sitting behind it.

She smiled as we walked up. "Good evening, my name is Kayla. How can I help you?"

"Do you have any rooms available?" I asked.

"Certainly. How many nights will you be staying?"

"Just one." Drake spoke from behind me.

I wanted to gag as I watched her eyes slowly roam over Drake's body. "Do you want smoking or nonsmoking?"

I looked at Drake expectantly; it didn't matter to me, but he smoked.

"Smoking is fine."

She started typing on the computer sitting in front of her. "I have three rooms available, two with twin beds and one with a queen. Do you want one of the twin-bed rooms?"

She looked hopeful that he would request one of the twin-bed rooms. I rolled my eyes as I pulled my credit card out of my pocket and slammed it down on the counter. "We'll take the queen."

Drake coughed to cover a laugh as she looked me over with

a smirk on her face. Without another word, she charged my card and handed us two key cards. "Follow the signs to the elevator, second floor, first hallway on your right. If you need anything, please let me know."

I bit back a reply that probably would have gotten us kicked out as I followed Drake down a hallway and into an elevator. He was grinning like an idiot until I "accidentally" stomped on his foot.

"Ouch! What was that for?"

"You were enjoying that way too much," I grumbled.

"I can't help it; you look so cute when you're fired up and trying to protect my virtue."

I tried to stomp on his foot again, but he pulled away as the elevator doors slid open.

"Don't be mad, it's sweet. It just shows how much you care."

"Right. I'm going to spend the next fifty years trying to beat off women who are old enough to be your mother."

He kissed my forehead as we walked down the hall to our room. "Don't worry, babe, I'm not into cougars."

I couldn't help but laugh as I put my card in the slot and pushed the door open. The room was small but clean, with a TV and microwave in the corner. I walked across the room to look out the window. There wasn't much of a view, unless you liked staring at a gas station and a grocery store.

I watched Drake's reflection in the glass as he walked up behind me and wrapped his arms around me. I snuggled back into his warmth as he kissed that sensitive spot behind my ear. I always felt safe when I was in Drake's arms.

"My mom called me tonight," I blurted out, effectively ruining the moment.

His whole body went rigid behind me. "What the fuck did she want?"

"Basically to tell me goodbye and how worthless I am. I'm pretty sure she was at a train station, so hopefully this time she'll be gone for good."

"For her sake I hope so; woman or not, if I ever see her again I'll knock the shit out of her."

"Drake! Don't say that!"

"We both know she deserves it. I can't believe a mother would do that to her own child."

"I know, but just let it go, okay? I don't need to worry about bailing you out of jail, do I?" I asked.

He kissed the top of my head. "Only if I get caught."

I laughed as I turned to face him. "Good to know. Jordan was hugging me tonight because she called me, just in case you're wondering."

"I was telling the truth earlier; I trust you. You don't need to explain yourself to me."

"I know, but I want to. I don't ever want you to doubt me." I kissed him softly as my hands slid under his shirt to the hard muscles of his stomach. They tightened under my touch and he shivered as he pulled away. He was obviously in need of a release as much as I was, if that was all it took to get him going. I smiled as I realized that was proof enough that he had been faithful while we were apart.

"I'm going to go take a shower," he said, clearing his throat, "probably a cold one. Stay here."

I raised an eyebrow. "Where exactly would I go? The gas station next door?"

"You know what I mean—don't sneak up on me in the shower. I'll lock the door if I have to."

I laughed as he grabbed clean clothes from his bag and walked into the bathroom. He always thought the worst of me; of course he was right this time, I was planning on attacking him in the shower. One way or another, I was going to get him to cave before the night was over.

I waited until I heard the shower running for a couple of minutes before stripping off my clothes and the bandage around my ribs. I walked quietly into the bathroom and stood by the shower stall. Drake had his back to me, and I grinned as I slid the door open and stepped inside. He jumped and turned as I ran my hands down his back.

"I thought I told you to stay," he grumbled as he rinsed off.

"I'm not a dog, first of all, and I don't listen very well anyway."

"Obviously."

I stepped under the water with him and began exploring the hard ridges of his stomach with first my hands, and then my tongue. Despite the hot water running over us, he shivered.

"Chloe, we can't. You're not healed and I don't want to hurt you."

"You won't hurt me; I know for a fact you can be gentle when you want to be," I said as I ran my tongue over first one nipple ring, then the other.

I tugged gently and he groaned. "You're going to drive me insane."

I ignored him as I licked my way back down his stomach to the deep V of his abdomen and then farther down still. I dropped to my knees in front of him, wrapping my hand around his arousal and squeezing. He leaned against the side of the shower stall as I started stroking him, picking up speed as I went.

His body stiffened as I wrapped my lips around his hardness and ran my tongue over his piercing. I knew he was extremely sensitive there and I intended to take advantage of that little fact. His breathing became ragged as I swirled my tongue around his tip and sucked him as deep as I could. His hips thrust toward me, trying to get me to take him deeper, as his hands gripped my hair to hold me in place.

Just as he was about to explode, I pulled away and he glared at me. "That's not playing fair."

"Never said I was going to play fair." I smiled coyly up at him.

He grinned as he wrapped his own hand around himself and started stroking roughly. "Neither did I."

My body instantly responded as I watched him pleasure himself. It was the single most erotic moment of my life, and I'd had several since we had been together. He closed his eyes and his lips parted as he worked himself to the brink again. I grabbed his hand and pulled it away, knowing that if I didn't stop him now my plan would be ruined.

"No, you don't. If you're going to finish, you're going to do it with me," I said as I stepped closer to him, our bodies sliding against each other as the water streamed over us.

He gripped my ass as he lifted me up and pushed me against the wall, his erection barely touching my entrance. "If I hurt you, tell me and we'll stop. Okay?"

I nodded as I squirmed against him, trying to push him inside of me.

He smiled as he leaned in and sucked on my neck. "Impatient?" His mouth moved to my nipple and all coherent thought left me. I clung to him as he slowly slid inside me. "Ah, you feel so fucking good. Always so tight."

He started thrusting, slowly at first, but picking up speed as he went. If there was a heaven, then I had found it; there couldn't possibly be anything better than the feeling of him buried deep inside me, stretching me.

With each thrust, his piercing brushed against my most sensitive spot and I felt my arousal building. His thrusts became harder and more erratic as he reached his peak, and I felt my body explode around him. I screamed out his name as I came and clawed at his back while my body tightened around him. That was all it took to set him off; his body tightened as he gave one final thrust deep inside me and came.

His chest was heaving from exertion as he slipped out and set me back down. My legs felt like jelly, and I clung to him so that I didn't slip on the wet shower floor.

"I don't care how many times we do that—it always feels amazing. No one could ever compare to you," Drake mumbled as he kissed my forehead. He opened the shower door and stepped out as he grabbed a towel and started drying off.

I smiled to myself as I grabbed his shampoo, since I had been in too much of a hurry to grab my own, and started washing my hair. I inhaled deeply as the smell engulfed me; Drake always smelled amazing. I rinsed my hair and finished my shower with that dopey smile still on my face. It made me happy to know just how much Drake craved me and the effect that I had on him.

I grabbed a towel from the rack and dried off before walking back into our room, still completely naked. Drake was on the bed with the remote in his hand, flipping through the channels on the television. He glanced up as I entered, and I watched as his eyes turned dark with lust. He lunged forward and grabbed my hands, pulling me down on the bed with him. I straddled him as he kissed me ferociously, taking my breath away.

"You can't be ready to go again." I mumbled against his lips.

"I've tried to control myself around you, but now that I've fucked you, my control is gone. I want you on this bed ten different ways, and I plan on making sure that happens before the night is over."

I felt myself grow wet at his words. His fully erect cock was pressing against my leg, and I bit my lip to keep from moaning as I positioned myself over him and slowly slid him inside. I was still sensitive from our time together in the shower, and the mere feeling of him sliding inside was almost enough to send me over the edge again.

His hips jerked up automatically and I cried out at the sensations the movement caused. He grabbed my ass as I started moving above him. I knew I was close, and I wasted no time going slowly or gently; my movements were rough and fast as his hips rose to meet me, thrust for trust. Within seconds, I felt myself floating away on an earth-shattering orgasm.

My body felt like dead weight as he flipped me onto my back and continued to pound into me to find his own release. He groaned as he came and let his body fall onto mine. I winced a little at the pressure on my ribs, but said nothing for fear that he would move away.

"I can't move," he groaned from above me.

"Then don't; we can just stay like this all night."

I felt him smile against my chest as his dick jumped inside me. "Don't get me started again just yet; I need a few minutes to recover."

I squeezed my internal muscles and he actually growled. "Dear God! Don't do that!"

I laughed as I relaxed and pushed him from me. "All right, I'll be good. Let me up so I can put some clothes on."

He wrapped his arms around me and held me down on the bed. "You won't be wearing anything for several hours if I have anything to say about it."

My laughter turned into a moan as he started kissing my neck. By morning he had his wish; we had christened the bed in far more than ten different ways.

CHAPTER SIXTEEN

CHLOE

I groaned as I opened my eyes and looked around our hotel room. My body ached everywhere from my nighttime activities with Drake. Speaking of Drake, I could feel him pressed tight against my back, and I snuggled in closer. He mumbled something in his sleep and wrapped his arm around me. I sighed happily; I never wanted to leave this bed.

Unfortunately, it was almost noon, and we needed to head back to the bus so that I could pick up Jordan and take him home. I rolled over and started running my fingertips along Drake's jaw and under his chin, trying to tickle him awake. He tried to brush my hand away, but I smiled and continued to tickle him.

His opened one eye and peeked at me through his lashes. "Will you quit? I'm trying to sleep."

"And I'm trying to wake you up. I guess that puts us at a draw."

He ran his hand down my side to my hip and started making small circling motions with his thumb. "There are better ways to wake me up, you know."

"Not when we have to be checked out of here in twenty minutes. So get up and get dressed."

"Fine," he said as he rolled out of bed.

I watched his naked backside as he walked to the dresser and pulled a clean pair of jeans from the bag sitting on top. My mouth hung open as he pulled them on commando style.

"Did you forget something?" I asked.

He smirked. "No, why?"

"You're missing your boxers."

"Nah, I figured I'd leave them off in case you wanted to tackle me on the bus or something."

"As fun as that sounds, I have to leave as soon as we get there. I'm sure Jordan is ready to go home."

He looked disappointed as he pulled a shirt over his head. "Right, for a second there I forgot you were leaving me again."

"I'm sorry, I promise I will come right back. I'll stay the night there, then head back to meet up with you tomorrow morning. After being apart as long as we have, less than twenty-four hours is nothing."

"I know. It still sucks, though."

I rose from the bed and walked over to him, wrapping my arms around his waist. "You won't even miss me."

"That's impossible. I miss you every second that you're away from me. It's like I can't breathe if you're not around."

I instantly melted into a puddle on the floor, and Drake had to grab a bucket and a towel to soak me up with; okay, not really, but I felt like I did.

"You give me the warm and fuzzies when you say things like that," I said as I leaned in and kissed him.

I slipped my tongue into his mouth, and he groaned as he

pushed me away. "Go get dressed or we're not leaving this hotel room. Do you need to wrap your ribs again?"

"Nah, I'm doing okay without it," I said as I grabbed my clothes from my bag and threw them on. After I finished getting dressed, I walked into the bathroom to brush my teeth and hair. When I was presentable enough, I walked back into our room and threw my things into the bag.

Within five minutes, we were packed and ready to go. I sat on the bed and flipped through my phone while Drake was in the bathroom. After a couple of minutes, I was about to get up and check on him, but he came out just as I stood up.

"What were you doing in there? Fixing your makeup?" I asked jokingly.

"Funny. Come on, let's get out of here."

I readied myself on the elevator ride down just in case the girl from the night before was still at the reception desk. Luckily, she was gone and an older man was sitting in her chair. I walked to the counter and checked us out while Drake carried our bags to the car.

The man smiled at me as he glanced at the clock. "You made it with three minutes to spare—that has to be a new record."

I laughed as he handed me the receipt. "Tell me about it."

I walked through the doors and to the car. Drake was tapping his fingers on the steering wheel impatiently as I slid inside.

"Took you long enough," he said as he pulled out onto the main road.

He seemed cranky, and I gave him a questioning look. "What's up your ass? You were fine five seconds ago."

"Nothing, I just hate taking you back to him."

I sighed and rested my head against the seat. I knew Drake was upset that I was leaving again, but the faster I got Jordan home and put some space between us, the better. I knew once he wasn't a daily fixture in my life that Drake would calm down.

The rest of the car ride was silent, with both of us lost in our own thoughts. Drake pulled into the lot and parked my car beside the bus. I opened my door to get out, but he grabbed my hand and pulled me back to him.

"I'm sorry, I know I'm being a dick. I just get so jealous when I see other guys with you."

"Drake, it's not every guy, it's Jordan. You couldn't care less when Adam and Eric talk to me."

"Because they're my friends and I trust them. No, I don't like Jordan, but he's definitely not the only one. When you're with Logan it bothers me too." He stared at the steering wheel as he spoke.

I really didn't know what to say to that; Drake was one of the most self-confident people I knew, and for him to be worried? Well, that just proved how much he really cared about me.

I threw my arms around him and kissed him deeply. "You never, ever have to worry about me wanting someone else. You're everything I want."

His lips turned up in a small smile. "I hope so."

"You are," I said as someone tapped on my window, and I jumped.

Jordan was standing beside the car, smiling down at me. He stepped back, giving me enough room to swing my door open and get out.

"It's about time. The band is cool and all, but I really want to get back to Danny. Kadi could be there trying to screw with him while we've been away."

That thought hadn't even occurred to me; I assumed that she would know that Drake would tell me everything and we would all be aware of her little plan.

"Shit, you didn't tell him?" I asked.

He shook his head. "I called, but telling him his 'kind of' girlfriend was just using him to get back at his cousin isn't exactly something you want to do over the phone."

"Go get your stuff and throw it in the car. We can leave as soon as you're ready."

"I'm packed. Let me just grab my bags and I'll be right back," he said as he turned and walked back into the bus.

Drake walked around the car and handed my keys to me. His eyes met mine as he brushed a stray lock of hair away from my face. The anger I had seen in his eyes earlier had all but disappeared now, and was replaced with warmth as he trailed the back of his hand down my cheek.

"Hurry back to me," he whispered.

"You know I will. I'll see you tomorrow." I stood on my toes and kissed him softly.

Jordan walked back outside to my car with his bag slung over his shoulder. "Let's get the hell out of here. I need the pool."

I stepped away from Drake, giving him one last lingering look as I slid into my car. I expected Jordan to get directly into the car, but instead he walked over to where Drake stood. I watched nervously as they spoke, afraid that Drake's newfound temper would make an appearance and they would start hitting each other.

I was shocked when Jordan held out his hand and Drake shook it. With that, he turned and walked back to the car. Drake watched him closely as he slid into the passenger seat and grinned at me.

"You can close your mouth now."

I realized I was staring back and forth between the two of them with my mouth hanging open. I snapped it shut as I started the car and pulled out.

"Want to tell me what that was all about?" I asked.

Jordan shrugged. "I didn't want this to be the last time we saw each other, and since your head is up his ass most of the time, I figured I should probably make amends with him so he doesn't keep you away."

I glared at him. "My head is not up his ass."

He snorted and gave me a bewildered look. "Whatever, you're like a lovesick puppy. It makes me want to gag."

I rolled my eyes as I hit the interstate and floored it. I wanted to make good time so that I would be able to make it back tomorrow.

"What's the rush? You're driving like a maniac."

"I just want to get back to him."

He laughed. "I rest my case. You said you're sleeping at Danny's house before you leave again, so it's not like it will matter what time we get there."

I realized he was right and I started slowing down a bit. "Yeah, that was kind of dumb, wasn't it?"

"It's all right. Your hair is blond, so use that as your excuse."

I reached across the console and pinched him. "Asshat."

The rest of the trip was uneventful; one stop to fill my car up and two Starbucks later, we were pulling up to the house. I got out and stretched, my body tight from the long drive. I sent Drake a quick text letting him know we'd arrived safely before following Jordan into the house. He stopped dead in the doorway to the living room and I bumped into him.

"Chloe, go back outside," he ordered.

Never one to listen, I refused and started trying to look around his large frame to see what was wrong. A string of curses left my lips as I saw Danny and Kadi locked in an embrace on the couch. Jordan tried to catch me as I slipped under his arm and into the room, but he wasn't quick enough. His fingertips brushed my shirt as I stomped over to them and grabbed Kadi by the neck, pulling her away from Danny.

I threw her into the nearby chair and glared down at her. "I can't believe you'd have the nerve to show up here after what you've done!" I shouted.

Danny jumped to his feet. "What the hell are you doing?"

Jordan walked into the room and put his hand on Danny's shoulder. "She's been using you. She was only here to break up Chloe and Drake."

Danny looked back and forth between the two of us. "Have you two lost your minds? She doesn't even know Drake!"

I looked down at Kadi, who was staring at the door, probably plotting her escape. "Oh, she knows Drake. She's one of his one-nighters from before we got together."

Kadi opened her mouth to speak but caught herself at the last minute. She turned her attention to Danny, giving him a pleading look. "Danny, they're crazy! I would never do that to you!"

"Quit lying—we saw the fucking pictures," Jordan growled.

"What pictures?" Danny asked.

"Who knows? You said they were with that band; they're probably both on drugs or something!" Kadi cried.

I laughed in her face. "Like anyone in Breaking the Hunger would be on drugs. If anyone is screwed up in the head, it's you." I turned to Danny. "She took pictures of Jordan and me together and showed Drake, trying to get him to break up with me. Unfortunately for her, Drake didn't fall for it."

I smirked as I said the last part and saw anger flare in her eyes. I'd hit a nerve, and I watched as she struggled with whether to tell me off or stick to her story of being innocent. I waited patiently, until finally she broke.

"I wasn't a fucking one-night stand! Drake loves me—he just can't see it because of you!" she spit out venomously.

Danny paled slightly as his mouth dropped open. "So they're telling the truth? Everything you've said to me was a lie?" he asked.

She sneered at him. "No offense, Danny, but you're not my type. You'd think you would have figured that out the third time I dumped you, but no, you keep coming back for more."

I heard a loud crack and was stunned to realize that I had slapped her. My hand stung as her cheek started to turn red.

"You bitch!" she screeched as she lunged at me. The air was knocked from my lungs, and I grunted from the pain that seared my ribs as I fell to the ground. She grabbed my hair and yanked as we tumbled around on the floor.

My ribs were screaming in protest as I threw her off of me and launched myself at her. I pinned her to the floor and punched her in the face. She clawed at my face and bucked, trying to free herself, but I was seeing red. That, coupled with the adrenaline coursing through my body, gave me enough strength to keep her pinned.

"Stay." *Punch*. "The." *Punch*. "Fuck." *Punch*. "Away from Drake, Danny, and Jordan." *Punch*.

Her head slammed back against the carpet and she moaned. I felt arms wrap around me as they lifted me away. I fought them, trying to get back to her.

"Chloe Bear, enough. You've almost knocked her out," Jordan said as he struggled to hold me back.

I let him pull my body tight against his as I stared down at

Kadi's bloodied face. I really had done a number on her; blood was pouring from her nose and a large cut on her cheek from one of my rings. One of her eyes had already started to swell shut and there were several bruises starting to show on her normally flawless skin.

Danny started yelling at her, telling her to get out of his house. She moaned as she tried to stand. She swayed from side to side, but no one offered to help her.

"You'll pay for this. I'll have you arrested!" she spit out as she clutched her side.

"I don't think you will. It'll be your word against ours. Plus, I'm sure Drake would be glad to press charges against you for stalking," Jordan said in a scarily calm voice.

Kadi's mouth gaped open as she processed his words. Her word wouldn't matter against ours, and we had several witnesses that could testify that she was stalking Drake. She was backed into a corner and she knew it. She sent us one final glare as she limped to the front door, slamming it behind her.

Danny walked past us, refusing to look at either of us.

"Danny, wait!" I called after him.

"Just . . . just leave me alone for a little while."

I bit my lip as I watched him disappear around the corner. "You should go talk to him, Jordan—he's really upset."

"Give him some time to cool off," he said as he turned me around to inspect my face.

I winced as he ran his finger along my cheek. "Easy, she got in a few punches too. Great, now I have bruises on top of bruises."

He laughed as he pulled his hand away. I must have had a cut somewhere on my cheek; there was a small amount of blood on his fingers that he wiped on his shorts.

"You look way better than she does, I promise."

I tried to laugh, but it shot pain through my ribs. I sucked in a breath and gritted my teeth to keep from crying out.

Jordan frowned. "What's wrong?"

"My ribs are hurting; I think I need a pain pill."

He lifted my shirt to my bra and ran his finger along my ribs. "You shouldn't have done that; you're still healing."

"Sorry, I'll try to make sure I'm not hurt next time I get into a fight."

He said nothing as he continued to run his fingers along my ribs. I started to take a step back, suddenly uncomfortable, when he looked up at me. My stomach dropped as I saw the need in his eyes. He lifted his hand and cupped my face.

"I don't like it when you're hurt."

"I'm fine. Stop worrying about me," I said nervously.

"That's impossible. Chloe, I don't even know how to say this. You're so important to me, you're in my head and no matter what I do, I can't get you out. I've tried to stay away and I can't." As he spoke, he lowered his head until we were nose to nose. "You could do so much better than him."

"Jordan, what are you doing?"

"I want you and I can't stand it anymore. I had to tell you, to let you know I'm an option."

He leaned in, pushing past the mere centimeters that were between us. His lips brushed mine softly. My eyes widened and I tried to push him away, but he refused to budge as he continued kissing me. I struggled against him, refusing to kiss him back. He became more aggressive, trying to part my lips, but I wasn't having it. Defeated, he pulled away.

"Don't do that ever again!" I yelled.

"You won't even give me a chance, Chloe! You cared about me before—what happened?"

"Jordan, there was a time when we might have been a possibility, but not anymore. I love Drake. I'm sorry if I'm hurting you, but I don't want you that way," I said softly.

The look on his face broke my heart, but I stood my ground. I felt tears running down my cheeks as he stared at me, a scowl on his face.

"He'll break you, Chloe. And when he does, I'll be here. Just please, don't forget that."

I watched as he walked out of the room without another word. I dropped down into the same chair I had thrown Kadi in earlier and covered my face with my hands. I had just lost Jordan and I knew it. It was as if I were reliving everything that happened with Logan, only this time I was doing the right thing.

CHAPTER SEVENTEEN

CHLOE

'm not sure how long I sat there until my phone started ringing. I pulled it out of my pocket and groaned at the unknown Maryland number flashing on my screen. It looked like Mom wasn't going to leave me alone after all. I resigned myself to the fight that was sure to ensue as I answered the call.

"Hello?"

"Is this Chloe Richards?" an unfamiliar male voice asked.

"Yes, who is this?"

"My name is Charles Rogers, I'm an officer from the Ocean City Police Department. Do you have a minute to talk?"

"Um, yeah, sure," I answered nervously. I knew this call had to have something to do with my mother. I assumed they had found her, but I still wasn't sure how I felt about that.

"Miss Richards, I don't know how to tell you this, but we think your mother was killed in an accident the other night. I'm sorry that we are just now contacting you, but due to certain circumstances we just now found you. Is there any way you can come down to the station and talk with me?"

At that moment, the world stopped rotating. The Earth

stilled as I realized my mother was really and truly gone from my life and that we would never make amends.

"Sure," I whispered, still in shock. "I'll be there shortly."

"I'll see you then, and again, I'm so sorry for your loss."

He disconnected the call, but I sat there with my phone still next to my ear. He had said she was in some kind of an accident. What if she was drunk and wrecked her car? Why hadn't I tried harder to get her to go into one of the programs my aunt had suggested? I felt as if her blood was on my hands.

I rose from my chair and stumbled my way up the stairs to the guest room Jordan was staying in. I was terrified that he would turn me away, but I needed him now more than ever. I knocked softly on the door. When no answer came, I turned the knob and pushed it open. Jordan was sitting on his bed with his back to me, staring out of the window.

"Not now, Chloe—leave me alone."

"Jordan, it's my mom. She's dead."

His head swiveled so fast, it looked like something out of a horror movie. It would have been comical if the situation weren't so dire.

"What did you say?"

"The police just called me. My mom's dead; there was some kind of accident."

I felt faint and my knees buckled from underneath me. He was off the bed in a flash and caught me before I hit the floor.

"Chloe. Chloe! Look at me!"

I raised my eyes to meet his. His face was full of concern as he lifted me and laid me down on his bed.

"Are you okay?" he asked.

"Yeah—no. I don't know. She was horrible, but she's still my mom."

My vision clouded as tears filled my eyes. He sat down next to me and pulled me into his lap. Sobs wracked my body as I let grief overtake me.

"Shhh, let it out. I'm right here," he whispered into my ear as he held me tight.

I clung to him as my tears soaked his shirt, but he never once complained. I cried until I felt that I had nothing left inside of me. When my tears slowed, I pulled away from him and wiped my eyes.

"I'm sorry," I hiccupped out.

"Don't ever be sorry for crying."

"I have to go to the police department. Can you drive me? I don't think I can drive."

"Of course. Let me get Danny and we'll all go."

He left me on the bed while he walked down the hall to Danny's room. They both appeared a couple of minutes later. Danny walked straight to me and wrapped me in a hug.

"I guess we're both orphans now," I whispered against his neck.

"Guess so. Come on, let's get you down to my car."

He held my arm as we walked to his car, helping me into the backseat before shutting the door and sliding behind the steering wheel. Jordan came out of the house a minute later and joined us. I stared out the window as Danny weaved through the congested tourist traffic and parked outside the police department. I brushed their hands aside when they tried to help me out and walked across the lot to the double doors. I had to be strong and stand on my own two feet.

An older woman with a no-nonsense appearance sat behind a desk just inside the entrance. She glanced up at us as we entered.

"Can I help you?"

"We're here to see Officer Rogers. My name is Chloe Richards and he's expecting me."

She picked up the phone and dialed a number. After a brief conversation, she hung up and pointed us to a row of chairs sitting against the far wall.

"If you'll have a seat over there, he will be out in a moment."

I watched from my seat as officers and other employees walked back and forth around the station. I had never been in trouble with the law, but cops always made me uneasy. I felt as if they were staring at me with eyes of accusation. Danny seemed at ease, but Jordan looked as uncomfortable as I was. He continuously tapped his foot on the floor as he followed their movements with his eyes.

A tall young officer with coal-black hair approached us. He had a kind face, and if not for his height, I would have assumed he was of Chinese descent.

He smiled at us as he approached. "Chloe?"

I stood and shook his hand. "That's me." I gestured to Danny and Jordan. "This is my cousin Danny and his friend Jordan."

He shook hands with both of them. "Nice to meet you. I wish it were under better circumstances. If you will follow me, please, there are some things we need to discuss."

He led us down a hallway to what looked like an interrogation room. I sat down at the table in the center of the room with Jordan and Danny hovering behind me, as the officer sat down across from me.

"Sorry about having to use this room. I don't have an office of my own, and I thought privacy would be the best thing."

"Not a problem," I answered.

He cleared his throat, looking uncomfortable. "I'm sure you have questions."

"Yes, I do. First of all, what happened?" I asked, already dreading his answer.

"Her death has been ruled a suicide; it appears she parked her car on the railroad tracks and waited. By the time the conductor saw her, it was too late."

The train's whistle: when my mother called me, I heard it in the background. She had spent the last moments of her life telling me how much she hated me. I stared at him as numbness spread across my body. Jordan rested his hand on my shoulder, trying to comfort me.

"She killed herself?" I managed to ask.

He nodded. "I'm so sorry for your loss. I know it must be hard to wrap your mind around something like this."

I only nodded, unable to find my voice.

"We would have contacted you sooner, but unfortunately she was driving a car that belongs to someone who is currently sitting in our county jail for public intoxication. After speaking with him and finding your mother's phone in what was left of the car, we managed to put the pieces together rather quickly and identify her—especially since she had a warrant out for her arrest with your name attached to it."

"I want to see her," I said suddenly.

"I, uh, I don't think that's such a good idea."

"Why not?" I asked. "She's my mother—I have every right."

I needed to see her, to make sure it was her. I already knew in my heart that it was, but I wanted that last validation.

"Chloe, I have to agree with Officer Rogers. Her car was hit by a train; nothing good can come from that," Danny said from behind me.

I winced, knowing he was right as I looked up at Officer Rogers. "Is that the reason?"

He nodded. "I'm sorry, Chloe, but I really don't think it's wise to put you through that."

Jordan gripped my shoulder tighter. "Just let it go, Chloe. She's put you through enough hell already; no reason to hurt yourself more."

All I could picture was my mother's lifeless body, mangled beyond recognition. The way she died seemed to suit her life: tragic and swift. I just wished she'd tried to turn her life around before it was too late.

"You're right. I don't think I could handle seeing that. Where do we need to go from here?"

"What do you mean?" Officer Rogers asked.

"I need to bury her; I don't know what I'm supposed to do," I said.

"Oh, she's been sent to the morgue at the county hospital. Just get in touch with them and the funeral home."

"Chloe, I'll handle everything for you, so don't stress," Danny said from behind me.

"Thank you."

"No thanks needed." He glanced up at Officer Rogers. "Is there anything else we need to go over or can I take her home?"

"We're finished here; you're free to go."

I thanked him one last time—for what, I'm not sure—and walked out of the room and back down the hall to the front doors. Jordan came up behind me and wrapped his arm around me as we walked to the car. After the incident earlier, I knew I should push him away, but I couldn't. I had grown to depend on him as a permanent fixture in my life over the last few weeks, and I wasn't ready to let that go.

Danny ushered me into my room and started calling the hospital and funeral home to make arrangements for my mother as soon as we made it back to his house. We had decided on the way home that, due to the situation, cremation was the best option. The mere thought chilled me to the bone, and I was glad that Danny was handling everything for me.

I picked up my phone and dialed Drake's number. My luck was shit, of course, and it went straight to voicemail. I left a message asking him to call me. There was no way I was going to explain everything to him over a voicemail.

I tried Amber next, and she picked up on the first ring.

"Hello?" she answered cheerfully.

I froze, unsure of how to tell her what had happened.

"Chloe? Are you there?"

"Yeah," I croaked out. I cleared my throat before continuing, "Yeah, I'm here."

She was on high alert. "What's wrong?"

"It's my mom," I choked out.

"Oh hell. What did she do now? I swear to God I'm going to punch that bitch in the face! I'm so sick of this shit!" she growled.

"You don't have to worry about that; she's dead."

The words still felt wrong as they fell from my lips. I didn't think that reality would ever set in.

"She . . . what?" Amber asked.

"She killed herself."

"I . . . Oh God, Chloe!" she cried. "Logan! Logan, get in here!"

I waited as she explained everything to him. Within seconds, he was on the line.

"Chloe? Are you okay?" he asked, his voice full of concern.

"No, not really," I answered truthfully.

"Where are you?"

"At my aunt's house. Danny and Jordan are both here with me."

"Give us a couple of hours to get packed and make the drive. What's the address?"

I gave him the address and he promised to hurry. I felt relieved that he and Amber were on their way; I needed all the support I could get. I hoped Drake would call me soon; I hated to pull him away from the band, but now I needed him too much.

A soft knock came at my door and Danny popped his head in. "Everything has been taken care of. I scheduled for Mom's preacher to come here for a small service once everything else has been taken care of, and they will contact me to collect . . . to collect her ashes."

"Thank you for doing this. I don't think I could've handled it all."

"We're family, the only family either of us has left. We need to take care of each other."

"We really are all alone now, aren't we?" I asked.

"Looks that way. Not that your mom was ever really there for you to begin with."

"I know; I just wish we could've fixed things between us. The last thing she ever told me was how much she hated me. What am I supposed to do with that?" I asked as tears filled my eyes.

Danny frowned. "Don't let that get to you. You're a wonderful person, Chloe, and if she was too stupid to see it, then that's her problem."

"Thanks, Danny. I don't know what I would do without

you and Jordan. I promise I'll come back as often as I can to visit you guys."

"I know you will. Can I ask you something?"

"Sure, anything."

He shifted from foot to foot nervously. "Is there anything between you and Jordan?"

I raised an eyebrow, surprised at his question. "Of course not. Why would you think that?"

"Just the way he acts around you, and you said Kadi had pictures of you two together. You can be honest with me. I won't judge you. I just don't want him to get hurt."

"There's nothing between us, I swear. The pictures Kadi took were innocent and she tried to twist them. Jordan is my friend, and that's all he will ever be."

He seemed satisfied with my answer. "All right, then. I'm sorry, but I had to ask."

"I understand—he's your best friend and you're just watching out for him. Are you okay after everything came out about Kadi?"

His face turned hard as he answered. "I'll be fine. You'd think after all the times she hurt me, I'd know better. I guess love really does make you blind."

"You don't deserve what she did to you. It's my fault that she even came here, and for that I'm sorry."

"Don't be. At least now I know what kind of person she is," he said as he gave me a weak smile. "Why don't you sleep for a little while. I know you're exhausted."

I really was tired. Drake and I hadn't slept for more than a couple of hours the night before and I was done for, body and mind.

"Yeah, I think that's a good idea."

He closed the door behind him as he left, leaving me completely alone and shut off from everyone. My eyelids dropped and finally slid shut. My mother's face was the last thing I saw before I slipped out of consciousness.

It was several hours later when I woke to the sound of my phone ringing. Still half asleep, I grabbed it from the nightstand and mumbled out a hello.

"Chloe, it's Logan. We're at the gate, but the guard won't let us in."

I groaned. "Let me talk to him."

I waited as Logan spoke to the night guard. A minute later the phone was passed to him. "Miss Richards?"

"Yes, Logan and Amber are my friends. Can you let them through, please?"

"Certainly, sorry to bother you."

I ended the call and stood, stretching my arms above my head. My body was stiff from the fight with Kadi earlier, and I bit back a moan from the pain the movement caused me. I hadn't bothered to shower or change my clothes before I went to sleep, and I felt grungy as I left my room and walked down the hallway to the stairs.

Logan and Amber were getting out of her car as I stepped outside. They both looked up at the sound of the door, and Logan ran toward me as soon as he saw me. He wrapped his arms around my body and pulled me close.

"I'm so sorry I wasn't here sooner," he whispered, his lips brushing my ear.

"It's all right. Jordan and Danny have been taking care of me," I said as I hugged him back.

Amber walked over to us and joined in on our hug. It felt great to have both of my best friends with me, and I realized just how much I had missed them over the summer. Amber and Logan had long ago become permanent fixtures in my life, and I felt at home with both of them holding me.

Logan pulled away first. "What happened?"

I felt awkward explaining my mother's death in the driveway. "Why don't we get your stuff carried inside and then I can explain."

He kissed my forehead and turned away. "Sure, but it might be a while. Amber packs like she's never going home."

Amber snickered as she released me. "Of course I do when I know you'll be around to carry it for me."

He scowled as he pulled two bags from the car. "Gee, thanks."

Amber and I walked to the car and each grabbed a couple of bags. The first one I grabbed was fairly light, but the second bag nearly pulled me down.

"Jesus, this thing weighs a ton!" I groaned as I started hobbling toward the house.

Logan held the door open for me as I passed by. "That would be Amber's. The other one is mine."

"Of course it is," I huffed as I set both bags down.

Danny and Jordan appeared from the living room and took in the bags at my feet. Amber and Logan were standing next to me.

"I take it we have guests?" Danny asked.

"Um, yeah. These are my best friends, Amber and Logan. Sorry I didn't tell you they were coming."

"Not a problem. While you're staying here, this house is yours too."

I smiled as I turned to Logan and Amber. "Guys, this is my cousin Danny and his friend Jordan."

Amber smiled sweetly while Logan shook both of their hands. He seemed to be studying them.

"Nice to meet you," Jordan mumbled before looking at me.

"You should have let me know they were coming. I could have let them in so that you could get some sleep."

"I'm fine. I really needed to see both of them."

He stayed silent as Danny crossed the room and grabbed a few of their bags. "Let's get you guys rooms." He glanced between Amber and Logan, "Do you each need a room, or would you prefer one together?"

Amber started blushing furiously as Logan laughed. "Nah, she steals the covers."

She punched him in the arm. "Shut up! We're just friends, nothing more."

Danny laughed at her embarrassment. "All right then, follow me."

Logan and Jordan split the remaining bags between the two of them and carried them up the stairs with Amber and me following closely behind. Danny stopped at the room directly across from mine and opened the door. "This one is free, as is the one beside it. Make yourselves at home."

They deposited Amber's bags inside and Logan carried his to the other room. I walked into Amber's room and sat on the bed as she started unpacking.

"Are you okay?" she asked as she hung some of her clothes in the closet.

"Not really, but I will be. I think I'm in shock right now more than anything. It just doesn't seem real."

She gave me a sympathetic look. "Understandable. I mean, she was horrible, but she's still your mom."

"You want to know what the last thing she said to me was? What a horrible person I am."

She walked over and threw her arms around me. "Oh, Chloe, you know that's not true."

"Yeah, but it's what she thought of me. She called me and told me that the same night she died."

"I feel bad speaking badly about the dead, but your mom was a crazy bitch. She tried her hardest to break you, and she didn't stop until she took her final breath. But you won, Chloe—in the end you won. You have an amazing boyfriend, friends, and family who love you more than anything, and that's something she never had."

Speaking of my loving boyfriend, I still hadn't heard from him. Amber released me and I pulled my phone out to check for any missed calls. There were none and I frowned. It wasn't like Drake to ignore me for hours, even when he had a show.

"Nothing I just said should make you frown," Amber complained.

"No, it's not that. I tried calling Drake earlier and he never called me back. It's not like him."

"He doesn't know yet?"

"No, that's why I was trying to call him. He still thinks I'm leaving tomorrow to meet up with him. I hope he's okay."

"I'm sure he's fine. He probably just turned his phone off or something."

I frowned; Drake never turned his phone off except for during shows, and he always checked it afterward. "Yeah, maybe you're right. I just really need him right now and he's nowhere to be found."

"I hope you're not talking about me; I'm right here."

I jumped at the sound of Logan's voice. He gave me a small smile as he entered the room and sat down next to us on the bed.

"No, she can't reach Drake and she's worried." Amber said.

"Oh," Logan said as he looked away.

I let the subject of Drake drop; it was obvious that talking about him made Logan uncomfortable. We sat in silence for a few seconds until Amber spoke up.

"So, do you want to tell us what happened?" she asked.

"She killed herself."

Amber's mouth dropped open and Logan's eyes widened.

"I . . . Oh, wow. I don't know what to say," Amber squeaked out.

Logan wrapped his arm around me and pulled me close. He squeezed my ribs, trying to comfort me, and I winced at the pain.

His brow furrowed as he noticed my discomfort. "What's wrong?"

It dawned on me that I hadn't told them anything about recent events—my aunt's deception, my mother's attack on me, Kadi's manipulation, my fight with her, the tension between Drake and Jordan.

I sighed as I ran my hand through my disheveled hair, unsure of where to even start.

"I haven't told you two anything that's happened this summer."

Amber crossed her arms over her chest and glared at me. "Am I going to be really mad at you when you do?"

"You will be."

I started at the beginning, telling them everything. Amber's face grew tight as I spoke and Logan's hold on me became stiff. He loosened it slightly when I got to the part about my cracked ribs. Neither of them interrupted, but I knew they were angry at me for keeping things from them.

Amber was glaring by the time I finished. "Why didn't you call us?" she yelled.

I stared at the floor in front of me. "I didn't want to bother you guys. It's my life and I need to deal with it on my own. Besides, I had Jordan and Danny around to help."

"Danny and Jordan are not your best friends!"

I backtracked, wanting to avoid Amber's rage. "I know that, but you were hours away. I figured it would be easier for you if you didn't know what was happening. I was thinking of you guys."

"That's bullshit, Chloe! You always do this to us; you keep us in the dark until the last possible minute. And it always turns out so well when you do that, might I add!"

Her gaze was on Logan as she spoke and I felt my face warm. How could she bring that up with everything else I had going on?

"That's not fair, Amber! I know what I did to Logan was wrong, and I'll regret it for the rest of my life!" I shouted, my temper taking over.

"Am I interrupting?" Jordan asked from the door.

I looked up to see him watching me closely. "You all right, Chloe Bear?"

I nodded. "Fine. We were just having a discussion about my poor decisions in life."

Jordan grinned as he entered the room and sat down in the chair by the desk. "I'd love to hear this."

Logan cleared his throat, looking uncomfortable. "I don't think that's such a good idea."

"Why not?" Amber growled. "Let someone else see how fucking stubborn Chloe is."

"Drop it, Amber—it's between Chloe and me. No one else." Logan emphasized the last part, and her eyes narrowed at him.

"We're all three best friends, so that makes me a part of it." She turned to Jordan. "Chloe here cheated on Logan with Drake. She kept everything to herself, just like she always does, and Logan paid the price."

Jordan's eyes searched mine, looking for confirmation. "Is that true?"

I cringed at the judgment in his stare as I answered. "Yes, I fucked everything up."

He frowned as he looked at Logan. "Drake has a way of really screwing things up, doesn't he?"

"Enough!" I shouted before Logan could respond. "You two can form an 'I hate Drake' club later. I have too much shit to deal with right now!"

I threw Logan's arm off of me and stormed out the door. I had no idea where I was going; I just knew I had to get away. I ran down the stairs and out the front door. I continued running until I had reached the edge of the property behind the house. My injured ribs screamed at me as I finally stopped running, clutching my sides and gasping for breath.

I stood there for a minute, trying to let my eyes adjust to the darkness. My breathing slowly quieted down and the silence of the night engulfed me. It reminded me of the serenity of the spot by the Cheat Lake that I shared with Drake. It felt right, and I let the atmosphere flow into my body. It soothed me, and I felt myself start to relax.

I sat down in the grass and leaned back against a small tree. There were several clouds in the sky tonight, blocking the moon and most of the stars, and I stared up at them until my eyes began to feel heavy. If only Drake were here, then everything would be perfect in my little world.

CHAPTER EIGHTEEN

DRAKE

I lost twelve hours. My entire body felt like it was on fire as I sat up in bed and surveyed my hotel room. I groaned as I took in the destruction I had caused the night before; my credit card was going to be maxed out by the time they charged me for all the damages.

Last night had been the worst trip of my life. I had found a dealer at the bar we were playing at, and he offered me a deal on LSD after I bought more cocaine. Of course my dumb ass had bought it.

The band didn't have another show for a couple of days, so we all decided to crash at a hotel for once instead of trying to sleep in a cramped bunk. I made some lame-ass excuse about being tired when we checked in and locked myself in my room. I had used acid a couple of times before and thought I could handle it, but what followed after I stuck that little piece of paper under my tongue was a disaster.

It had started out fine, but after a couple of hours, things started to change. As I watched the swirling colors of the bedspread, Chloe and Jordan popped into my head. They were standing by the pool, locked in a passionate embrace. That one image set me off, and I literally saw the air around me start crackling with my energy.

The pale red walls changed to the color of blood and started dripping onto the floor. I grabbed a towel from the bathroom and tried to wipe the blood up, but there was too much. The towel was saturated with blood and my hands were covered in it. I wiped them on my jeans and my shirt until they were red as well, but my hands wouldn't come clean.

I ran to the bathroom and jumped into the shower after I stripped my blood-soaked clothes off. There was a bar of soap on the side of the tub and I grabbed it. I scrubbed my skin furiously as the water around me turned red. I panicked as the water pouring over me turned red as well. I dropped to my knees in the tub and closed my eyes.

"It's not real. It's not real. It's. Not. Real," I chanted.

When I opened my eyes, the red water had disappeared, along with the blood that had covered my body. I breathed a sigh of relief as I shut the water off and grabbed the extra towel from the hook. I wrapped it around my waist as I stumbled back into my room and sat down on the bed. My relief was short-lived as I noticed the walls were still covered in blood. I was in one of those hotel rooms that was expensive enough that nothing was bolted down, so I grabbed the lamp beside me and threw it at the wall.

The sound of it shattering as it hit the wall echoed over and over in my head until I felt as though my ears were bleeding. I reached up and felt for blood, surprised when there was none.

After that, things had gotten even crazier, and judging by the room in shambles around me, I didn't remember most of it. Besides the shattered lamp, I had managed to damage most of the room. The mini-fridge door was lying on the floor; I had somehow torn it from its hinges. The hair dryer from the bathroom was on the bed beside me, with the cord missing.

I scratched my head, trying to figure out how I'd managed that one. The nightstand drawer was on the floor, broken into pieces, and the curtains had been ripped from the window and shredded. There were other things scattered around the floor, but I didn't even bother to look at them.

I glanced at the clock on the nightstand that had somehow survived my assault on the room and groaned. It was pushing two o'clock, and I knew everyone else had to be back on the bus by now. I had no clue as to why they hadn't stopped by to get me up on their way out.

I stood slowly, making sure that everything was in working order. When I didn't find my legs broken, I sighed in relief. I put on a pair of jeans and a shirt before walking into the bathroom and collecting my clothes from the night before. I groaned as I noticed that I had somehow smashed the mirror above the sink.

I could almost hear my credit card crying in my wallet as I threw my dirty clothes in my bag and walked out the door. The woman at the front desk eyed me closely as she handed me my receipt. I was used to the unwanted attention, but after last night, I wasn't in the mood to deal with it.

"When you manage to put your tongue back in your mouth, you might want to send someone up to clean my room. And yeah, I know I'll be billed for damages," I bit out.

Her mouth dropped open and I couldn't help but laugh as I turned and walked out the front doors. The hotel was only a couple of blocks away from where we had left the bus parked. The summer heat had me sweating before I'd even made it a block, and I regretted not just throwing on a wife-beater and shorts. My hair was plastered to my forehead by the time I made it back to the bus.

The guys were sitting at the table playing cards, but Jade was nowhere to been seen when I entered the bus. Both of them turned to look as I climbed aboard.

"I have a question for you," Adam said.

"What?" I asked as I stifled a yawn.

"Why do you even have a cell phone?" he asked, raising an eyebrow.

"Um, so I can call people. And so that Chloe can send me naked pictures. Why?"

"I don't see how either of those things matter, since you never bother to take it with you or keep it turned on if you do." He pulled my phone from his pocket and held it up. "I could have looked at every picture on here, naked Chloe included."

I walked to the table and snatched it out of his hand. "But since you like your face the way it is now, I know you didn't."

He chuckled. "No, I didn't. But if I didn't like Chloe so much I probably would have." Then he told me, "Jade kept trying to call you until I noticed your phone plugged in by your bunk. After that, she got kind of pissy."

"Why? You guys knew where I was."

"We beat on your door for a good ten minutes this morning. There was no answer, so we assumed you had already left. Chloe called Jade when we got back here, and that's when we realized we'd lost you again," Eric said.

"Not that we told Chloe that; she'd kill us," Adam murmured.

"Wait, Chloe called Jade? When?" I asked.

Eric and Adam glanced between each other. "This morning, right after we got back to the bus. She was worried because she couldn't reach you."

I cursed, hating the fact that I had made Chloe worry. I had been in too much of a hurry last night, trying to get away from everyone, to remember my phone. I was more worried about my damn drugs than I was about Chloe.

"Did she say what she wanted?" I asked.

Instantly, I knew something was wrong as Adam looked away. "Just call her."

"Tell me what's wrong first!" I shouted.

Adam glanced at Eric. "*You* do it. I suck at this shit."

Eric and I watched as Adam made a hasty exit off the bus before I turned to look at Eric. "Well?"

He sighed. "Chloe called this morning because she couldn't reach you. I guess she tried since early last night. She finally was worried enough to call Jade to check on you. By that time, we realized we had lost you again, but we didn't want to worry Chloe, so we told her you were still back at the hotel sleeping."

"Okay, but why did Adam just make a quick escape?"

"You're going to be mad at yourself when I tell you."

"I'm already mad at myself for making her worry. Just tell me, damn it!"

"She won't be coming back today; her mother killed herself. She's really upset, but Danny is taking care of everything for her, and Logan and Amber made it to the house late last night. She's not alone, but she needs you there."

I cursed and kicked the seat beside me. Pain shot through my foot, but I ignored it. I had been off getting high, while she was alone with Logan and Jordan. I had left her alone with both of the assholes while she was completely vulnerable; I might as well have tied a bow around her too. And her mother? What the hell had happened there?

"Where's Jade?" I asked.

"Out looking for you. She's been gone a while, though, so she should be back anytime."

"I hope so; we need to go. Like now."

Eric spoke, but I had suddenly turned deaf as I watched the walls of the bus tilt and whirl. I shook my head, trying to clear it, and they slowly moved back into place.

That was the thing I hated most about LSD. While I might not be high on it any longer, it would randomly pop back into my life for weeks after I had taken it.

I felt slightly dizzy as I dropped into the seat next to me.

Eric looked at me with concern. "You all right?"

"Fine, just a little dizzy," I said as I closed my eyes and waited for the dizziness to pass.

My eyes flew open as the bus door banged against the wall. I blinked several times as Jade came running up the steps.

"Oh, thank God. If I had to tell Chloe we lost you again, she might have never forgiven me!" she said as she hugged me tightly.

Adam walked in behind her and closed the door. "Told you he was in here." He gave me a pointed look. "Damn crazy woman."

I laughed as Jade pulled away. "Yeah, I'm here. Now can we get on the road?"

Eric walked to the front and sat down in the driver's seat. "Sure. Now go call Chloe."

I jumped up from my seat and walked to my bunk, dialing her number as I went. She answered on the first ring.

"Drake? Oh, thank God! I was freaking out!" she yelled into the phone.

I pulled the phone away from my ear as I winced. "Ouch, yes I'm here. I'm so sorry, baby, I left my phone in the bus to charge and forgot to grab it before we went to the hotel."

"It's all right. I just thought something had happened to you."

"Don't worry about me. Are you okay?" I asked.

She was silent for a minute before answering. "Did Jade tell you?"

"Yeah. I'm sorry I wasn't there for you. We're on our way back now."

"The whole band?" she asked, sounding surprised.

"Well, yeah. They all want to be there for you and besides, how else would I be getting there? You want me to walk the whole way?"

"Oh, right. *Duh*. Sorry, my mind isn't working right now," she said as she laughed at herself.

"It's fine. We're in northern Pennsylvania right now, so it'll be a few hours before we get there."

"Hold on a second," she said as I heard voices in the background. "Okay, I'll be down in a minute," I heard her say.

I waited impatiently, hoping that the person she was talking to wasn't Logan or Jordan.

"Sorry, I'm back. Jordan said Danny needs to talk to me, so I have to go. Call me when you're almost here."

"All right—love you," I said unhappily. No matter what either of them said, I wasn't happy with Jordan being around her, especially now that she was hurting and vulnerable.

"Love you too," she said as she hung up.

I sighed and threw my phone on the pillow beside me. Now I played the waiting game, stuck on this damn bus while Chloe needed me. I felt my anger at the entire situation boiling over, and I punched the side of the bus.

Adam appeared beside me and leaned down to look into my bunk. "What's wrong with you?"

"Nothing, I'm just stuck on this fucking bus while Jordan and Logan take care of Chloe for me, that's all," I said, kicking the side of the bus this time. I hoped that if I left a dent, they didn't notice and take it out of my deposit when I returned it.

"Dude, take a chill pill. Chloe's a good girl; she won't do anything behind your back. Hell, I'm not even dating her and I trust her." He scratched his head with a baffled look on his face, surprised by his own admission.

I couldn't help but laugh at his surprise. "Are you crushing on my girl, Adam?"

"Nah, but if she's ever up for a threesome, let me know."

I glared as I punched his leg.

"Shit, I was just kidding!" He jumped back, out of my range.

"Anyway, it's not Chloe I'm worried about. It's Jordan and Logan; they both hate me and want in her pants. That makes for a bad situation waiting to happen."

"Amber is there with her, isn't she?" he asked.

"Yeah, why?"

"Because she'll watch out for her. That girl can bust some balls when she needs to." His gaze turned thoughtful as he thought about Amber, "I wonder if she wants to hook up while I'm around. With all your shit lately, it's been too long since I got laid."

I rolled my eyes. Amber and Adam had been hooking up way before Chloe and I had gotten together, and she was the only girl I knew who was a repeat for him. I never asked, but I was sure there was something else going on between those two besides just sex. Adam would deny it, of course; the guy was worse with commitment than I was.

"You'll have to take that up with her."

"Oh I will, not that I think she'd turn me down. I mean, come on, she's had me before. She knows what she's been missing since I left."

"Just don't piss her off, all right? That makes it rough on Chloe and me."

"Whatever. Amber's not the clingy type, so I don't think you have to worry about that," he said as he turned and walked away.

Despite what he said, I was worried. If they ended up hating each other, it would put Chloe right in the middle, since she was with me and I came as a package deal; you get me and the band follows.

My thoughts drifted back to Logan and Jordan, and I clenched my teeth in anger. If either of them touched her, I'd kill them. As I lifted my hand to run it through my hair, it brushed the side of my pants. I had a fresh bag of cocaine and an itch I needed to scratch. It would be just the thing to take the edge off.

I rose from my bed and slipped into the bathroom. I pulled the bag from my pocket and grabbed the mirror and dollar bill from their hiding place under the sink. Not that they would be much evidence, but I had made sure to hide them away from anything the band used often.

I set them on the counter and made two lines across the surface of the mirror before putting the bag back in my pocket. After rolling the dollar, I leaned down and snorted both lines quickly, my eyes watering. I wiped the mirror clean and stuffed it back under the sink with the dollar, then sat on the floor and leaned back against the sink.

I was just starting to feel the effects when the door swung open and Eric walked in. I cursed myself for not locking it as he caught sight of me, sitting on the floor with bloodshot eyes. We both were frozen as we stared at each other.

"Are . . . Are you all right?" he asked.

"Yeah, I'm fine. Just needed to be alone," I answered lamely.

"You know you could have done that in your bunk, right? Why are your eyes red? Have you been crying?" he asked.

"What? No, I just had something in them and came in here to flush them out. Who's driving?"

"Jade took over for me. Anything you want to talk about? You know I'm not here to judge," he asked, undeterred.

I mentally groaned. If he figured out what I was doing, he would tell everyone else and it would be blown out of proportion. They would tell Chloe, too, and it would all be over.

"Nope, I'm fine. Like I said, just something in my eye."

He watched me closely as I stood and walked past him out of the door. I breathed a sigh of relief when he walked into the bathroom and shut the door behind him. Crisis averted. As long as no one found out I was using again, everything would be fine.

I sat down at the table with Adam and watched out the window as the miles disappeared below the bus. I felt light and even a bit happy from the cocaine and with every mile that passed, my heart began to lighten. I would be with Chloe soon and everything would be all right.

Eric returned from the bathroom and took over for Jade. She came back and sat down with us, a deck of cards in her hand.

"Who wants to give me some money?" she asked cheerfully.

I groaned and laid my head on the table. I was running

through money a lot faster than I wanted to think about and I couldn't afford to lose another hundred bucks to our resident card shark.

"Not today. I'm going to owe you a house by the time summer is over with," I said.

"Me either, you cheat!" Adam said from beside me.

She pouted. "I do not cheat; you two just suck at cards. Eric too."

"I heard that!" Eric yelled from the front.

"Fine—we won't bet actual money, we'll just play for fun. Deal?"

I looked at Adam, who shrugged his shoulders. "Sure, why not?"

Jade smiled broadly as she dealt us both in. Adam and I spent the next couple of hours having our asses handed to us by her in poker. I had never seen someone who was so good at cards before.

"You should go to Vegas and play. You'd probably make more money that way than being in a band," I grumbled.

She laughed. "What would be the fun in that when I have you guys here to murder?"

Adam threw his cards on the table. "I'm out, damn it!"

I threw mine down as well. "Jade wins. Again."

I glanced out the window and grinned as I realized that we were only about twenty minutes from Chloe. I stood and all but ran to grab my phone off my pillow. I dialed her number, excitedly bouncing back and forth as I waited for her to pick up.

"Hello?"

Jordan. Any happiness I felt left me as I heard him answer her phone.

"Where's Chloe?" I bit out.

"She's sleeping. Why?" he asked in a too calm voice.

"I'm almost there and I wanted to let her know."

"Hold on a sec—let me see if I can wake her up."

I heard him set the phone down. "Chloe. Hey, Chloe Bear, wake up," he whispered.

I heard her groan and I almost threw my phone across the bus. He was there with her while she was sleeping. A few seconds later, he picked the phone back up.

"I can't get her to wake up. I'll try again in a couple minutes; I'll make sure she's up by the time you get here."

"Are you in bed with her?" I asked, using my own deadly quiet voice.

All noise on the bus ceased as Jade and Adam listened in.

Jordan was silent for a minute before answering. "I am, but it's not what you think."

"Then what the fuck is it? This is the second time I know of that you've been in bed with her!" I shouted, not caring who heard me.

"Calm down. She was having a nightmare when I came in to check on her. I lay down with her to help calm her down. She was asking for you, but since you weren't here I had to do your job. Again."

"Well, isn't that convenient for you. And what the fuck is that supposed to mean, doing my job again?" I asked as I heard the blood pounding through my veins.

"You know exactly what I'm talking about. You've been off playing band while I've been here taking care of her. I just wish she'd open her eyes and realize that she's wasting her time with you."

"She isn't wasting her time with me—I love her and she fucking knows that! If she had told me what was going on, I would have been there in a heartbeat. She told me to stay away."

"Then maybe she realizes that I'm more than capable of taking care of her."

"What happened to that truce you tried to call in the parking lot? I knew it was bullshit then and look, I was right. All this time, you've wanted her."

"Of course I want her! You're with her, so I don't have to tell you how amazing she is, inside and out. I'd be stupid not to want her!"

He kept his voice low as he spoke, and I knew he was trying not to wake her.

"Is she aware of this?"

"Yeah, she is. Of course she shot me down for you." He sounded bitter, and I smiled.

"Good to know. She'll be thrilled when I let her in on this little conversation."

"Fuck you, asshole, I'll deny it. Tell her and I'll just use it as more ammo against you."

I knew he was right; Chloe had been patient with me, but she knew I hated her spending time with him. She would think it was just another way I was trying to keep her from him.

"He doesn't have to tell me—I heard everything." Chloe said, a bit muffled through the phone.

My heart leapt and I laughed like an idiot. "Fuck, yes!" I shouted as I fist-pumped. "Give Chloe the phone!"

Jordan didn't say a word as he put her on.

"Drake?" Chloe asked.

"Who else, unless you have another boyfriend he's trying to steal you away from?" I asked sarcastically.

"Funny. Where are you?"

I glanced out of the window. "About ten minutes away."

"I'll call the guard station and let them know it's okay to let you through. I'll meet you out front."

I smiled as I dropped my phone into my pocket. I had no doubt Chloe was ripping into Jordan right about now. Too bad that I was too far away to hear any of it.

CHAPTER NINETEEN

CHLOE

Where should I even start?" I yelled.

Jordan stood and walked across the room. He sat in the chair next to the desk and gave me a pleading look. "I'm sorry, all right? I didn't mean to say what I did—he just went off and I snapped. He's an asshole, Chloe! Why can't you see that?"

"I'm so sick of you talking shit about him, Jordan! I love him and I will always love him. I want *him*, not you, or Logan, or any other guy out there!"

"He's going to hurt you! I've told you that over and over yet you still can't see it!" Jordan shouted back, getting angry.

"If he hurts me, he hurts me. But it's not your job to watch out for me. I told you before if you couldn't accept him, then I didn't want to be around you, and I meant it. Just stay away from me, Jordan."

Tears filled my eyes, but I stood my ground. Drake had been right about Jordan all along and I had refused to see it. I loved Jordan, but not in that way, and if he couldn't accept Drake, then I couldn't accept him as a friend any longer.

"You don't mean that, Chloe," he whispered.

"Yes, I do. If you can't accept Drake, then I can't accept you."

He stared at me, disbelief written all over his face. "Fine, if that's how you want it. From now on, go to him when you need something, not me!"

He stood and threw the door open. I watched as he turned and gave me one last look before slamming the door behind him.

I had stood while we fought, but once he left, the fight in me left as well and I crashed onto the bed. Was it too much to ask for a simple relationship with a guy? First Logan, and now Jordan. I snorted; at least I didn't have to worry about Danny trying to hit on me. Then I shuddered; that was not somewhere I wanted to go.

I glanced at the clock and jumped from my bed; Drake and the band would be arriving any second. I looked horrible: my hair was tied back in a messy bun and I was wearing an old Nine Inch Nails shirt that had seen better days and cut-off shorts. I didn't care, though; my only thought was to get downstairs to Drake.

I made a mad dash down the stairs and out the front door, reaching the driveway just as the bus was pulling up. My heart soared as I watched them approach; Drake was finally here and everything would be all right. I turned as Amber stepped outside to join me, followed by Logan and Danny. Jordan was noticeably absent.

The bus hadn't even come to a complete stop when the doors opened and Drake came tumbling off. I felt like I was in one of those old movies as I ran to him and met him halfway. He picked me up and spun me around, laughing.

"I missed you so much, Chloe, even if it's only been a day."

I kept my arms wrapped around him as he lowered me to the ground. I felt safe with his arms around me, his smell engulfing me and overloading my senses.

I buried my head in his chest. "I missed you too. I'm so glad that you're here now."

"I won't be leaving again until you're ready to go with me, even if that means cancelling every show we have left. I'm sick of this being-apart shit we've done all summer," he whispered into my ear.

His breath tickled against my skin, making me shiver with desire. The heat that was always present between us was still there, despite our audience. I pulled away, needing to keep my body under control, as Jade and the guys stepped off of the bus.

They all gave me a sad smile as they walked over to us.

"Hey, girl," Jade said as she stepped around Drake to hug me.

I hugged her back until she released me and then first Adam, then Eric, replaced her. I was a bit shocked by Adam and Eric being affectionate, but I tried to hide it. Apparently, my surprise was written all over my face, because they both started laughing as Eric pulled away.

"Don't act so surprised—you kind of grew on us," Adam said between chuckles.

I laughed as Drake threw his arm around my shoulder and steered me back into the house. Amber and Danny smiled at us as we passed, but Logan kept his face carefully blank. I hated how having Drake around stressed him out. Except for Drake, Logan was the most important guy in my life, and I wanted him to be happy.

"I assume you will all be staying for the next few days?" Danny asked from behind us.

Everyone nodded as they followed us into the house.

"That's fine with me, but I don't have enough rooms for everyone. A couple of you will have to double up," Danny said.

"I call Chloe!" Drake joked from beside me.

"Darn," I grumbled, "I wanted Jade."

Jade laughed as she walked over and kissed me on the cheek. "Just come to my room after he goes to sleep. What he doesn't know won't kill him."

I burst out in a fit of giggles as Adam, Logan, and Drake's mouths all dropped open.

"Oh, hell no! If there is girl-on-girl action, I want to watch!" Adam shouted.

Amber rolled her eyes as she smacked him across the chest. "I think you'll be too busy with me."

He grinned. "Right. I volunteer to room with Amber!"

"Jade can stay with me if she wants," Logan said from behind me.

I turned to look at him, surprised. He and Jade had always gotten along well enough, but I didn't realize they were close enough to share a room.

"Thank you, Logan, I appreciate that. I thought I was going to get stuck with Eric, and he kicks in his sleep," Jade said.

Eric snorted. "Do not."

Logan avoided my gaze as he and Jade walked up the stairs together. Even though they kept several feet between them, I couldn't help but wonder if something was going on there. I wanted Logan to be happy, and I couldn't think of anyone nicer than Jade.

"Well, *that's* surprising," Drake murmured next to me.

"All right, looks like you're getting the extra room, Eric. I'll show you where it's at," Danny said as he followed Logan and Jade up the stairs, Eric right behind.

"Yeah, Adam and I are going to go get caught up," Amber said with a grin.

"Hell yeah we are. But Chloe, if you and Jade decide to go all girl-on-girl, let me know. I'll be glad to help!" Adam yelled as Amber pulled him up the stairs.

I laughed as I watched them go. It was nice to have everyone I cared about back together again.

"Looks like it's just you and me, love," Drake whispered against my ear.

"No complaints here," I said as I turned my head and caught his lips with my own.

"Let's go to your room."

I nodded as he grabbed my hand and pulled me up the steps behind him. As we turned the corner and stepped into the hallway, he stopped dead in front of me and I crashed into him. I opened my mouth to ask what he was doing when I saw Jordan standing a few feet away, locked in a stare-down with Drake. I could feel the tension in Drake's body as the seconds ticked by, and I knew he was waiting for Jordan to make a move.

Jordan broke the stare-down and turned his attention to me. "Can we talk?"

"I don't think so. You said what you had to say earlier," Drake said.

"I wasn't asking you, I was asking Chloe," Jordan bit out as he glared at Drake.

"Well, I was talking to you. Chloe is aware of how you feel and she chose me, so back off."

"Chloe," Jordan pleaded, "please talk to me. I just need a minute."

Drake stepped toward him, glaring. "I told you—back off."

"Stop it! Both of you!" I said as I glared at them. I was not going to stand around while they tore into each other. "Jordan, I said what I had to say earlier, so please leave me alone."

"I don't want to leave things like that. You're important to me. I just . . . Can we talk about this privately?"

Drake smirked. "Say what you have to say, but I'm staying. You've had enough alone time with her already."

Jordan opened his mouth to speak, but I cut in. "He's right. If you have something to say to me, you can say it in front of him."

Jordan looked back and forth between the two of us. "Fine. I don't like the way we left things earlier. I was a jerk and I know it. I don't like Drake and I won't pretend that I do, but I won't push you for anything else. You're my friend first and foremost, and I don't want to lose that."

"I don't know what you want from me, Jordan. I've done nothing but be a friend," I said.

"That's all I'm asking for. I want things to go back to the way they were before I tried to kiss you." Drake opened his mouth to speak, but Jordan shot him a look. "Keyword: *tried*. She shot me down and gave me the whole 'Drake is the love of my life's speech, so chill. She didn't cheat on you."

"You still tried to kiss her, asshole!" Drake yelled.

"Yeah, I did. But I'm trying to make amends, so shut up." He looked at me. "Can we just go back, Chloe?"

"I don't know, Jordan. Just give me some time, all right? I'm still mad at you for what you said to Drake earlier."

I had grown close to Jordan over the summer and I didn't want to lose him as a friend, but my relationship with Drake was more important.

"Fair enough; just remember that Drake isn't the only one who cares about you. We've been friends for a long time, way longer than you two have been together, and I don't want to lose that over something stupid."

"You won't—just give me a couple of days. My mom just killed herself and I'm trying to deal with that. I don't need all of this shit thrown at me too," I said, exasperated.

"I'll leave you alone, but you know where to find me when you're ready to talk."

Defeated, he turned and walked down the hall. I watched until he disappeared into his room and shut the door behind him. I knew that he was hurt, and it broke my heart.

Drake tugged on my hand. "Come on."

I followed him into my room and collapsed across the foot of my bed. "That sucked."

Drake didn't reply, and I rolled onto my back to look up at him. He was still standing by the door with an annoyed look on his face.

"What's wrong?"

"Why didn't you tell me he kissed you?"

"Are you serious right now? He kissed me the same day I found out about my mom; it kind of slipped my mind."

"Oh, sorry."

"Not that I could get a hold of you anyway," I added, giving him a pointed look.

He glanced down at the carpet as he ran his hands through his hair. "Sorry about that."

"It's all right. I'm not mad, I was just worried."

"Do you have feelings for him?" he blurted out.

"For Jordan? Of course I don't! Did you just miss the entire conversation five minutes ago? Why would you even ask me that?"

"Because I know you well enough to know when something's bothering you. I watched your face while he walked away from you; it killed you to send him away. If you want him, don't let me stand in the way."

"I can't even believe we're having this conversation right now! I do not want Jordan! I only want you!"

"Are you sure? Because I'm not going to be a blind idiot like Logan was, living in my own blissful existence while you're off screwing around behind my back."

I saw red. Not only was he implying that I would stay with him while cheating with Jordan, but he was also calling Logan an idiot.

"Fuck off, Drake. You cannot talk to me like that, and Logan doesn't deserve to be portrayed that way! He trusted me; that doesn't make him an idiot!"

"Sorry, I'm just pissed off, okay? I love you and I don't want to lose you. I suck at this shit."

"Yeah, you do," I grumbled.

He shot me a look and I rolled my eyes. "I love you too. What I did to Logan was wrong and I don't ever intend to do that to anyone else, especially you."

"I just don't want to hold you back."

"You're not. Like I said, I love you and I would never do anything to screw that up."

He crossed the room and climbed onto the bed, hovering above me. "I don't want to screw this up either. I know I'll do stupid shit to piss you off from time to time, but promise me you won't leave me because of it."

His mouth hovered just above mine and I watched his lips move as he spoke. "Promise me, baby."

"I won't. Nothing could tear us apart."

"I'm holding you to that." He grinned as he lowered his mouth to mine.

. . .

The next few days passed in a blur of both laughter and tears. Things were still tense between Jordan and me, but with the band around I found myself laughing a lot more, especially when Adam opened his mouth. The tears usually came when I was alone in bed with Drake late at night. He would hold me until my tears dried and more often than not, I fell asleep cradled against his chest.

Danny kept his word and handled every detail regarding my mother's arrangements. He even pulled a few strings to speed up the process a bit. Less than a week after her death, Danny had picked up her ashes and a small service was held in her honor. I knew none of her friends, not that I would have invited them anyway, so the service was small, with only my small group of friends in attendance.

I had never been religious, but Danny had requested that a preacher perform her services and I had agreed in order to please him. Danny had a temporary tent placed in the field behind the mansion, and as I sat in the front row next to Drake, listening to the preacher talk about eternal life, forgiveness, sacrifice, and redemption, I prayed for the first time in my life.

I prayed that if there was something after this life that my mother would find it and the peace she had never managed to find here, and that all of her sins would be forgiven. I knew it was asking a lot, but I hoped that my prayer was enough.

I didn't realize I was crying until Drake reached up and wiped both of my cheeks with a tissue. The tenderness of such a small gesture warmed my heart, and I reached over and squeezed his hand as a thank-you. He gave me a small smile as he took my hand in his and kissed it.

Danny had left the decision of what to do with my mother's ashes up to me. At first, I had been clueless as to what I should do with them, but after a drive to the beach yesterday afternoon, I knew what she would have wanted. Despite her addictions, she was a free spirit, and I couldn't think of anything better than to have her drifting across the ocean, carried around the world by the tide.

After the preacher finished his services and left, Danny and I drove to the bay and boarded his private yacht. I had requested that everyone but him stay behind; this was something I needed to do alone, but since I couldn't drive the boat, Danny had agreed to go with me. Not only was it his boat, but he understood better than anyone what I was going through and I needed his comfort.

I sat on the deck with the urn clutched tightly in my hands as I watched the shore disappear behind us. He continued to take us farther out to sea until the shore was no longer visible. He shut off the engine and sat down in the seat next to me without speaking.

"I don't think I can do this." I whispered.

"Take your time, Chloe. We can stay out here as long as we need to."

"Thank you, not just for this, but for everything you've done for me."

"We're family, and I know you'd do the same for me. I love you."

"Love you too."

We sat in silence as the boat swayed back and forth gently.

My mind moved at warp speed as I thought of all the moments my mother had hurt me. I tried to ignore them, to focus on happier thoughts with her, but the sad truth was that there were few. And never once had she ever told me that she loved me, or even that she was proud of me.

A tear slipped down my cheek as I stood and walked to the edge of the deck. I removed the lid and stared down at the urn in my hands. This wasn't just goodbye, it was peace. I held the urn over the edge and tilted it to the side, letting the ashes slowly slide out. A breeze caught them and carried them away as I poured, until there was nothing left.

I stared down at the empty urn in my hands before throwing it into the ocean. There was no comfort in its presence, only an empty shell and a reminder of the pain my mother had caused. I watched it hit the surface of the water and sink down into the dark depths below. As it sank, I let it take all the pain and regret with it. I would leave my pain here, in the middle of the ocean, and start over again.

I hugged myself as I turned to face Danny. "I'm ready."

"Are you sure? We can stay for a while if you'd like."

"No, there's nothing here and there never was."

He stood and wrapped his arms around me. "All right then, let's go home."

He started the engine and took us back to shore. I stared straight ahead, refusing to look back. I was leaving it all behind.

We docked and I helped him to secure the boat, before making the drive back home. The car ride home was as quiet as the trip back to shore in the boat, and I appreciated that Danny was trying to give me space.

Drake was standing outside as we pulled up to the house,

and I smiled at the sight of him. Regardless of where life took me, I knew he would always be by my side. As soon as Danny parked, I jumped out of the car and ran straight into his arms.

He stumbled back from the impact. "You okay, babe?"

"I am now."

"Glad to hear it. Let's go in. Allison has dinner ready for everyone."

We walked inside, with Danny close behind. As soon as I stepped into the house, my stomach growled in response to the smells coming from the dining room. Everyone was already sitting around the table eating as we entered.

I smiled as they all looked up. "I hope you saved something for us."

Adam snorted. "It's every man for himself around here. I don't think I'll survive once I have to start eating Drake's Pop-Tarts on the bus again—this food is the shit."

"I knew it was you who was stealing them! You asshole, I asked if it was you and you denied it!" Drake said, pretending to be outraged.

"No, you asked if I touched your shit, which I didn't. I ate your Pop-Tarts."

They continued to bicker back and forth as we walked to the table and sat down. Allison had gone all out, making all of my favorites. The table was piled high with homemade mashed potatoes and gravy, fried chicken, shrimp linguini, crab legs, fresh dinner rolls, ribs, and two key lime pies.

Drake looked disgusted as I added a little bit of everything onto my plate.

"What? I'm hungry."

"That has to be the most repulsive combination I have ever seen."

"It's not like I'm going to eat it all together," I said as I rolled my eyes.

"It's still nasty. I'm not kissing you after you eat all of that."

I laughed. "Whatever. Your idle threats won't stop me."

As I ate, I watched Jordan from the corner of my eye. He was a few seats down from me, deep in conversation with Danny. Drake and I had talked last night, and we had decided that the band and I would leave early tomorrow so that they didn't have to miss any more shows. I needed to fix things with Jordan before I left.

When we finished dinner, I stood and walked over to where he and Danny were sitting.

"Can I talk to you for a minute?" I asked.

Jordan seemed surprised, but he nodded as he stood to follow me from the room. Drake was watching us closely, and I stopped beside him.

"I need to patch things up with him. Just give us a couple of minutes alone, okay?"

He gave me a curt nod, but said nothing.

I sighed as I led Jordan from the room and out the patio doors to the pool. I knew I had upset Drake, but Jordan deserved better than to be left hanging.

I was still wearing a knee-length skirt from the services, so I sat down at the edge of the pool and stuck my feet into the warm water. Jordan sat down beside me and leaned back on his hands.

"You wanted to talk?" he asked.

"Yeah. I just wanted to tell you how sorry I am over everything. I shouldn't have pushed you away these last few days. I care about you, but just not in that way."

"I know that, and I was an idiot to push you for more. I can see how much you love Drake and I just wanted that with you. You're unlike anyone else and I can't help how I feel about you, but from now on it won't be an issue."

I reached over and squeezed his shoulder. "I'm glad that you understand where we stand. I didn't want to leave tomorrow if we weren't okay."

His shoulder tensed under my hand. "You're leaving tomorrow?"

"Yeah, the band has to get back on the road, and Drake won't leave without me."

He brushed my hand away as he stood. "I see. Make sure you come back to visit when he lets you."

I watched him walk back into the house with a heavy heart. Regardless of what we both said, there was no way we would ever really be okay as long as I was with Drake, and I had to accept that. Drake was the most important part of my life now and if Jordan couldn't accept it, then so be it.

CHAPTER TWENTY

CHLOE

There was something wrong with Drake, but I couldn't put my finger on it. I had been on tour with the band for just over a week and everything had gone smoothly, apart from Drake. His moods were starting to give me whiplash; one minute he was normal, cheerful Drake, and the next he was yelling at me and storming off over the littlest things.

The worst fight, and the stupidest as well, was when I had tried to be nice and clean the bus for them while they were practicing in a bar before a show. I scrubbed every inch of the bus, from the makeshift kitchen to the bathroom, and had even run to the local store and stocked up on everything from toilet paper to his worshipped Pop-Tarts.

The rest of the band had been grateful for my hard work, but Drake had flipped out and started yelling at me. Shocked at his outburst, I had stood frozen while he screamed at me. When he was finished, he stomped off to the bathroom and locked himself in there for over an hour. When he came out, he apologized over and over, but I ignored him. I was hurt, but I was mad, too. I had tried to do something nice for him and he'd reacted with anger.

At first, I had assumed his anger was from my attempt at making amends with Jordan, but that didn't seem to be the case. He wasn't lashing out only at me, but at the band as well. Eric had all but thrown him off the bus when he and Adam had almost come to blows over who was going to drive. I knew they were as concerned as I was, but we were lost as to how to help Drake. Whenever one of us would try to talk to him about the changes we had seen, he would either get angry or blow us off.

We were only a couple of weeks away from the end of their summer tour and I was secretly glad. I hoped that once we were back home, Drake would return to normal. Tonight they were playing in one of the biggest bars on the tour, in Trenton, New Jersey. The bar itself was easily three times the size of Gold's back home, and word had spread quickly that Breaking the Hunger would be here.

With only half an hour until they started their set, the room was filled to capacity. The bar had reserved a table next to the stage for the band, and I sat with them, watching the bar skanks and sipping my beer. There had been a few who were brave enough to approach Drake while he sat beside me with his arm around my shoulders, but he quickly got rid of them. I had to admit, that was a major plus side to Drake's newfound temper. I couldn't help but smile as he not-so-politely told them all to fuck off.

Drake kept his arm around me until it was time for them to take the stage. He had been in a bad mood most of the day, so I was surprised when he bent down to kiss my forehead before leaving me alone at our table. I watched as he followed the other band members onto the stage and took his place in the front.

He still looked every bit the badass rocker I had met almost a year ago, but I could see how tired he was. Living on a bus and the events of this summer had taken a toll on him, both mentally and physically.

He introduced himself and the band before Jade started into the first song. Their performance was good, but not one of their best. I nearly had a heart attack when Drake stumbled and almost fell, but he quickly regained his footing and continued on with the song as though nothing had happened.

I glanced up when the chair beside me was pulled out and a guy sat down next to me.

"Why are you sitting over here all by yourself?" he asked.

"Um, just watching my boyfriend onstage." I emphasized the word *boyfriend*, hoping he would take the hint.

"Oh, which one is he?"

I pointed to Drake. "The one singing."

"He's got a hell of a voice. Kind of reminds me of a mix between Three Days Grace and Seether, which are two of my favorite bands."

"Yeah, he does."

"I'm Ron, by the way. Do you mind if I sit with you until they're done? I'd love to meet them."

"Nice to meet you, Ron, I'm Chloe. I don't mind. I'm sure they'd like to meet you since you're not a screaming fan girl."

He laughed. "No, definitely not a screaming girl."

My reply was cut off by the shrill sound of a microphone being thrown down. I glanced up to see Drake jumping from the stage and rushing over to me. My eyes widened as he grabbed Ron and pulled him from his chair. I scrambled out of my chair as he threw him on the table and slammed his fist into Ron's face.

"Stay the fuck away from my girlfriend!" Drake shouted as he landed another punch.

"Stop!" I screamed. I tried to grab his arm to keep him from hitting Ron again. Before I even realized what was happening, Drake spun around and shoved me away. I lost my balance and tumbled to the ground.

Drake froze as he stared down at me. "Oh my God, Chloe, I'm so sorry."

Jade rushed to my side and helped me up. "Are you all right?"

"Fine," I growled.

Drake reached out for me, but I pushed him away. "Chloe, I'm so sorry."

"Just stay away from me right now." I pointed to Ron, who was sitting on the table, holding his face. "You hit an innocent guy who was sitting with me so that he could meet you, and then you pushed me down. I don't know what your problem is, but I've had it!"

I turned and stormed away as one of the bouncers rushed over to the scene Drake had caused.

"We don't put up with this shit, especially from the performers. Pack your stuff up and get out!" I heard him roar when he reached Drake.

The bar was deathly quiet as I walked through the crowd. They parted easily for me, and I was out the door in seconds. I ran to the bus and jumped on, with Jade right behind me.

"I can't believe him!" I shouted.

"I know, honey. This isn't like him," Jade said sadly.

"He just beat up some random guy and got you guys kicked out of the bar. Was he like this before I got here?"

"He's been a little off for a while, but it's getting worse."

"What's wrong with him?" I asked as I started to cry.

I felt like I was losing him, and I was powerless to stop it. He was slowly slipping away, and he refused to open up to me so that I could help him.

Eric stepped on the bus, looking more pissed off than I had ever seen him. "We have a serious problem."

"You think?" I grumbled as I rubbed a sore spot on my bottom. "Where is he, anyway?"

"He helped pack everything up and then disappeared."

"I don't know what to do, Eric," I said.

"I do," Adam said as he boarded the bus as well. "Let me beat the shit out of him."

"Adam, you're not helping." Jade said with a glare.

"I think I know what's going on with him, but I hope I'm wrong," Eric said as he sat down at the table.

"What? Tell me and we'll fix it," I pleaded.

"This isn't something you can fix."

"Damn it, Eric, spit it out," Adam growled.

"I think he's using again."

"Using? You mean *drugs*? Drake wouldn't do that," I said, confused.

"I didn't think he would, but all the signs point in that direction. The mood swings, the random outbursts of anger, him disappearing constantly; it all fits. I knew him before he went to rehab and it was almost exactly like this."

I dropped into the seat across from him. "There's no way he would do that. He knows how I feel about drugs after everything that happened with my mom; he knows I'd leave. I won't go through that again."

"I think he's right, Chloe. I've been thinking the same thing, but I was afraid to say it," Jade said sadly.

"You're all wrong. He wouldn't do that!" I all but shouted.

I jumped from my chair and stormed back to Drake's bunk to grab my purse.

"Where are you going?" Adam asked as I walked to the door.

"To a hotel. I can't deal with this right now."

I exited the bus and ran for my car. I drove around town for a while, trying to clear my head. There was no way that Drake would ever start using again; Eric had to be wrong. Drake knew about my past, and he had seen firsthand how screwed up my mom had been because of drugs. Knowing how much I hated them, there was no way that he would risk losing me; we loved each other too much.

I finally pulled into a run-down hotel just a few miles from the bus. I told myself it was because I didn't want to have to hunt to find my way back in the morning, but the truth was that I wanted to be close in case Drake called. Yes, I was really angry with him for tonight, but I wanted him to open up to me. Maybe after tonight, he would realize he needed to do so.

After paying for the night, I carried my bags inside and looked around the room. I cringed and rethought my decision to stay here as I took in the dingy space. The room was clean enough, but it was aged. The walls were a bit stained and the wallpaper was peeling in places. I glanced at the bed; it seemed okay, but I was definitely wearing pajamas to bed just to be safe.

I took a quick shower and checked my phone, but there were no missed calls. Defeated, I crawled into bed and pulled the covers up. Maybe tomorrow; it was a new day, after all.

. . .

There were still no missed calls when I woke the next morning. My hope deflated when I still hadn't received a call after I was dressed and driving back to the bus. Amazingly enough, the bus was still parked in the lot. I had been afraid that the bar would force the band off their property.

The bus was quiet as I stepped inside. Jade was sitting at the table with her laptop open in front of her. She glanced up and gave me a weak smile as I closed the door behind me.

"Morning."

"Morning. Did he show up?" I asked, afraid to look back and see Drake's bunk still empty.

She sighed. "Yeah, he came back in the middle of the night. He was drunk, and he flipped out when he realized you'd left. He thought you had left him period and started to go after you. Since he could barely stand up, we convinced him to sleep it off and that you would be back in the morning."

"I assume he's still sleeping?"

"Yeah, and he probably will for a while. I'd let him sleep; it's not going to be pretty when he wakes up."

"I won't wake him, but I'm going to check on him," I said as I walked quietly to his bunk.

He was lying in bed in only his boxers, with his mouth hanging open. I couldn't help but smile at how cute he looked. I stepped closer and tripped over something on the floor. I threw my hands out and to keep myself from falling and glanced down to see what the culprit was. Drake's shirt and pants were tossed down beside the bed and I reached down to pick them up.

I grabbed his shirt first and almost gagged; it smelled like he had taken a bath in Jack Daniel's. I grabbed his pants next and threw them and the shirt in the bag he used for dirty laundry. A small bag fell from his jeans and onto the floor. My heart stopped as I reached down to pick it up.

"No," I whispered as I stared at the white powder inside. "How could he?"

So this was it; this stupid little bag was why he was putting everyone through hell. Drake had his faults, just like everyone else, and I looked past them. But this—this I couldn't ignore. I had spent my entire life being physically abused by a drug addict, and I wasn't going to spend the rest being verbally abused by another one.

My eyes fell on Drake's sleeping form and I lost it. "Un-fucking-believable!" I screeched. Eric and Adam were sleeping only a few feet away, and they both woke up when they heard my shouting.

"Whadafuck?" Adam mumbled, still half asleep.

Eric sat up in bed and looked at me. "What's wrong?"

"You were right. This"—I kicked Drake's bunk as I held up the bag for Eric to see—"asshole is using cocaine."

Jade rushed back to us, but stopped dead when she saw the bag in my hand. "Oh, no."

"Oh, yes," I growled.

I leaned down and shook a still sleeping Drake roughly. How he had slept through my shouting, I'll never know.

"Wake up, asshole!" I shouted.

He groaned and rolled over, but continued to sleep. My patience was running out and I slapped his bare arm; next would be a kick to a certain area he was extra fond of.

"Wake! Up!" I shouted into his ear.

His eyes opened slowly. "Chloe?"

"Good job, you know who I am. Now get up."

He slowly sat up and peered at me through bloodshot eyes. "Not so loud—my head is killing me."

"It's *really* going to hurt after I get through with you." I threw the bag at him. "Look what fell out of your pocket."

His eyes widened and he glanced back and forth between the bag and me. "That's not mine."

"Don't lie to me, Drake, I'm not stupid! It fell out of *your* pocket!"

Eric stood and put his hand on my shoulder. "Hey, calm down."

I turned to glare at him. "Stay out of this. Actually, I want you guys to give us a minute alone."

"I, uh, you're kind of mad right now. I don't think that's such a good idea," Eric said.

"No, I want to be alone with him. Please."

Eric seemed unsure, but Jade nodded. "We'll be outside. Just yell if you need us."

I waited until they left to turn back to Drake. Neither of us spoke as we stared at each other and my eyes welled up with tears, both from anger and hurt.

"How could you?" I whispered.

"I didn't . . . ," he started, but I held up my hand.

"No, just stop. Tell me the truth."

He stood and reached out for me, but I pushed him away. "Chloe, I'm sorry. I didn't mean for it to happen."

"That's a lie. If you didn't want it to happen, you wouldn't have started using to begin with. You've gone years without using; I thought you were done with this shit."

"I was—I mean, I am. Everything got to me and I wanted a release. I never meant to keep using, but things just kept getting worse."

"Drugs are not a release, they're a prison. How long?"

He looked away and I counted to ten in my head to keep from screaming.

"How long have you been using again?"

"Since the night Kadi showed up with the pictures."

"Jesus, Drake!"

"It's not a big deal, all right?"

"*Not a big deal?* Are you kidding me? You know what I went through with my mother, and I'm not about to go through it again with you!"

"I'm nothing like her; I would never hurt you like that!"

"You already did, Drake. You've been lying to me the entire time, and don't even get me started on your anger issues. I won't do it again. I want you to get help."

"What do you mean, help? I don't see what the big deal is, Chloe—I've got it under control."

"No you don't, or you wouldn't still be using. I want you to go to rehab again. Please, for us."

"I'm not going to rehab, Chloe! You're overreacting to all of this!" he shouted, finally losing his temper.

"Then stop using right now!" I shouted back.

"I will when we go back home, I promise!"

"Bullshit, Drake, you can't stop. Either you go to rehab or we're done!"

His mouth opened and closed, but no words came out.

"I mean it, Drake: either you get your shit together or I'm walking out the door right now and I won't be back."

"You don't mean that, Chloe. You wouldn't just leave me like that—you love me."

"You're right, I do love you. But I have to do what's right for me, too. I can't be with you if you won't stop, Drake. I'm sorry, but I can't do that again."

"Just wait until we finish the tour, and I'll go. I swear to you I will."

"No, I won't wait that long. Either you go now or it's over."

"Damn it! Damn it! Damn it!" he shouted as he kicked the bag next to him and the contents scattered. "Why are you doing this to me?"

"Because I love you, and I want you to get help! You haven't been on them long and it shouldn't be that hard to stop."

"I can't do rehab; just let me do this on my own. Please."

I shook my head. "I'm sorry, Drake, but if you won't go, then it's time for me to leave."

"You wouldn't really leave me, Chloe. Think about it. I love you—hell, I want to marry you someday!"

That hurt. I knew he was serious and I wanted to marry him one day too, but it wasn't going to happen. He needed help, and this was the only way I could think of to make him see that.

"Goodbye, Drake. I love you." I stepped closer to him and kissed his cheek.

"Chloe, please don't go," he pleaded, but I ignored him as I walked off the bus.

Jade, Eric, and Adam were all standing next to the door. They looked up as I stepped down onto the pavement.

"Everything okay?" Eric asked.

I was on the verge of tears as I shook my head. "I can't do it all over again. If he won't get help, I can't be with him."

"Oh, honey, come here." Jade held her arms out and I fell into them. "Don't cry; he'll get his shit together. You're too important to him."

"I hope you're right, but I don't know. He just let me walk away. I'm going to miss you guys so much," I sobbed.

"Shhh, it's all right," Jade said as she rubbed my back.

I pulled away from her and wiped my eyes. "I have to get out of here. Just watch out for him, okay?"

Eric nodded as he hugged me. "Of course we will. You take care of yourself."

"I will. I think I'm going back to Danny's; Charleston is too far to drive from here."

I stepped away from Eric and started toward my car, but Adam stopped me. He surprised me by wrapping his arms around me.

"Regardless of whether Drake is being an idiot or not, you're still part of this band," he said as he squeezed me tightly, "even if you can't play an instrument and you sing through your nose."

I laughed. "Thanks, Adam—that means a lot coming from you."

"Just don't get used to it. I don't do this mushy shit."

I waved at them as I stepped away from Adam and got in my car. They stood by the bus and watched until I disappeared around the corner. As soon as they were out of sight, I lost it. I pulled into a parking lot and put the car in park as sobs shook my body.

I had done the right thing, but it killed me. Drake was my life and now he was gone, just like that. I didn't know where to go from here; since I had been with him, all visions of my future included him. I hoped that once he realized that I was serious, he would get help so that he didn't lose me.

I waited until my sobs quieted to hiccups before pulling back onto the road. It was a long way to Ocean City and I wanted to get there as soon as possible. I knew Danny wouldn't mind me staying with him again, but I felt horrible for abusing his hospitality. I hoped to stay there for only a few days and then head back to Charleston with Amber and Logan. They had decided to spend a couple of weeks in Ocean City to enjoy the beach, and Danny had offered to let them stay at his place while they were there.

I grabbed my phone off the console and dialed Danny's number.

"Hello?"

"Danny? It's Chloe. I need a place to stay."

CHAPTER TWENTY-ONE

CHLOE

Six Months Later

I blew a strand of hair that had fallen loose from my ponytail out of my face as I left my class of the day and walked to the parking lot. After throwing my books in the backseat, I sat behind the wheel and started my brand-new car. I had decided to trade my old car in for a new Kia Sorento at the beginning of the school year, using a small amount of the money my aunt had left me.

Winter in West Virginia could go from warm and sunny to cold and snowy in a matter of hours. If I wanted to make it from the house I shared with Amber and Logan off campus to my classes when the roads were bad, I knew I needed something with four-wheel drive.

The three of us had decided that we were tired of sharing a bathroom with other students and started looking for a house to rent as soon as we got back from Ocean City. We found one just a couple of miles away from the main campus with a reasonable rent. As soon as the ink was dry on the lease, we had picked up my stuff from Drake's house and taken it to our new home.

When everything was packed and loaded into my car, I left my key on the kitchen counter and walked away from the house and from Drake.

That was almost three weeks after my breakup with Drake, and I hadn't heard a word from him. With every day that passed with no word, my hope had dwindled. He knew by then that I was serious, but had obviously decided that the drugs meant more to him than I did.

A week before school started, Jade had called me with some news. The band had been contacted by a studio in Los Angeles that wanted them to come out and record a few tracks to see how they sounded. While I was glad that things were starting to look up for them, I was also disappointed. Jade said they had all accepted the offer, which meant Drake would be in Los Angeles working on his music instead of returning to school. I had hoped that if Drake came home, maybe he would see reason and seek the help he desperately needed.

Jade and I had kept in touch through the first month of school, but with both of our schedules full we had quickly lost contact. I hadn't heard from her since September, and the last time she called, she said Drake seemed to be using more instead of trying to get better. The band had been pushing him to stop, but with the potential of a recording contract hanging over all of them, they didn't want to push him away and ruin all their dreams.

I pulled into my driveway and parked my car. One of the things that had drawn us to this house was the fact that it had private off-street parking, something of a novelty in a college student–packed town.

Since it was a Friday and I had no weekend classes, I left my books in the car as I walked into the house. Amber and

Logan were sitting in the living room watching some stupid reality television show. Amber was addicted to reality TV, and I couldn't help but laugh at the expression on Logan's face as he watched it with her. His eyes found mine as soon as I entered the room.

"Thank God, a reasonable person. Can you convince her to change the channel to something worth watching? At this point, I'd take the cooking channel over this shit."

I laughed as Amber stuck out her tongue at him. "And miss all the miserable faces you're making? Not a chance."

I sat down next to Amber and pretended to have my eyes glued to the television. I hated reality shows as much as Logan did, but it made them worth the trouble just to watch him squirm.

"This is what I get for living with two women!" he groaned as he stood and walked out of the room.

I turned to Amber and grinned. "I hate this shit too."

She laughed. "Yeah, I don't like this one either, but it seemed to annoy him the most."

"We're horrible," I said as we collapsed against the back of the couch in a fit of giggles.

"I know, but it's so worth it to annoy him," Amber gasped out.

I loved living with Amber and Logan, and not just for the good parking and private bathroom. Coming home to them was the favorite part of my day, and it had helped me through dealing with the loss of Drake.

I had been nervous about living with Logan considering our past, but we had sat down and talked about everything a couple of nights after we moved in. He had sensed my wariness and wanted to put me at ease. While he admitted he still cared about me, after everything that had happened between us, he never wanted to go down that path again. To say I was relieved at his confession would be an understatement.

One of my fears after Drake and I split up was that Jordan or Logan would try to start a relationship with me, but I should have known better. Jordan had taken care of me after I arrived back at Danny's. I had been a blubbering mess, but he didn't seem to mind as he held me close and let me cry into his shirt on more than one occasion.

Amber, Logan, and I had spent a couple of days at Danny's before leaving for West Virginia, and never once had Jordan pushed the issue with me. He knew that I wasn't looking for that type of relationship and had respected me enough to understand. We never spoke again about his feelings toward me, but I think he finally accepted that we would never be more than just friends.

I still spoke with both him and Danny several times a week and had spent most of my Christmas break at the mansion with the two of them. Amber, Logan, and I had even made the long drive out to their school during football season to watch Jordan play.

I knew next to nothing about football, but I was smart enough to know that he was good, really good. Even though he was only a sophomore in college, he had already been contacted by a couple of NFL scouts about possibly joining their ranks after he graduated. I was so proud of him when he told me, and I could tell just how excited he was about the whole thing.

Since my aunt left me more than enough money to cover my basic living expenses, I decided not to go back to my old job. I used the extra free time to study for my classes, and I had managed to pass every single class last semester with As and Bs.

I had made school my number one priority and threw myself into the work to distract myself. It worked most of the time, but not a day went by that I didn't think of Drake.

The fact that he hadn't called even once was what hurt the most. It was as though I had meant nothing to him, and it made me question every aspect of the relationship we had shared. They say time heals all wounds. The first couple of months after our split, I had been depressed, to say the least. Amber and Logan had stayed by my side, though, and with their help I had slowly started to become the old Chloe. I hadn't made it quite there yet, and I wasn't sure I ever would. A broken heart was a hard thing to come back from.

Amber had forced me into a few blind dates, hoping to get me out of my slump, but nothing ever came of them. While most of the guys were nice, I couldn't help but compare them to Drake in every way. Needless to say, none of them even came close. Some asked me for a second date, but I politely declined, much to Amber's fury.

I just wasn't ready to jump into another relationship, and I didn't think I would be ready for a very long time. I was on campus daily with literally thousands of men and none of them caught my attention in the least. I couldn't help myself; I looked for Drake in every face even though I knew he wasn't coming back.

I sighed as I realized I was thinking about Drake again. It seemed even bad reality television couldn't help me escape.

"Can we change the channel before my eyes start bleeding?" I begged.

"Fine. Let's see if there are any good music videos playing," Amber said as she started flipping channels.

She stopped at one of the music channels that actually played music. I relaxed as Stone Sour started blaring from the television. There was nothing like music to take your mind off your problems.

Amber and I talked while we watched the video. When it finished, another video I didn't recognize started playing. I leaned forward, anxious to see who had come out with a new one. A few seconds in, the camera flipped to the lead singer and my heart stopped.

"Oh fuck," Amber muttered as she grabbed the remote to change the channel.

"No, leave it on," I mumbled as I kept my eyes glued to the television.

Drake was staring right back at me, giving me his trademark sexy smile. I couldn't seem to tear my eyes away, even when the camera switched to Jade beating the hell out of her drums. My heart was beating wildly as I willed the camera to pan back to Drake. I got my wish a few seconds later and my breath caught in my throat.

He looked amazing, which surprised me. He had lost a little weight since the last time I'd seen him, but he had bulked up a bit as well. The shirt he wore clung to his chest and stomach, showing just how much muscle was hiding under there.

I had envisioned him pale with bloodshot eyes, but he was just the opposite. He had never been pale to start with, but now his skin was tanned and his striking brown eyes were clear. It seemed that drugs and time away from me had been just what he needed to look even better.

Amber and I sat in silence as the video ended and the host appeared onscreen.

"That was the brand-new band Breaking the Hunger, with

their first video. I have to admit, I can't wait to see what else these guys have in store for us! We'll be right back after the commercial break."

Amber shut off the television and turned to me. "You okay?"

"Yes. No. Hell, I don't know. I never expected to see him again," I mumbled.

"I know. I should have changed it."

"No, it's fine. I have to face it sometime. I just didn't expect him to look that good."

"Me either. Are you sure he's on drugs? Because he certainly doesn't look like he is."

"I'm sure, Amber. I found the cocaine and I talked to Jade."

"How long has it been since you talked to her?" she asked.

I shrugged. "A couple of months ago. Why?"

"Did you think that maybe he's cleaned up since then?"

"If he did, why hasn't he called me?" I asked as another thought crossed my mind. "Unless he did and decided he still doesn't want me."

Tears sprung to my eyes and Amber hugged me. "Don't assume that, Chloe. Why don't you call Jade and see what's going on?"

"I don't want to bother her," I said as I wiped a tear away.

That was a lie; I wanted more than anything to pick up my phone and demand an answer from her, but the thought of Drake being clean and still not wanting me was enough to send me into a new state of depression.

"Then text her. You know Jade wouldn't mind."

"I guess I could. That way if she's too busy or she doesn't want to talk to me, she can just ignore it."

I pulled my phone from my pocket and took a deep breath as I sent her a text.

Me: **Hey Jade, long time no see. I just wanted to let you know I saw your video and it rocked! Xoxo**

That seemed good; I had tried to contact her without mentioning Drake, so hopefully she would reply.

A few seconds later, my phone dinged with an incoming text.

Jade: **Chloe! I've missed you, how have you been? It just started playing a few days ago, I'm so excited! We've been working on our first album!**

Me: **That's great! I'm so proud of you guys. How is . . . everything?**

Jade: **Eh, I can't really say much, Chloe. I'm sorry, but I love you both and I don't want to be caught in the middle.**

Me: **I know, and I'm sorry I asked.**

Jade: **It's ok, I wish I could tell you. But I can't so I won't. I have to go, but I hope to see you soon!**

I raised an eyebrow. She hoped to see me soon? I didn't see that meeting anywhere in our future. I loved Jade like a sister, but I didn't think I could stand to be around her right now. She would be just another reminder of Drake, and I didn't think I could handle it after seeing him again tonight.

"Well, what'd she say?" Amber asked.

"Uh, nothing, really. She doesn't want to be 'in the middle of us.'"

"Well, that sucks. Want me to text Adam?"

"No!" I shouted. "Just leave them out of it."

Amber and Adam had surprised me. They hadn't seen

each other in months, but they still talked occasionally. Adam wasn't the type of guy to talk to any girl, and I had started to wonder if he wasn't interested in Amber for more than just sex. I had mentioned this to Amber one day, but she just shrugged it off.

I had to admit that I was a bit jealous that she was still in contact with the band, but I never said anything. I didn't want to ruin her happiness just because I had lost my own. Besides, I knew she would tell me if Adam mentioned Drake, so apparently he never did.

Amber picked up her phone and started scrolling through her contacts.

"What are you doing?" I shrieked.

"Um, ordering pizza. I'm hungry, so sue me."

"Oh, sorry. I thought . . . never mind." I mumbled.

"Whatever, freak."

"Bitch," I growled as I threw a pillow at her.

"Hey! I'm on the phone here!" she bellowed as she threw the pillow back at me.

I laughed as I caught it and stood up. "Get it with sausage. I'm starved."

I waited until she started placing her order before slamming the pillow in her face and running from the room. I could hear her cursing and the mumbled apologies to the guy at the pizzeria as I walked down the hall to my room; nothing like embarrassing your best friend to lift your spirits.

. . .

The next two weeks seemed to go in slow motion. It didn't help that every time I turned the radio on, Drake's song was playing. I decided that listening to my CD collection was a lot safer after the third day straight of hearing his voice coming out of the speakers in my car.

Classes were starting to get tougher, and I threw myself into them with everything that I had. I was taking much harder courses this semester and they helped keep my mind off Drake. Any distraction was welcome at this point; that stupid song had brought everything back to the surface.

Amber was still breezing through with the easiest classes that she could get away with. Her mom was ready to strangle her for not taking school seriously, and the phone calls between the two of them were hilarious. Her mom called at least once a week to yell at her about applying herself to her studies and for some of the charges that were showing up on her credit card. My personal favorite was the six-hundred-dollar charge for an autographed poster of Avenged Sevenfold.

Since she had so much free time, Amber was constantly trying to drag me to parties. I hated going to parties, mainly because every guy there seemed to assume that I was there to hook up with someone. It had taken a drink to the face for the last one to take the hint; after that, Amber decided to let me stay home more often.

Logan, being the overachiever that he was, was taking several of the same classes as me and we spent most evenings on the couch working on a paper or studying for a test. It felt nice to have our old connection back after all those months of awkwardness.

I still thought of my mom from time to time. Danny had given me a picture of her that my aunt had from their childhood, and I kept it in the drawer beside my bed. I pulled it out once in a while and stared at the innocent child my mother had once been. I like to picture her that way, instead of the horrible person she had become. After all, everyone was innocent in the beginning, and my mother had been no different.

It was Friday night again, and I had decided to spend the evening on the couch with my collection of Johnny Depp movies. I popped a bag of popcorn and grabbed the blanket from my room before putting in the first movie and settling onto the couch.

Logan had gone back to his job at the shop and was working late. Amber was running around the house, trying to get ready for another party.

"Are you sure you don't want to come with me?" she pleaded. "I bet you would find a hot guy to bring you out of your dry spell."

"I'm perfectly happy being in a dry spell as long as Johnny Depp is here to entertain me," I said, and stuck my tongue out at her.

"Oh come on, you haven't had sex since Drake. You've got to be going nuts."

I winced at the mention of sex. I didn't even want to date someone, let alone get all naked and sweaty with him.

"Sex is for chumps. I have popcorn."

She laughed as she slipped her feet into a pair of heels. "Popcorn, right. You have fun with that while I'm out finding a cute guy to get naked and sweaty with."

"I will," I said as I turned my attention back to the television.

Amber sighed as she walked back to her room. "I give up."

I rolled my eyes as I stuffed more popcorn in my mouth. I knew she was only looking out for me, but her constantly playing Cupid was starting to drive me nuts. I did have to admit that I missed sex, but I wasn't ready to take that leap just yet.

While I knew I could go find some random guy that I'd never have to see again for a one-night stand, that wasn't my style. Besides, sex was the only thing that I had left from my relationship with Drake, and I wasn't ready to let that go just yet. Call me crazy, but I liked knowing that Drake was the last person I had been with.

Just as the movie was starting to get good, someone knocked at the door.

"Amber!" I yelled, not wanting to pause the movie.

"What?" she yelled back.

"Someone's at the door! Answer it!"

"I'm peeing. You get it!"

I groaned as I reached for the remote and paused Johnny. Another knock came at the door as I threw my blanket and stood.

"Hold your ass, I'm coming!" I shouted as I walked to the door.

I had no idea who it could be, and frankly I didn't care. Whoever was there was interrupting my quality time with the closest thing I had to a boyfriend.

I threw the door open and glared at the figure standing on our porch. "Yes?"

The figure turned around and my heart stopped. My mouth hung open as I stared at Drake standing there, completely at ease.

"Hi, Chloe," he said, giving me a small smile.

At that point, I did what any self-respecting crazy woman would do. I slammed the door in his face and ran toward my room. I nearly knocked Amber down as I ran past her when she came out of the bathroom.

"Ahhh!" she shrieked as she grabbed the wall to steady herself. "What the fuck, Chloe?"

The doorbell rang again and my head snapped up to look at the door. "Don't answer it!"

"What? Why? Who is it?"

I shook my head as I grabbed my doorknob and ran inside my room. I fell onto the bed and hid my head under the pillows. There was no way that Drake could be standing at my front door after over six months of nothing from him. I had no idea what he wanted and I didn't care. Him showing up here would only end with me being hurt all over again, and I couldn't take that. My heart couldn't take that.

I pulled the pillows off my head and strained my ears, trying to listen for Amber or Drake's voice, but I heard nothing but silence. I hoped that Amber had kicked him off the porch and shoved her four-inch spike heels up his ass to get the point across. I loved Amber; she always looked out for me in her own way.

I smiled as I pictured Amber trying to beat the crap out of Drake. Too bad I was hiding in my room; that would have been something I wanted front-row tickets to see.

I jumped when someone knocked on my door. Amber swung the door open and gave me a small smile.

"You okay?" she asked as she walked across the room and sat at the foot of my bed.

"I'm fine. Did you get rid of him?"

"Yeah, I took care of it for you. I don't want you hiding in here all night while I'm out; come back to the living room and get your Johnny on."

I laughed as I sat up. "I wasn't hiding."

"Did you forget that I witnessed your mad dash down the hallway?"

"I wasn't hiding . . . I was escaping," I grumbled.

She laughed as she pulled me to my feet. "Whatever. Now go bond with your popcorn and Johnny before I drag you to the party with me."

That was all it took to get my feet moving; I did not want to spend my night surrounded by drunken idiots. I let Amber drag me back down the hallway and into the living room. She stood in front of the chair as I plopped down on the couch and grabbed the remote.

"Thanks for being here for me, Amber. I don't think I would have made it through these last few months without you."

"Uh, no problem. Listen . . ."

"I'm serious. We both know I was a fucking wreck and you helped me get my shit together. If there's one thing I've learned from all of this, it's that men are total and complete dicks," I said as I clicked play and watched Johnny start dancing across my screen.

"Well, see, Chloe . . . ," she started again, but I cut her off. It felt good to just put everything out there.

"Take my word for it: men are nothing but cold-hearted bastards. Look at Drake. I loved him more than anything, and he just let me go. I hope he's enjoying the good life out in Los Angeles without me; I hope he finds some nasty groupie that gives him every STD known to man."

"Chloe, shut up!" Amber shouted.

"No, let her finish. I'm curious as to what else she has to say about me," a voice said from behind her.

I froze at the sound of Drake's voice. Amber moved away from the chair and I started cursing when I saw him sitting there with a grin on his face.

"In my defense, I tried to warn you." Amber said.

"I thought you said you got rid of him!" I groaned.

"I said I took care of it. There's a difference."

"Whatever. I'm done talking now; both of you can go jump off a bridge."

"No, keep talking, I'd love to hear what else you wish upon my poor dick. That kind of hurts, you know; I'm quite fond of that certain body part," Drake said as he smirked at me.

I couldn't believe him; he was sitting in my house making smart-ass comments, pretending as if the last six months had never happened.

"I want him out, Amber, *now*," I growled. I couldn't believe that she had done this to me. I had been praising her not five minutes ago, and here she was, stabbing me in the back.

"Just hear him out, please. If not for him, then for yourself; you deserve that much," she pleaded.

I stared back and forth between the two of them. My mind screamed at me to make him leave before he could do any more damage, but my heart was begging me to let him stay and listen to what he had to say.

"You have five minutes; after that I'm kicking you out," I said.

"Works for me. I'm late for my party, so I'll catch you two later," Amber said as she winked at me.

I glared at her. I had thought she was on my side this whole time, yet here she was, standing up for Drake.

Drake waited until she walked out the front door before he turned to me. "Did you really want me to catch a bunch of sexually transmitted diseases?"

"You're wasting your five minutes; I'm waiting," I said as I crossed my arms over my chest and glared at him.

CHAPTER TWENTY-TWO

DRAKE

I couldn't help but smile at Chloe's stubbornness. It was one of my favorite things about her, after all. I knew coming back here was a gamble, but I couldn't stop myself; I had to know if she still wanted me.

"I'm not going to lie; I was hoping you would welcome me back with open arms."

"Sorry to disappoint you. Why are you even here? Shouldn't you be out snorting cocaine and banging groupies? I figured you were living the typical rock-star life by now," she snapped.

"Yeah, I guess I deserved that, didn't I?" I asked. She raised an eyebrow but said nothing as she waited for me to continue. "And I assumed it would be obvious why I was here. I've missed you."

"You've missed me? If you missed me so much, why didn't you call me even once over the past six months?"

"Because I couldn't. After you left, things started to get worse and I started using more. Then Eric got the call about the label out in L.A. wanting us to come out, and my life went crazy from there."

"I was waiting for Jade or one of the guys to call me and tell me you were dead from an overdose, Drake. All this time, I've secretly worried about you and you couldn't take two seconds out of your busy life to let me know you were okay? That's bullshit."

"At least that means you still care," I mumbled, feeling like the biggest ass ever. I hadn't wanted to stay away from Chloe, but I'd wanted the drugs more than anything.

"I did care; not anymore, though. I've seen you, so you can go now."

"Don't you want to hear anything that I came here to say?"

"Not really, Drake. You ripped my heart out once already; I don't need to go through that again."

"I never meant to hurt you, honest. You're the most important thing in the world to me, but my judgment was clouded. I just miss you so much, and I know that I fucked up."

"I don't know what you want me to say to that, Drake. I already made myself clear back on the bus; I don't want anything to do with you while you're on drugs. I can't stop you from destroying your life, but I can still save mine," she whispered as a tear slid down her cheek.

I wanted more than anything to wipe it away, but I knew she wouldn't let me. That wall she used to keep people away was up, and this time it was for me. I hated to think that I had hurt her to the point where she would never let me in again.

"I'm clean, Chloe. I have been for a little over a month now."

"What? Why didn't you try to reach me, then? Is it because you finally figured out you could do better than me?"

"You know better than that, Chloe. I love you. Basically, the band and our manager threatened to fire me from the band if I didn't get clean. I had already lost you, and they were the only thing I had left that mattered. I checked myself into a two-month program and I've been clean since I was released."

"So let me get this straight: you cared enough about the band to go into rehab, but I wasn't enough of a reason when I walked away from you?"

"No, it's not like that, Chloe. I knew I was in trouble, and it was just the final straw. I wanted to stay in the band, and I wanted to win you back."

"How do I even know you're telling me the truth about all of this? And if it is true, that means you've been out of rehab for a month without contacting me."

I knew she wouldn't believe me, so I had come prepared. I stood as I reached into the inside pocket of my jacket and pulled out a piece of paper. "If you want proof, then here it is. As for why I'm just now showing up, I wanted to make sure I could handle the outside world without falling back into my old habits. I didn't want to come back and tell you I was clean, only to disappoint you again."

She stood up and came a few steps closer to me, but only close enough to grab the paper out of my hand. I waited while she read what I hoped was my saving grace; it was my certificate of completion from the rehab center I had stayed at in L.A.

"You really did it, then?" she asked as she stared down at the paper in her hands.

"Yeah, I did. You were all I thought about while I was in there. I screwed up so bad with you, Chloe, and I want to make it right; I want to make *us* right."

"It's not that simple, Drake. You really hurt me. You let me walk off that bus without even trying to stop me. I'm glad that you got help, but I don't think I can go through that again."

"I'm so sorry for what I did, Chloe. I promise you that I will never do anything like that again."

"How can you be sure, Drake? You're just starting out in an industry that is full of drugs and sex. Can you really walk side by side with temptation on a daily basis and not give in? Drugs will be easy to get and women will be lining up for you, worse than they were when we were together. I can't handle that kind of life. I won't share you with them."

"Then come with me. Stay by my side every night so that you know you can trust me," I said.

"*What?*"

"I said come with me. That's why I came back, Chloe; I want you back and I want you by my side through all of this."

"You can't just walk back into my life and expect me to drop everything for you, Drake. Even if I did want to give us another chance, I have responsibilities here: school, my part of the rent for this place."

"So stay here until you're finished with school for the year. Then you can take online classes and come on tour with us. Thanks to me, we're still in the studio recording tracks for our first album, and we will be for a few months. We won't start touring until several months from now."

"This is insane, Drake!" she shouted.

"Please, Chloe—I love you. I want to spend every second of my life with you from now until the day I die. I can't live without you," I pleaded.

This had gone so much better in my head. While I knew she would be angry, I had hoped that I wouldn't have to resort to groveling to get her to take me back. But if I had to, I would. I would rather die than spend one more day without her.

"I don't want to get hurt again Drake," she whispered. "I can't take it."

I grabbed her and pulled her into my arms. She struggled at first, but I held on tight, refusing to let her go. "I will never hurt you again, Chloe. Never. Let me prove it to you."

I pressed my lips to hers and kissed her like I was dying, like it was the last kiss we would ever share, because it might just be our last. She might slap me when I let her go and never speak to me again. If she did, I wanted to remember the feel of her lips against mine for the rest of my life.

Despite what she said, her body responded to me instantly as she wrapped her arms around me and kissed me back, showing me just how much she still wanted me.

I groaned as her lips parted and I slipped my tongue inside her mouth, flicking my tongue ring against her tongue in a way that I knew drove her crazy.

She moaned in response before quickly pulling away. "What are we doing?"

"I'm not sure what *you* were doing, but I was kissing the woman I love."

"I love you too, Drake, and I do want to be with you. There's no way that I can deny that now, but if we do this again, we're going to take it slow and start over. I don't know how this is going to work with you being so far away, though."

A smile broke out across my face; if I had known all it would take to change her mind was a kiss, I would have done that first.

"We'll figure it out—we always do," I said as I kissed her softly. "But I can't agree to the taking-it-slow part."

"Why not?" she asked, confused.

I reached into my pocket and pulled out a small box. "Because the first thing I did when I checked out was stop at the jewelry store and pick this up."

Her mouth dropped open as I lowered myself to one knee and opened the box to reveal a sparkling diamond ring. "Oh my God."

Before I met Chloe, if someone had told me I would be down on one knee asking the woman I love to marry me, I would have kicked his ass. Before her, marriage had been nothing more than a trap that others fell into. I was too smart for that, or so I thought.

"Chloe Marie Richards, I never thought I would ever be one of those dumbasses who love a woman so much they want to tie themselves to her forever, but here I am, down on one knee, trying to think of something sweet and romantic to say. As you can tell, I'm failing miserably, so will you please put me out of my misery and say yes if I ask you to marry me?"

She laughed as I stared up at her. "I don't know . . . You'll have to ask me to find out."

"I thought I just did."

"No, you asked me if I would say yes if you asked me to marry you; it's not the same."

I groaned. "You're not going to make this easy on me, are you?"

"After the last six months? I think not; you're lucky I haven't thrown you out yet."

"Fine. Chloe, will you please marry me? I promise to love and cherish you forever and always, and I promise to give you lots of mind-blowing sex every day."

"Even when we're ninety and walking with canes?" she asked with a serious look on her face.

"Damn it, quit stalling! Will you marry me or not?"

"Well, since you asked me so nicely, I guess I have to now," she said as she laughed.

"That was a yes, right?"

"That was a yes."

I let out a breath I hadn't realized I'd been holding as I pulled the ring from the box and slipped it onto her finger. "Thank God."

"Aren't you going to kiss me or something now? You're not very good at this, you know."

"I was getting to that part, smart-ass," I said as I stood back up and pulled her into my arms. "I can't wait until you're Mrs. Drake Allen. Hell, maybe even one day we will have two-point-five children and live in a log cabin by a lake."

She grinned. "I never understood that whole point-five thing, but I wouldn't mind kids someday. I love you, Drake; I don't think I could be any happier than I am right now."

"Me too, baby, me too," I said as I attacked her mouth. I was going to make up for every lost moment with her, even if it took me all night, or all year. I didn't care. I had her in my arms and there was nothing in this world that would ever tear us apart.

I knew we had a lot to figure out, especially with me living in Los Angeles now, but I wasn't worried. Sometimes life throws you curve balls, but other times it seems like everything falls into place. I was determined to make sure Chloe had her happily-ever-after, starting right now.

CHLOE

Six Years Later

I think I'm going to be sick," I groaned as I stood backstage with Amber and Logan.

"Just take a deep breath—it'll be fine. He's going to flip!" Amber squealed as she hugged me.

I did as she instructed, trying to calm myself as I watched Drake, no more than ten feet away, perform to a crowd of thousands. After I finished my classes my sophomore year of college, I had moved out to California to be with Drake. Since then, we had been back to West Virginia only a few times, and tonight was one of them. Drake was playing to a sold-out crowd right in his hometown—Morgantown.

I decided that here was the perfect place to clue him in on a little secret I had been keeping from him. It seemed only fitting to do so in the place where it had all started, where our life together began.

"He's getting ready to start the next song. Are you ready?" Amber asked.

"No, but I already made the sign, so I can't turn back now," I said as I grabbed my sign from behind the curtain and clutched it to my chest.

"Right, because the time and effort you put into it is too much to waste," she teased.

"Bite me," I grumbled as I took another deep breath and raised the sign above my head.

I stood there feeling like an idiot as I waited for Drake to look my way. Finally, halfway through the song, he looked over at me. He smiled as he glanced at the sign I was holding and then looked away. I waited for it to register, and ten seconds later it clicked.

Drake stopped mid-song and turned to look at me again. "*What?*" he bellowed into the microphone.

The band stopped playing and turned to face me as the coliseum went dead silent. Before I realized what he was doing, Drake walked across the stage and stopped in front of me.

"Seriously?" he asked.

"Seriously," I said as I grinned.

He grabbed me and threw me over his shoulder as he walked back onto the stage.

"Put me down, Drake Allen!" I shrieked.

"Sorry for the interruption, guys, but it seems I have an announcement to make," Drake's voice boomed from the speakers.

"Oh no," I groaned as he sat me on my feet.

"I'm sure you all know her by now, but in case you don't, this is my lovely wife, Chloe."

I blushed as a few members of the crowd whistled at me.

"All right, back off. She's taken, and she has just informed me that I'm going to be a dad. Now, I don't know about the rest of you, but I think that's pretty fucking cool!"

The crowd went wild as Drake pulled me close and kissed me in front of thousands of people.

"I'm going to kill you for this. I've never been so embarrassed in my life!" I cried as I felt my face warm.

While Drake was used to being the center of attention, I tried to hide from the media and fans as much as possible.

He laughed as he kissed me again. "I'm so happy, baby; you're going to make a great mom."

"I think you're going to make a pretty amazing dad yourself. Now go sing before the natives get restless. We can talk about this later."

He laughed as he released me and turned back to the crowd. "All right, are you guys ready to tear down this fucking place?" he screamed.

The crowd roared as I ran offstage and into Amber's arms.

"That was the funniest thing I've ever seen in my life!" Logan said as he howled with laughter.

"Shut up or I'll throw you out there!" I said.

Amber kept her arms around me as Logan wrapped both of us in a hug. There was nothing like having the three, now four, most important people in my life all together at once.

And I had to admit as I watched Drake mesmerize the crowd, life was pretty good. I had two of the best friends in the world, an amazing husband who loved me more than I deserved, and a tiny bundle of joy on the way. What else could a girl ask for?

RESOURCES

For more information on some of the topics covered in this book, please check out the following links:

Childhelp National Child Abuse Hotline: http://www.childhelp .org/pages/hotline-home

Drug Abuse Hotline: http://drugabusehelpline.net/

National Suicide Prevention Lifeline: 1-800-273-TALK (8255)

No one should ever have to suffer alone.

SHOUT-OUT!

I really don't think I could name everyone that I want to send my thanks to at this point—there are enough of you to put in a book!

First—to all of the bloggers whom I've met since *Torn* was released in January. You've welcomed me into this crazy author/ blogger world with open arms and I'm proud to call several of you my friends.

Second—to my fans. I have received SO MANY comments and emails, and I want you to know just how important those are to me. I always have a silly grin on my face when I read them, so thank you for that. You've pulled me out of some really bad moods more than once.

Third—to my book club for making me laugh until I cried. No words can express how much I love you all.

Fourth—in a category all her own, Dirty Molly. You have sent me some of the most AMAZING fan art a girl could ever ask for. And yes, I know you're blushing right now.

Fifth—to my parents. I couldn't have done any of this without either of you. And the fact that you've dealt with me on a daily basis for the past twenty-two years without murdering me, well, that deserves a medal. I love you both.

Thank you to every single one of you reading this. You've touched my life so much. I love you all!

ABOUT THE AUTHOR

K.A. Robinson was born and raised in West Virginia, where she still lives, next door to two of the most wonderful parents she could have ever asked for. When she's not writing, she continuously has her nose buried deep in a good book. Most of her favorites are new adult, dystopian, or paranormal. She works full-time at a Kubota Tractor dealership. She is happily married to her high school sweetheart, together with whom she has a two-year-old son. She has major weaknesses for Starbucks and for Cocoa Pebbles.

For more information, please visit her Goodreads page at:
K.A. Robinson Goodreads Author Page

Or her Facebook page at:
http://www.facebook.com/KARobinson13

Or her Twitter:
https://twitter.com/KARobinsonAutho